# DEATH DIVE!

The bullets tore through Brauer, slapped against Ludecka's back armour and ripped into both legs. They ruptured the port inner-wing fuel tank and shattered the control pulley to the rudder. They punctured the tank in front of the instruments, and the cockpit was sprayed with oil. Out of control, the Stuka rolled on to its back . . .

# Sea Wrack

## RAYMOND HITCHCOCK

SPHERE BOOKS LIMITED
30-32 Gray's Inn Road, London WC1X 8JL

First published in Great Britain by Michael Joseph 1980
Copyright © Raymond Hitchcock 1980
Published by Sphere Books Ltd 1982

To Ann and Michael,
with love and gratitude

TRADE
MARK

Set in Times by The Yale Press Ltd. London SE25

Printed and bound in Great Britain by
Cox & Wyman Ltd, Reading

# PROLOGUE

'During August [1940] the corpses of about forty German soldiers were washed up at scattered points along the coast between the Isle of Wight and Cornwall. The Germans had been practising embarkations in the barges along the French coast. Some of these barges put out to sea in order to escape British bombing and were sunk, either by bombing or bad weather. This was the source of a widespread rumour that the Germans had attempted an invasion and had suffered heavy losses, either by drowning or being burnt in patches of sea covered with flaming oil. We took no steps to contradict these tales, which spread freely through the occupied countries in a wildly exaggerated form and gave much encouragement to the oppressed populations.'

Churchill — *The Second World War,* Volume II (Cassell Ltd), confirmed in substance by Attlee in a written Parliamentary answer, 18 November 1946.

'After examination of our documents in consideration of the cemetery of Cannock Chase where about 2,700 German soldiers of the Second World War rest in peace, we were only able to identify seven soldiers who were washed up on the coast of England in August 1940.'

*Deutsche Dienststelle für die Benachrichtigung der nächsten Angehörigen von Geffallenen der ehemaligen deutschen Wehrmacht,* German Department for the Notification of the Nearest Relatives of Victims from the Wehrmacht, in a letter to the author, dated 2 May 1978.

All seven listed by the Deutsche Dienststelle were *airmen* of the Luftwaffe. What then happened to the forty German *soldiers'* bodies from the invasion barges? There is no record of them in the war diaries of the British divisions guarding the south coast at the time. The Imperial War Graves Commission has no knowledge of them, nor the German equivalent, the Volksbund Deutsche Kriegsgräberfürsorge. In spite of the statements of two British Prime Ministers, did they ever exist?

1

# CHAPTER 1

Simon Manning got out of the Métro at the Opéra, walked down the Boulevard des Capucines to the Place de la Madeleine and thence into the Rue du Faubourg St Honoré. He carried a brown suitcase made of pressed cardboard and tied with string. Under a light fawn mac that had lost its weatherproofing, he wore a Harris tweed jacket with leather arm and elbow patches, and his grey flannel trousers were loose, baggy and frayed at the heels. The soles of his brown shoes were coming away from their uppers, and under a sweat-stained grey trilby his head had been shaved.

Simon walked up the steps of Number 39 and demanded to see the British Ambassador. The receptionist offered him the Consul-General's office and he said No. A clerk asked for his passport and he handed it over. He was asked what his business was and said he had just come out of Germany. The clerk blinked, told him to wait and he waited. After half an hour he was taken up a wide flight of stairs and shown into a large room with a window on to the street. The man behind the desk, too young to be the Ambassador, indicated a chair and he sat. The man was flicking slowly through the passport.

'Simon Irving Manning, born 20 May 1908 in the city of Durham. A British subject. Height, six feet and half an inch, eyes brown, hair dark brown.'

Simon nodded.

'An archaeologist with no "special peculiarities".'

Simon nodded again.

The First Secretary scratched his domed forehead and smiled. 'And you claim to have just come out of Germany?'

'Yesterday.'

'How, may I ask?'

From his pocket Simon took an American passport. 'On this.' Simon was forced to get out of the chair to hand over the passport. The First Secretary examined this new piece of evidence.

'Mr Richard James Cotton, same photo, much the same signature, also born 20 May 1908, only this time in West 24th Street, New York. Issued, I see, in America by the State Department.'

'In fact supplied by the Abwehr.'

'Indeed, the Abwehr,' said the First Secretary. 'Would you care to explain why the German Intelligence Service should give you an American passport?'

Simon explained. It took half an hour and during that time the First Secretary sat back in his chair, his eyes closed, his hands together on his chest. When Simon finished, the First Secretary slowly came back to life. He picked up the American passport, flicked through it again, and stared at the emaciated, dishevelled creature in front of him.

'You must admit, old man, it's a damned odd story. A civilian coming out of Germany after eight months of war, saying he's been hobnobbing with Admiral Canaris, their Intelligence Chief, been given a load of red-hot information about concentration camps and SS squads murdering Jews in Poland, then demanding to be taken to the PM.' He stopped, shook his head at the enormity of it all, then said, 'Before we can do a thing here, we'll have to tell London. See what they make of it. I'm sure you understand.'

Simon pointed at the telephone on the desk. The First Secretary slowly shook his head.

'You've got two passports,' he said. 'Two passports. That in itself is most irregular.'

Simon got up from the chair and grasped the edge of the First Secretary's desk. 'For Christ's sake, I've got information that could be devastating if used properly. Documented evidence of Nazi atrocities in Poland. The systematic murder of Jews, gypsies, aristocrats, officer POWs and priests.' He laid his suitcase on the First Secretary's desk, untied the string and raised the cracked brown lid. From beneath a crumpled shirt, he extracted a file a quarter of an inch think. The First

Secretary stared at the file, slid his tongue over his lips, then held out his hand.

'Perhaps we'd better keep it in the safe.'

Simon shook his head. 'Get me to London tonight.' He shut the case and retied the string. 'I'm giving that file to the Prime Minister.'

The First Secretary wilted, shocked by such naïvety. 'I don't think you understand, old man. The PM is a VIP. If we let every Tom, Dick or Harry ...' He tailed off under Simon's stare and got slowly to his feet. They stood facing each other, the immaculately dressed diplomat and the unshaven, ill-kempt man in the fawn mac. Then the First Secretary opened the desk drawer, took out a key and a bundle of notes. 'Luckily we've got an empty flat. You can stay there tonight. And get yourself a decent meal, you look as if you need one.'

Simon took no notice of either key or money. 'The night boat.'

'My dear fellow,' said the First Secretary, coming round his desk to open the door, 'I've explained. We have to ask for instructions, particularly these days. After all, there is a war on, and there are Fifth Columnists about. And your case isn't exactly straightforward. A civilian internee coming out of Germany with the sort of information you claim to have. And holding two passports!' The First Secretary jingled the key: 'Be a good fellow. The address is on the label. It's off the Avenue Foch. Not a bad area. Have a good sleep, that's what you need, a good sleep. You'll feel better after a good sleep. There's coffee in the cupboard.'

Simon did not move.

'Are you by any chance interested in military information?' he asked with as much sarcasm as he could muster.

'My dear fellow,' said the First Secretary, smiling, 'what a droll sense of humour you have. Of course we are. We have military attachés for that very purpose.'

'Would it surprise you to know that the roads of West Germany are choked with lorries, the railways blocked with troop trains?'

'We do have our own sources of Intelligence, thank you,' said the First Secretary politely, and gave the key another jingle.

Simon stood staring in disbelief.

'I haven't just been to see Snow White!' he shouted. 'I've been in Germany. In Berlin with two of Hitler's top men in OKW!'

'That all has to be checked,' said the First Secretary, unruffled.

'People like you are going to lose us this bloody war!'

'You're tired and hungry,' said the First Secretary. 'We can talk about all this tomorrow when you're feeling better and we've heard from London.'

Simon hesitated, then took the key and money but kept his hand out. 'My passport?'

The First Secretary shook his head. 'We'll look after them both. Just for the moment. I'm sure you understand.'

A mist filled Simon's head. He fought to stop himself crashing his fist into the face in front of him.

'You bastard!' he breathed, and the First Secretary drew back, surprised and hurt.

'There's no need to be offensive.'

Simon stared at the man, then shook his head.

'You must try and see things from other people's points of view,' said the First Secretary. 'This is nothing personal, that I can assure you. It's simply that we have our own way of doing things.'

Simon stood swaying with the weightlessness of exhaustion.

'A good sleep,' said the First Secretary, 'that's what you need. You're all in. Come back tomorrow, old chap. By then the picture will be a lot clearer.'

Simon staggered down the stairs and out into the street. It wasn't until he was in the fresh air again that he realised that the First Secretary was the first Englishman he had had a conversation with for nearly a year.

# CHAPTER 2

Cuthbertson was lying on the bed when Sinclair got up and began dressing. Cuthbertson watched him for a while and said, 'You've got pimples on your back, Ross.' He listened to Sinclair's laugh, then poured himself another drink. As Sinclair was putting on his jacket, a brown OHMS envelope fell on to the carpet. Sinclair picked it up and put it on the bed.

'Nearly forgot,' he said. 'Came in this morning. From the First Secretary in Paris. I think you ought to read it now.'

Cuthbertson glanced at his watch. Sinclair opened the envelope, took out a single sheet of ruled foolscap, written in ink on both sides, and thrust it under Cuthbertson's nose. It was a précis of the information carried by Simon Manning. Cuthbertson dropped back against the pillow and began to read.

'Damned lucky it came through my hands first,' said Sinclair, watching Cuthbertson's face. 'If it's true, it's an appalling story. I'd call it political dynamite!'

When he reached the signature, Cuthbertson sat up and said, 'Anyone else seen it?'

Sinclair shook his head.

'Thanks, Ross, thanks very much,' said Cuthbertson, gripping Sinclair's arm. 'And don't worry, I'll look after it.' He put the foolscap sheet back into the envelope, slipped it into the inside pocket of his jacket and quickly began to dress. Sinclair, surprised and uneasy at Cuthbertson's calm, asked his next move.

'February 1933, remember, Ross?' said Cuthbertson sternly. ' "This House will *not* fight for King and Country." We meant it then, it was an act of faith. One doesn't give up one's faith just because of a few difficulties. Civilisation can yet survive. Even with all that's happening, it's not too late. We must take the broad view. See Europe as a whole, not just pieces of it. Fortunately we still have friends in the right places.'

Aghast, Sinclair indicated Cuthbertson's inner pocket. 'That report says that the Jews of Poland are being *exterminated*.'

7

'The air's full of rumours,' said Cuthbertson urbanely.

'We can't just forget it, suppress it,' said Sinclair. 'It wouldn't be possible. It wouldn't be right.'

'Who's saying anything about forgetting it or suppressing it?' said Cuthbertson, laughing. 'All we do is continue the process you started. Channel it correctly. That is, if we still believe in peace with Germany?'

Sinclair shook his head. 'Of course I believe in peace with Germany, but if that gets out, if someone like Winston or Eden hears about it, all hell'll be let loose.'

'Doubt and despondency belong to the other side, Ross,' said Cuthbertson. 'We must see that it doesn't get out. That people like Winston and Eden don't hear about it. And with your help, they won't.'

'There's still this Manning chap over in Paris,' said Sinclair. 'He wants to bring the whole file over here. We can't keep him away for ever. Then there's the First Secretary.'

'Trust me, Ross,' said Cuthbertson gently. 'Just trust me, that's all.'

Sinclair gave a faint smile.

They walked down the stairs together, an incongruous couple, Cuthbertson slight and sandy-haired, Sinclair stocky and dark. They parted on the pavement even though they were both going back to Whitehall.

Simon slept for fourteen hours. When he awoke, he shaved, dressed and walked until he found a restaurant he could afford. He had his first decent meal for months and returned to the embassy in a state of contentment. The First Secretary was polite, almost friendly, but said he had heard nothing from London: 'Give them a chance old man. They've got a lot on their plates these days.' He gave Simon a handful of francs, made him sign for them, and told him to go to the cinema.

Simon dropped into the chair, thrust out his legs and stared at the First Secretary.

'Funny world, yours,' he said. 'Never had anything to do with it before. You're not interested in the Polish massacres...'

'My dear fellow,' said the First Secretary, holding up his hand, 'what a terrible thing to say.'

'You're not interested in troop concentrations. Would you

by any chance be interested in a few words uttered by the Chief of German Intelligence on the forthcoming offensive?'

The First Secretary smiled. 'You are a persistent fellow. It's simply that we know our business, that's all. I assume you're talking about "Fall Gelb", "Case Yellow"?'

Simon looked puzzled.

'The attack in the west,' said the First Secretary. 'We've had warnings of that for a long time. The Dutch Military Attaché came in with one this morning. First we were told it was to be last November, then suddenly it jumped to May and we heard it was to be the 5th.'

'Sunday!'

The First Secretary glanced at the calendar on his desk. 'Absolutely correct.'

'And we're going to stiffen our upper lips and await the onrush of the German hordes? Clean our boots while the world falls about us?' asked Simon sarcastically.

'You completely miss the point,' said the First Secretary. 'We and the French are ready. This time the Hun'll get a very bloody nose!'

'He didn't get much of a bloody nose in Norway.'

'Norway in no way compares with France.'

'I was specifically warned to get out of Belgium and Holland as quickly as possible.'

The First Secretary smiled. 'Let me assure you, Manning. Belgium possibly. The Germans do have a penchant for invading Belgium, although whether they dare upset world opinion a second time, I doubt. But Holland, no. The Dutch Government has received a written assurance from the German Foreign Office that their neutrality will be respected.'

'And you believe it?' asked Simon, astonished.

The First Secretary nodded. 'It didn't come from Hitler but from their diplomatic service.'

Slowly Simon got to his feet. 'You have heard from London, otherwise you wouldn't have trotted out all that information about "Fall Gelb" and the diplomatic note. Not to me. It means you know I'm clean.'

The First Secretary opened his mouth, stayed poised like that for a while, then said: '*The Lady Vanishes*, made by that chappie Hitchcock. It's on at that little place in the Champs-

Elysées. If you haven't seen it, you'll enjoy it. Should interest you. All about getting out of Nazi Germany.'

Simon walked out and back into the street.

Before finding the Minister, Cuthbertson made some inquiries. When he did get to the Minister's office, he was about to leave for the House.

'I think you should read this, Minister,' said Cuthbertson, holding out the OHMS envelope. 'It's extremely important.'

The Minister looked towards the hatstand, but Cuthbertson's inflexibility won. The Minister took the paper and read it. When he finished, he peered over the top of his glasses, shook his head and said: 'If true, a terrible story. Shocking.'

'Also most inopportune, Minister, as I think you'll agree,' said Cuthbertson. 'It's politically hazardous whichever way you look at it. If the information is genuine, it makes one wonder at K's motive. He might almost be trying to embarrass us.'

The Minister scanned the paper again and nodded. 'Made public it's hardly likely to sweeten the path to peace.'

'According to the First Secretary,' said Cuthbertson, indicating the paper, 'this fellow Manning actually undertook to hand the wretched file to the PM personally.'

The Minister shook his head. 'Neville wouldn't want to see it. Not at the moment.' He paused, then said, 'Anyone else seen it?'

'Only my contact at the FO. He won't talk.'

The Minister gave Cuthbertson a sharp glance. After a while he said, 'Things must be pretty bad in Poland for K to send this.'

'Everything has still to be verified,' said Cuthbertson coolly.

The Minister grunted and asked what they knew of Manning.

'He's British all right,' said Cuthbertson. 'Thirty-one, single, reputedly an expert on Angles and Jutes. He was digging in North Germany, and instead of getting out like everyone else, seems to have got himself interned. On the face of it, that's a little suspect. Until we sort things out this end, I've instructed our people in Paris to keep him there and trail him. I thought it best.'

The Minister agreed and stared down at his pad.

'You know, Cuthbertson,' he said at last, 'I think we've got to accept that there'll never be peace with Hitler. The idea would stick in too many gullets. He may go down with some of the aristocracy, but not with many others.'

'Hitler's not the only person in Germany, Minister,' said Cuthbertson, alarmed. 'What about Göring, the Generals...?'

The Minister glanced towards the door. Cuthbertson saw the signal but waited. 'Perhaps we can discuss it first thing tomorrow, Minister? We ought to have an agreed approach.'

The Minister nodded and put the paper in his case. Cuthbertson went back to his own office and rang Sinclair. He arranged to meet the FO man in the shadow of the Needle.

They walked fast, Cuthbertson as usual setting the pace. The Palace of Westminster lay in front of them, and when Cuthbertson raised his umbrella, pointed and began talking excitedly, the buildings were a perfect setting.

'A month of dramatic change, Ross. Half Norway lost, one messed-up evacuation after another. And now, all the indications are that the German push in the west is close.'

Sinclair nodded. 'The Air Ministry are getting some good photos of tank concentrations.'

'The Schlieffen Plan, only this time with panzers,' said Cuthbertson thoughtfully. 'Everything repeats itself.'

At the sandbag-shrouded Cenotaph they stopped. Already, after just one winter, the bags were beginning to rot. Sand was trickling out. Cuthbertson couldn't resist sticking the ferrule of his umbrella into the fraying fabric.

'Another thing we've got in common, Ross, this memorial. My father was killed at Third Ypres, yours on the Somme. Neither has a grave. Of course, a lot of idiots think this war is the second half ' — he shook his head — 'as if the whole thing was a perpetual, inevitable, bloody stupid game.'

They resumed their walk in silence. Instead of going back to his office Cuthbertson glanced at his watch, then led the way across the park. As they neared the lake he began talking again. 'It's not too late even with everything changing. We've got to be adaptable, that's all. We've got to be prepared to go on even under a new Government, under a new PM.'

'Halifax won't be too bad,' said Sinclair.

'It might not be Halifax,' said Cuthbertson. 'It could be Churchill.'

Sinclair shook his head. 'He couldn't even get the support of his own party. And he's partly to blame for Norway.'

'If it is to be Churchill,' said Cuthbertson, his voice rising, his eyes half closing, 'then, by God, things will hum. It'll be all out, full scale, bloody crazy war! And there'll be unrestricted bombing, Ross, do you realise that? The Germans won't hold back with Churchill at the top.' He swept the point of his umbrella across the familiar skyline. 'The Luftwaffe will be over St James's Park . . . over the Mall . . . Piccadilly! The buildings of London will crumble under an avalanche of high explosive. And we shall be stupid enough to try and do the same thing to Berlin. That's what Winston will want.'

Once Sinclair, like Cuthbertson, had had no doubts. Now, like so many of his countrymen, he too was feeling the change of mood.

'No one can be dogmatic about these things,' he said cautiously. 'Situations change. What was valid seven years ago isn't necessarily valid today. Up to a point one must be practical.'

Cuthbertson stopped, turned his head and stared. Contempt, almost hatred, on his face.

'Our hopes,' he said icily, 'all those lovely words about civilisation ...' Then his voice rose as the excitement and anger returned. 'Truth doesn't change, Ross. "Truth is truth to the end of reckoning." Seven years, seventy years, seven hundred years, makes no difference. War is a crime against humanity. Those who participate in it are criminals.'

Sinclair glanced round the park. He had always been a little afraid of Cuthbertson, and now he was beginning to fear for his reason.

'Take it easy,' he said. 'You need a bit of leave, that's all.'

Cuthbertson nodded.

'Paris,' he said quietly, 'Paris in the spring, before the battle starts. Pity we both couldn't go.'

# CHAPTER 3

Simon was in the wide open spaces of the Place de la Concorde when it began raining hard. His shoes soon became pulp, and with sodden feet he ran north to the boulevards and the shops. With his remaining money he bought a cheap new pair of hideous continental brogues, then hurried back to the flat. Inside, out of the deluge, he had a moment of intense excitement. He kidded himself that tomorrow the embassy must have word from London, and by midday he would be on his way from the Gare du Nord. Indeed, his information was so important they might even send a plane for him.

He lit the gas fire, laid his clothes out in front of it and went into the bathroom to dry himself. He was suddenly conscious of himself in the mirror. He had seen himself in the mirror last night when he had had his first real wash, and he had seen himself this morning when he had shaved. This was different. He had time. He stared at his sunken eye-sockets, hollow cheeks, gaunt jaw and shaven head. Even the blue of his eyes had faded in the last eight months. He was not a pretty sight nor a hopeful one. He closed his eyes. All the euphoria, all the excitement of getting out of the rain, had vanished.

He made a cup of coffee, took it to the window and pulled back the net curtains. In pants and vest he stared out at the wet roofs opposite, at the glistening grey slates, at the pigeons huddled for shelter on the ledges. He looked down, past the dripping façades, and the bundles of bright spring leaves that burst sodden from the neat little plane trees that rose from their circular gratings, to the torrent in the gutter. Other than the falling rain the only other movement was a woman hurrying by, bent forward beneath her umbrella.

But for his own pale reflection in the window, the features mercifully blurred, he would have doubted his continued existence. His clothes were wet and threadbare, he had no passport, and the total of his other possessions were 228 francs, 30 centimes — barely one pound, five shillings at current rates

— a fountain pen and a wrist-watch that miraculously still worked. And, of course, the cardboard suitcase with the file. Suddenly he began laughing. There was no one to share the joke but he laughed. In his tatty, disintegrating child's suitcase he had twenty-two pages of closely typed German that were as potentially devastating as a plague virus or a new poison gas. Yet the British didn't seem to want to know.

It was growing dark early. He glanced at his watch. The SS Oberscharführer who had driven him out of Dachau to the forest landing-strip had returned it with his clothes. That had been the start of the night flight to Berlin wedged into the Fieseler Storch next to the Hauptmann of cavalry: the sight of the Havel through the arc of the propeller, the blackness of the Berliner Forst, the journey from Tempelhof to the Tirpitz Ufer in the big black BMW 335, and the astonishing meeting with the slight, lisping, Konteradmiral Wilhelm Canaris and the tall, stiff-backed officer introduced simply as 'Generalmajor X'.

Staring across the grey, rain-washed Paris skyline, he saw the stark office; the maps; the long desk with its single light and model cruiser; the three chairs; the black telephones; the two cabinets by the wall; the cot with folded blankets and the sleeping dachshund in the corner; the uniformed portraits; and the photo of Hitler with the Kriegsmarine. Only the Red Queen and the Mad Hatter had been missing. The proof of that room and that evening lay in the cardboard suitcase, otherwise he might have doubted the visit himself. Indeed, but for the file the extraordinary events of the last seventy-two hours would already have begun to pass from memory towards myth.

He went back to the gas fire, turned his steaming jacket and trousers and wondered what wartime England was like, and when he would see it.

The Minister's feelings on leaving the House were shame at the muddle in Norway and despair at the progress of events in England. A change of leadership now seemed a possibility. If Chamberlain did go, the Minister prayed that the King might send for Halifax. The thought that Churchill might be PM he didn't allow to enter his head.

In the car going home he read the sheet of foolscap again. As Cuthbertson had said, it was an embarrassing document. It was also a disturbing one. If it was to be believed, a race was being deliberately extinguished. An action so horrific that if it were known it was as likely to hinder the chances of peace as promote them. He wondered why Canaris had sent the information. It wasn't as if Britain could do anything about events in Poland. Denmark and Norway had proved what the Minister already knew. They were all impotent in the face of German power.

At home in the bath, with a double whisky on the cork seat of the chair beside him, he realised that he was worrying less about Canaris's action than the pricking of his own conscience. When his wife, moving in their bedroom, creaked the floorboards, he called out to her. She came into the bathroom and started tidying the towels.

'How would you balance cries from the Polish forests,' he asked, 'with the lives of aircrew in obsolescent aircraft? What can we do?'

'I would pray for time, dear,' said his wife 'As you did at Munich.'

The Minister smiled. Time was another thing they didn't have. But mention of Munich took him back eighteen months.

'We're still nowhere near ready for this war. Remember the idiots who talked about fighting in September '38? When our front-line squadrons had Hawker Fury biplanes 120 miles per hour slower than the Messerschmitts they would have to oppose?'

She did remember.

'Nasty word, appeaser,' said the Minister. 'Cruelly simple, cruelly unkind.'

His wife gave him a reassuring kiss on the forehead and went back into the bedroom.

He moved his toes above the water and thought of the relative strengths of the air forces today. Six squadrons of RAF fighters in France, thirty-one in England. 500 first-line, eight-gun monoplane fighters. Against that, the latest figures on the Luftwaffe showed 1,700 fighters, 2,300 bombers, all tested and tried in Spain. Sensible people didn't play games with odds like that. He caught the soap and soaped his chest.

'What does your young friend Cuthbertson say?' asked his wife. 'You usually find him a help.'

Of course it was useful having a man of Cuthbertson's outlook, but they were odd bedfellows. Cuthbertson saw all this quite differently. The man was an idealist. All war was wrong, but war with Germany was a sin. In Cuthbertson's case, neither expediency nor memory had driven him to his beliefs. Cuthbertson could pronounce on the morality of war between the two great Aryan powers without having gone over the top at Thiepval at dawn on 7 August 1916. The Somme and Passchendaele were the Minister's conditioning. If you were going into battle, make sure you could win it, or at least survive.

'Bit of a fanatic, Cuthbertson,' he said. 'Rather colours his judgement.'

'You're always saying you can only do the possible,' said his wife, 'and your aeroplanes can't possibly reach the Polish forests.'

'They can get to Berlin.'

'Does that help?'

He didn't know. He lay back in the soothing water, raised an arm towards the glass on the chair, noticed the 24-year-old bullet scar above the elbow, remembered the other scars below the water, and thanked God that Cuthbertson had had the sense not to circulate the report.

# CHAPTER 4

At seven in the evening, two men came to the Paris flat. One was the First Secretary, the other Cuthbertson. They were polite, and settled around the kitchen table, their briefcases laid in front of them. Simon expected his ticket and passport and asked for them. The First Secretary glanced at Cuthbertson, and Cuthbertson said, 'It's not quite as simple as that, Manning. The whole affair is, to say the least, unusual and delicate, as I'm sure you'll agree.'

Simon kept his temper and said that they'd checked on him.

'This information you have,' said Cuthbertson, 'this file on the Einsatzgruppen . . . the death squads . . . London have seen the First Secretary's précis.'

Simon nodded. Cuthbertson's manner suddenly changed. Gone was that amateurish gait, that upper-class bumble with which he had started the conversation. Now he spoke crisply, officiously.

'Why didn't you get out of Germany before hostilities began? You must have had the opportunity. Nearly everyone else managed it.'

'I've explained all that,' said Simon wearily.

'I'd like to hear it,' said Cuthbertson.

There was a long silence, then Simon said, 'I was excavating at a site we call Site B. Angles' inhumations, mid-fourth century. South-east of Flensburg, right out in the wilds, miles from anywhere. We never saw a newspaper and never heard the wireless.'

'And not expecting war between Great Britain and Germany, and being a dedicated scholar, you didn't go back with those others of your countrymen in that last week in August?'

The words were spoken with great sarcasm. Simon ignored them.

'This business of Dachau and the Gestapo,' said Cuthbertson. 'You seem to have got out of Dachau easily enough.'

'I think Canaris got me in and got me out. It sounds bizarre, but he wanted me to see the inside.'

'Good friend of yours, K.'

'K?'

'Canaris.'

Simon shrugged. They were trying to discredit him. He had no idea why.

'The Admiral seems to have contacts with British Military Intelligence,' he said. 'Why not ask him about the Gestapo?'

'How do you know he has contacts with British Military Intelligence?' asked Cuthbertson quickly.

'He told me he'd checked on me.'

Cuthbertson drummed his fingers on the table, then said: 'What do you know of the war?'

'Very little. What I gleaned in camp. What Canaris told me.'

'What did K tell you?'

'The RAF drop leaflets. We have the BEF in Northern France and a division in the Maginot Line, the latter for propaganda purposes. From time to time they patrol through the vineyards. The poilus stay well underground. The Germans call it the "Sitzkrieg", we call it "The Phoney War". Only on the sea is there any activity. On land, for another few days, it's "All Quiet on the Western Front".'

'Why do you say "for another few days"?' asked Cuthbertson. 'Did K tell you that too?'

'Not directly, but he hinted. I saw the troop movements on the way out. Besides, several times Canaris said that time was not on our side.'

'Our side?' asked Cuthbertson.

'He and some of the generals want to make an honourable peace with Great Britain. I understood you knew that.'

'What exactly is in the file?' asked Cuthbertson.

Simon glanced at the First Secretary. 'You said London had read his précis.'

'But the First Secretary didn't actually see the contents, did he?' said Cuthbertson, glancing at his companion. 'There may well have been points you forgot to mention. If you ran over it again?' He looked round the room for the cardboard suitcase.

Simon got up, went into the bedroom and came back with the case. He took out the file, opened it, and sat with it on his lap. 'Copies of orders from the Inspectorate of Concentration Camps . . . copies of orders from Hauptabteilung 1/5 concerning the use of camp labour . . . regulations for punishments . . . photos and construction drawings of the Dachau "Dog Kennel", and the Buchenwald "Cowstalls".' He looked up and said, 'The "Cowstalls", of course, are designed to facilitate nape-of-the-neck shooting,' then went back to the file. 'The SS's own statistics for deaths, numbers executed . . . details of the proposed 14fl3 SS medical commissions. That's a top secret programme of medical experiments to be carried out on selected prisoners. Indeed, a complete dossier on the four main concentration camps within the German Reich: Dachau, Sachsenhausen, Buchenwald and Ravensbrück.'

Simon looked up. Cuthbertson was frowning.

'Hot stuff?' said Simon. Cuthbertson did not reply.

18

'There's more to come,' said Simon, turning the pages of the file. 'Details of the Einsatzgruppen. The extermination squads, formed by a certain SS Obergruppenführer Reinhard Heydrich. Their uniform, identity marks, the SD diamond on their left sleeve, the names of the five commanders. Each group is about 500 strong. They went into Poland on the heels of the Wehrmacht. That means they've had nine months to operate.'

'And it is alleged that they're killing Jews, gypsies, intellectuals, aristocrats, officer POWs and priests, is that it?' asked Cuthbertson, with the trace of a smile.

'They *are* killing them,' said Simon firmly.

'How do you know? You weren't in Poland.'

'They're being shot *en masse*,' said Simon, clenching his fists. 'Jews mainly. Often in hundreds, and buried *en masse*.' He swept his hand across the page. 'Everything's here. Dates . . . numbers, eyewitness accounts. Even signed confessions by two SS who found the work "psychologically disturbing".'

'You believe it all?' asked Cuthbertson.

'Having been in Dachau for a while myself, yes.'

'Hearsay evidence,' said Cuthbertson with an impatient gesture, 'nothing more.'

Simon turned to the last six sheets. ' "Some Thoughts on the Treatment of Foreign Populations in the East". Himmler's own treatise written less than two months ago. There you'll find outline proposals for the total destruction of all racial minorities, deportation, sterilisation, the lot. The east is to be populated solely with the SS and their Slav serfs.'

They sat looking at one another. Simon closed the file and put it back in the case. Carefully he retied the string. Cuthbertson smiled and said, 'Tell me, Manning, why do you think K should have chosen you as the bearer of such startling information?'

Simon shrugged. 'I haven't the faintest idea.'

'Didn't it surprise you?'

'It wasn't in my hands. I was simply taken to his office in the Tirpitz Ufer, presented with the file, told the contents and pledged to take it to the Prime Minister.'

'And that visit was your first sight of K or the Abwehr?'

Simon nodded.

'You're sure of that?'

'Of course I'm sure.'

'When Canaris gave you the file did he explain his motives? After all, he is Germany's spymaster!'

'Yes, I remember his words. He said that if this conflict was allowed to continue, much more of Europe would be plunged into darkness. Deeds would be perpetrated in the name of Adolf Hitler that would take generations to expunge. He also said if the information in the file was not seen by the world now, sentiment might not allow it to be seen for a very long time. By then it would be too late.'

'How much do you know of the peace-moves inside Germany?'

'Very little. Canaris and the Generalmajor were obviously part of the conspiracy. I thought they stuck their necks out a long way.'

'They appeared very keen for an honourable peace?' asked Cuthbertson quickly.

'They insisted that the British Government could rely upon them. That once they had got rid of Hitler, they had the elements of a new government.'

Cuthbertson got up, picked up his briefcase and moved towards the door. The First Secretary did the same. Simon suddenly realised that the visit was at an end.

'What the hell's going on?' he shouted, trying to follow them. 'What about me? What about the file?'

Cuthbertson went out without a word. It was the First Secretary who turned, smiled and said, 'Terribly sorry, old man, but just at the moment going home is right out of the question. And it's no good heading for the ports, they'd never let you through.'

Simon went down the stairs arguing with them, and the First Secretary begged him to be quiet. He went back up to the flat and watched them emerge on to the pavement and hurry into the waiting car. Power, he decided, must be corrupting both sides in the war.

# CHAPTER 5

In his office in the Tirpitz Ufer, Konteradmiral Wilhelm Canaris lifted his gaze from the mass of papers on his desk, rested his chin in the palm of his left hand and stared at the dates on his calendar. Within two or three days, depending on whether Hitler changed his mind yet again, the old Western Front would once again be in flames. The successes in Poland, Denmark and Norway had already weakened the conspiracy. Victory in the west might well finish it off.

He went back to his papers, signed a few, then put down his pen. He was tired, worried and found it hard to concentrate. He stared at his dog, sleeping in its usual place in the corner. Why was the Englishman, to whom he had entrusted the dossier with the secrets of the Einsatzgruppen, still in France? The head of the Intelligence Bureau of the Oberkommando der Wehrmacht thought about it, but could find no good reason. The English were neither particularly stupid nor particularly deceitful. They were, however, slow, and perhaps all he was observing was that tardiness. He was still considering the Manning problem when his clerk announced a visitor. A young man, seventeen years Canaris's junior, strode into the room.

Canaris rose and held out his hand. 'My dear Reinhard, what a surprise. Come and sit down.' The voice was slight, the words spoken with the trace of a lisp.

For a moment the two men stood facing each other: the Admiral, compact, more Latin in appearance than Teuton, dressed in the dark blue of the Kriegsmarine, wearing on his cuff four gilt rings; Heydrich, tall, handsome, blond-haired, wearing the black uniform of an SS Obergruppenführer. Then Heydrich's blue eyes closed slightly and a flicker of annoyance crossed the long, classical face. The visitor glanced at the same leather chair in which Simon had spent that extraordinary hour, and very deliberately remained standing.

'You asked for the release of an Englishman, Manning, from Dachau.'

Canaris sighed. The subject dismayed him, so did the prospect of a difficult meeting. But nowadays most of his meetings with Heydrich were difficult. 'I put my request through the usual channels,' he said quietly.

Heydrich, always angered by Canaris's composure, scowled. 'Manning was flown here to your office, then he crossed the border into Holland.'

Canaris nodded and waited.

'The man's an Englishman,' said Heydrich. 'That automatically makes him an enemy of the Reich.'

Canaris sat down. Heydrich, looking down at the little Admiral apparently so unconcerned behind his desk, tightened his lips. Canaris, used to the gesture and understanding it, smiled.

'Manning can be very useful to us,' he said, nodding. 'With "Case Yellow" imminent, we need all the links with England we can get. It's foolish to make the war more difficult when it's possible to attain one's objectives peacefully. Manning will get in touch with the English appeasers.'

Suddenly they were back fifteen years on the training cruiser *Berlin*. Standing, uncertain, was the young cadet, and lecturing him from behind the desk was the First Officer. It only needed Heydrich's excellent violin playing and Frau Canaris's adoration to complete the memory. But that was all before Himmler had cast his spell.

Canaris tilted his head. It was a friendly gesture. In spite of his genuine loathing for the SS and a sadness that Heydrich should have been so easily beguiled by the Death's Head, there still lingered a fondness for the young man.

'I hope that assures you, my dear Reinhard, that the Abwehr are quite capable of looking after all aspects of the Manning affair.'

'Are you saying that he is now an Abwehr agent?' asked Heydrich.

'Let's just say he is now a friend of the Abwehr and therefore, of course, of the Reich and the Führer.'

Beneath the black-peaked cap the eyes remained unresponsive, the mouth hard. Heydrich had little further need of the Admiral's friendship. The time for Canaris to go on winning was almost past. Germany had room for only one spymaster.

With each day of the war, the power of the SS grew and that of the Abwehr diminished. Very soon, the Sicherheitsdienst would be the only Intelligence service in the Reich.

Heydrich glanced quickly around the room. The tip of his tongue flicked between his lips. As he started to speak, his body shook. 'You know and I know, Admiral, that your interest in this Englishman, the reason you asked for his release from Dachau, was not so that you could make him a double agent for your Abwehr, nor that he might be a link with the English appeasers!' His voice rose towards hysteria. 'You want Manning as your liaison between England and that miserable clique of generals who are disloyal to the Führer!'

'An accusation you would find impossible to substantiate,' said Canaris, flushing.

Heydrich stood, fists clenched, swaying. Canaris pushed back his chair, stood up, wiped his hand across his forehead, and said, 'Do drop these damned silly histrionics, Reinhard, please. You are a tactician. A man in your position should be a strategist.'

Heydrich flushed. Canaris went to the door and opened it.

'You might like to know that the Führer has personally ordered me to build up our espionage network in England, in preparation for the aftermath of "Case Yellow". He believes that Manning will be the cornerstone in that build-up.'

Heydrich gave a crisp Nazi salute and strode out. Canaris waited ten minutes, then rang Generalmajor Weber and suggested that they should ride together in the Tiergarten.

It was raining hard when they met. Canaris knew it would be another difficult meeting and for a while said nothing. They rode side by side, the wet dripping from their caps, their topcoats glistening. Canaris fought off the despair which events and the weather were enveloping him in, and when they were quite alone he brought his horse close to the Generalmajor's and broke the news of Manning's delay in France and Heydrich's visit.

The Generalmajor's normally rigid Junker exterior shook. The muscles in his thin cheeks twitched. 'If the Gestapo...' he began hoarsely, when Canaris interrupted.

'The Gestapo can't do anything at the moment.'

The Generalmajor lowered his voice and asked the question which Canaris knew must come. 'And the dossier?' Canaris hesitated, then said, 'We believe Manning still has it with him.'

'It was meant to be in England days ago!' cried the General-major. 'It was to go straight to Chamberlain!'

'The Englishman and the dossier are under the protection of the British Embassy in Paris,' said Canaris equably, then added with far more confidence than he felt, 'The British are simply taking their time in checking his security.'

The Generalmajor was not at all reassured. That this Eng-lishman was privy to the conspiracy was bad enough. Already the Generalmajor greatly regretted the meeting and the hand-ing over of the dossier. To learn that Heydrich was on the scent and Manning not yet in England completed the destruction of those frayed nerves.

'It was a most dangerous and foolhardy move, Wilhelm,' he said angrily. 'You've made us all far too vulnerable.'

'You agreed to everything at the time, Herr General,' said Canaris. 'You were present at the meeting with Manning. You agreed that there was no other way of proving events in Poland.'

The Generalmajor wiped the rain from his face and said nothing.

'You also agreed that only detailed information of evident authenticity would make the British realise that for the sake of humanity they must support us against the regime. Make the eventual peace with us.'

'Perhaps you've misjudged the British,' said the General-major tetchily. 'Perhaps they don't want your information.'

Canaris shook his head. 'We've been into all that too. They declared war for Poland. All winter there have been queues in London to fight for Finland. It's the British character to tilt at windmills. But there is a contradiction, also in our favour. They yearn for peace. They'll never forget the Somme, Passchen-daele and the U-boats.' He paused for a moment, then said, 'Whichever way you look at it, it's very much in their interests to deal with us. They're not ready for this war, nor have they yet got America in.'

'Whatever you say, Wilhelm, your dossier in Europe puts us all in great peril.'

'In matters like this I trust our enemies,' said Canaris.

The Generalmajor gave Canaris a quick glance. 'If you were simply dealing with your friends in British Military Intelligence I might agree. But you're not. You're dealing with the British Government.'

The Generalmajor cantered away, his horse's hooves showering the mud behind him. After a hundred metres he drew rein and waited for Canaris to catch up. 'Anyway, it's quite the wrong time for this operation,' he said, staring into Canaris's eyes. ' "Case Yellow" is imminent. Hitler's train left Finkenkrug for his new headquarters at Meunstereifel yesterday. Göring's train left Oranienburg two days ago.'

'The advent of "Case Yellow" doesn't dissolve us, Herr General!' cried Canaris, shocked. 'Our purposes are still valid. To remove Hitler, bring peace and save Germany.'

'It's too late, Wilhelm,' said the Generalmajor. 'Events are about to overtake you. You must get one of your men in Paris to remove Manning and destroy that file. Otherwise the Gestapo, and perhaps even the British, will make us all regret it.'

'Manning will be in England in twenty-four hours,' said Canaris. 'Now we've got this far, it's criminal to turn back!'

'It's madness to go on!' said the Generalmajor, glaring at the little Admiral. 'Manning dead and that dossier destroyed. Otherwise we're finished.'

Canaris knew it was useless to continue the argument at the moment. Angrily he saluted, turned his horse's head and cantered away. When he passed a detachment of the Waffen-SS 'Liebstandarte', and the Obersturmführer at their head gave the order, 'Eyes right!', Canaris was abruptly reminded of realities. His anger faded. He felt bitter with the British for being so obtuse and dilatory, and sad with Weber for being so faint-hearted. The British he still couldn't understand. Unless they had no faith in the conspiracy. But it was so evidently in their interests to support internal opposition to Hitler, Canaris dismissed the thought as ridiculous. As for Weber, in retrospect Canaris saw that the Generalmajor's action was not wholly unexpected. The foot that Weber kept in the Hitler camp had been growing bigger each day. How his voice had risen when he had talked of 'Case Yellow'! Not only had the conspiracy been forgotten but even the threat from Heydrich. As for himself, Canaris knew he was too deep in plot and counter-plot to change course, even had he wished to.

Back in the Tirpitz Ufer, Canaris revived himself with a cup of black coffee and sat seeking for a light amidst the gloom. He could find none. In spite of all the glorious victories and the prospect of more to come, he felt no inclination to change his firm belief, uttered the day Poland was invaded, that this war could only mean the end for Germany. He badly needed the comfort and support of his bluff Oster. He rang the bell on his desk.

'Come in, Hans, sit down and shut the door.'

The artillery colonel sat and waited. Like Weber, he had much of the elegance and arrogance of the old school.

'Were we wrong to send the dossier with Manning?' asked Canaris.

'Wrong, Herr Admiral?' said Oster, puzzled. 'Are you thinking of the oath to Adolf Hitler, the Fahneneid?'

Canaris shook his head. 'That's something we each have to live with. I was thinking of our strategy. Weber has taken fright. He now calls our action in giving Manning the dossier "a most dangerous and foolhardy move".'

'Dangerous, yes, Herr Admiral,' said Oster. 'What in our business isn't dangerous? But foolhardy...' He shrugged. 'It can't be foolhardy to get rid of the Corporal.'

'Weber also now thinks the information might diminish the English desire for peace.'

'Those are the deeds of the Nazis!' cried Oster. 'The English can still make peace with *us*!'

'If they really believe in us,' said Canaris quietly.

'They showed their commitment by sending us terms via the Vatican,' said Oster hotly. 'They know we have plans, people in high places.' He paused for a moment. 'They can't dismiss us when we have generals like Beck and Halder, the chief of the Army General Staff!'

'Good old Hans, that's what I wanted to hear,' said Canaris, cheered. 'But it doesn't alter the fact that we've taken too long.'

'Mistakes, bad luck, but we'll get him,' said Oster grimly.

'"Case Yellow" is imminent.'

Oster nodded. 'The swine has left for the west,' he said, 'with Jodel and Keitel yapping at his heels.'

'Too many of the generals are now yapping at Hitler's heels,' said Canaris sadly, then added, 'But I suppose one shouldn't blame generals too much for being enticed by the prospect of more victories. Especially when they can't see further than their noses.'

'Fools, that's what they are, Herr Admiral,' said Oster bitterly.

Canaris sat looking at the papers on his desk. After a while he said, 'Have we been asked to provide any Dutch, Belgian or French military uniforms?'

Oster shook his head. 'Just the frontier police and customs officers you know about, Herr Admiral.'

'So unlike Poland, Hans, "Case Yellow" looks like being a more or less straightforward attack? No SS tricks?'

'It would seem not, Herr Admiral.'

Canaris looked up. 'It will be the eighth or tenth. I think it must now be the tenth.'

Oster smiled. 'I'm dining with the Dutch Military Attaché tonight, Herr Admiral.'

Canaris held up his hand. 'Please, Hans, I'd rather not know exactly what you say to your friends just at the moment.'

The Saxon understood and smiled. Canaris put his elbows on the desk, stared straight ahead and said, 'And what about Manning?'

'He was still in Paris this morning,' said Oster. 'No sign of him going. He walks to the British Embassy every day, is there half an hour, then spends the rest of the day at the cinemas or art galleries. We don't think he's got a passport, and he's being kept very short of money.'

'Weber wants him "removed",' said Canaris quietly.

'I don't see what we can do. We can't order the British to take their own national back to England.'

'If MI5 thought he was an Abwehr agent,' said Canaris, 'he'd be a useful man to let in the country and trail.'

Oster thought for a moment, then said, 'That could jeopardise the validity of the dossier, Herr Admiral.'

Pain filled Canaris's face. 'God knows, it's the very last thing

I want to do, **Hans. But** with "Case Yellow" upon us and the Gestapo interested, we may be forced to take that risk.'

After a while Oster nodded.

# CHAPTER 6

Cuthbertson and the First Secretary arrived just as he was about to go out for supper. He went back upstairs with them, and this time they sat in the sitting room with the view of the rooftops. Cuthbertson opened his briefcase and took out a sheet of paper which he laid on the small table.

'I think we have the solution,' he said cheerfully, turning the paper round so that Simon could read it. 'It's simply standard wording binding you, under the Official Secrets Act, not to disclose the contents of the information in your possession to any unauthorised persons. Sign that and you'll be in England within twenty-four hours.'

Simon glanced at the paper with its Cabinet Office heading.

'Purely routine,' said Cuthbertson. 'Nothing more.'

'I don't see how this helps,' said Simon, reading the paper. 'Keeping my mouth shut doesn't have much to do with getting Canaris's file to the Prime Minister.'

'Sign that,' said Cuthbertson. 'Come back to England with me tomorrow and watch it go into the machine.'

'We have what are called "normal channels",' explained the First Secretary, and with that facetious remark the slender bonds of trust between them withered away. Simon pushed back his chair and glared.

'Ever been in Germany, Cuthbertson?'

'Before the war. 1932. Three weeks on the Rhine...'

'Ah,' said Simon with icy sarcasm, 'Rhine maidens! I wasn't quite so fortunate. For the last month all I saw were black-uniformed sadists of the SS Totenkopfverbände, the Death's

Head . . . Alsatian dogs and emaciated wrecks in striped pyjamas.'

'My dear fellow . . .' said the First Secretary, as Simon jumped to his feet.

'Nothing's grinding through your bloody "usual channels"!' he shouted. 'And I'm not signing any miserable piece of paper. In Poland the Nazis are beginning the systematic extermination of a whole race, and you don't want to bloody well know!'

Cuthbertson shook his head. 'What nonsense! We're as distressed by your information as you are. That's why we're here.'

'I'll deliver it myself,' said Simon quietly, 'as I promised. The information in that file should be shouted from the rooftops, not smuggled in like a dirty book!'

'Really, Manning,' said Cuthbertson, putting his hand on the sheet of Cabinet Office paper, 'you're making a mountain out of this, piling up no end of difficulties for yourself. This isn't anything personal, just a formality. In wartime we have to take particular precautions, as I'm sure you must understand.' He tapped the paper. 'Now be a good chap and sign.'

Simon had no idea why they should be obstructing him, or why information that could be such a valuable weapon in the hands of the Allies should appear almost an embarrassment.

'I'll hand the file to Mr Chamberlain,' he said wearily, 'then I'll sign your wretched paper.'

Cuthbertson got up and the First Secretary followed.

'Just now,' said Cuthbertson, 'you said that the news of the death pits and the Einsatzgruppen should be shouted from the rooftops. Maybe if it was, the war would be prolonged. The people you appear to be so concerned about, the Jews of Poland, would suffer even more. Have you thought about that one, Manning?'

With that they both picked up their briefcases, and as they moved towards the door Cuthbertson added: 'I'll leave you the paper. You'll soon come to your senses. You can't exist long in Paris without money and a passport, the French police wouldn't like it.'

This time Simon didn't bother to go to the window and watch them get into their car. He cut the lining of his jacket at the top, slipped the file inside and went out to supper.

Late in the evening, much to his surprise, Cuthbertson came back alone. He immediately apologized for his ill temper on leaving, and Simon was sufficiently moved to offer him a cup of coffee.

'The truth is, Manning,' said Cuthbertson, balancing his cup on his lap, 'you're in a bit of a fix. You may not realise this, but having had that chat with K you're tainted.'

Simon said nothing, just waited.

'I'm quite certain that meeting was all perfectly innocent,' said Cuthbertson, 'exactly as you told us. Nevertheless, any contact with German Intelligence inevitably puts a chap in quarantine.'

'You checked me out,' said Simon.

'Ah, but that was what we knew about you in England. Now you've seen K,' he shrugged, 'naturally it alters everything.'

'It doesn't alter the fact that I've a file for the Prime Minister.'

'No, but it means that if you were to come to England, without an escort, you might be in considerable jeopardy. After all, we still execute spies, you know.'

Cuthbertson was smiling. A halting, icy chill went through Simon. He tried to speak but his throat was dry.

'You see, old man,' said Cuthbertson, watching Simon's face, 'when I said you were in a bit of a fix, I wasn't exactly pulling your leg. K badly wants a few new agents in England. We've picked up all his old ones.'

'You know bloody well I'm not an Abwehr agent!' said Simon.

'It wouldn't be up to me or what I think,' said Cuthbertson. 'It would be up to MI, a judge and jury. And with feelings as they are ... That's the terrible thing about war, people become so irrational.'

Simon got up and started pacing the room. Cuthbertson watched without showing any emotion. Suddenly Simon stopped and said, 'You know bloody well I'm no one's agent! So what the hell's it all about?'

'I'm simply trying to help,' said Cuthbertson affably, 'by suggesting that for the time being you stay where you're relatively safe in France.'

'You could get the French to pick me up any day.'

Cuthbertson didn't answer. After a while Simon said, 'And you take the file back?'

'Of course,' said Cuthbertson. 'After all, I am an executive of HMG. Not a hostile body.'

Simon dropped into the chair and closed his eyes.

'We have a bond you may not know about,' said Cuthbertson.

Simon opened his eyes in disdainful surprise.

'After your own frightful experiences, and all you've learned of events in Poland, it's not unreasonable that you've come to hate the Nazis.'

Simon muttered his agreement.

'However, as I'm sure you'll have realised after your little chat in the Tirpitz Ufer, not all Germans are evil. Fortunately there are other, far better influences at work. You yourself were impressed with the officers' conspiracy and their desire for an honourable peace with Great Britain.'

'Where exactly is this leading?' asked Simon wearily.

'My dear Manning,' said Cuthbertson in a strange, high-pitched voice, 'you don't seem to understand. The greatest paradox of life is that the only thing worth fighting for is peace. You, of course, being something of a scientist were at the other place, but no doubt you've heard of the "King and Country" debate?'

'Bit late, isn't it, quoting that now?' said Simon.

Cuthbertson shook his head. 'Even in the depths of war one must always be on the watch for the chance of peace. After all, war never achieved anything. Sooner or later there has to be peace. In this particular conflict, things are even more clear-cut than usual. Europe is the cradle of our civilisation. K was right when he said we can't afford to let it fall further into anarchy and chaos. It's absolutely crazy that the two great Aryan countries should be tearing each other's throats out.'

Simon had never heard this Cuthbertson. He tried to see the man's face, but it was in the shadow of the lamp.

'You completely ignore Nazism,' he said.

'There's something far worse than that,' said Cuthbertson. 'Bolshevism. That's why peace is so important. The moment Britain, Germany and France have exhausted one another, the Bolsheviks will sweep into Europe destroying everything that's left, like the Goths and Vandals before them.'

'What about Hitler's pact with Stalin?'

Cuthbertson laughed. 'An expedient. Germany's anti-communist. We should be helping them to face the Reds!'

There was nothing funny anywhere, but Simon began to laugh. Cuthbertson seemed upset.

'It's nothing like as odd as you appear to think,' said Cuthbertson petulantly. 'It's simply a matter of being logical and farsighted.'

'This bond,' said Simon. 'Mine isn't peace at any price, you know. I wasn't for Munich. You stop the killings in Poland, then I might be a little more with you.'

'We can't stop the killings in Poland,' said Cuthbertson. 'That's if they're happening. Only the Germans themselves can do that. And for them to act in that way they mustn't feel threatened.'

'And who exactly is threatening them?' asked Simon astonished.

'The countries encircling them,' said Cuthbertson blandly.

Simon got up and started pacing the room again. 'Do you want me to stay here in France because if I go back to England I'll be accused of being an Abwehr agent, or because it appears to suit your purposes to keep events in Poland away from those who would presumably know how to use the information?'

'For everyone's sake,' said Cuthbertson, 'including the Polish Jews.'

He got up, picked up his briefcase and went to the door. 'Think about peace, Manning, and everything will make sense. And don't go too far away.'

'You forget,' said Simon, 'I haven't a passport.'

Cuthbertson thought about that for a moment, nodded, and let himself out.


'Case Yellow' started in the early hours of 10 May. Over Holland there was no thunder of guns, and at first not even the crackle of small arms, just the drone of low-flying aircraft. In the early dawn, people in the Hague looked up and pointed. Formations of Ju52s, dark grey against the sky, appeared over the rooftops. They passed slowly across the arc of the streets, and just before they disappeared beyond the further houses the

32

first 'roses of death' spewed out. In a few minutes the distant skyline was dotted with slowly descending petals. It was a rare and beautiful sight, but for those standing, staring at a battalion of Fallschirmjäger jumping upon the three airfields that surrounded their city, the novelty of the occasion was lost. That they were witnessing the first mass airborne attack in the history of warfare was academic. Their only emotions were bewilderment, anger and fear.

In Belgium, paratroops and gliders fell out of the same darkness and with the same silence upon the fortress of Eben-Emael guarding the crossing of the Albert Canal. For those living near the frontiers between Luxembourg and the sea, it was the roar of the Luftwaffe, the crack of the guns of the assault troops, and the rumble of the ten panzer divisions that drowned the dawn chorus. For Simon Manning, it was the shouts in the streets below his window, the banging of doors and the wireless.

The First Secretary was busy but not particularly worried. The most difficult task was getting reliable information. So far as he could make out, the BEF, the French 7th, 1st and 9th Armies had, as agreed, instantly put Gamelin's Plan D into operation. Even now they were moving out of their prepared positions along the French frontier and into Belgium. By tonight there should be the first shock of arms.

He greeted Simon by raising a hand. Simon stood clasping the front of the desk. 'The Germans won't invade Holland! They have given their diplomatic word. And they're unlikely to incense world opinion a second time by invading Belgium!'

'All right,' conceded the First Secretary, 'you look like being right about Belgium and Holland, but you don't think the Allies haven't full contingency plans for just such an event, do you?'

'I dare say there were contingency plans for Norway and Denmark. They didn't do much good.'

'My dear fellow,' said the First Secretary, aghast, 'I've told you before, Norway and Denmark are in no way comparable with Belgium, Holland and France. There's not only the BEF, but the whole French Army.'

Simon was not reassured. The phone rang. The First Secretary picked it up. When he put it down, Simon said, 'What about me?'

The First Secretary looked vague.

'I presume this makes all the difference?'

'Difference?' said the First Secretary, puzzled.

'The war starting in earnest. There's no point keeping me immobilised here any more.'

'Cuthbertson's coming back ...'

Simon shook his head and held out his hand.

'Passport and ticket. That's all I want.' When the First Secretary remained motionless, Simon called out, 'For God's sake, man, with all this on, your people in London have forgotten that I even exist!'

'Cuthbertson won't forget,' said the First Secretary. 'Never! And I'm still responsible for you.'

The phone rang again. The First Secretary picked it up, put a hand over the mouthpiece and opened his drawer. He took out a bundle of francs, held them out to Simon and said, 'Come back tomorrow. It should be a lot quieter.' Then he waved Simon out and spoke into the phone.

Simon bought a newspaper, tramped back to the flat and listened to the wireless. But for Holland it looked as if the Germans were getting a bloody nose. He was frustrated and angry, yet at the same time cheered that the war had at last started. When he heard that the British Government had fallen and that Churchill had taken over, he felt the first real optimism since he had run in out of the rain.

# CHAPTER 7

Cuthbertson was as surprised by the Minister's demeanour as the Minister was surprised and shocked by Cuthbertson's. To the Minister, it was as if Cuthbertson hadn't heard of the invasion of France and the Low Countries, the fall of Chamberlain and the ascent of Churchill. To Cuthbertson, the Minister seemed to be trimming his sails prematurely.

'Our friend Manning, Minister,' said Cuthbertson, bringing the Minister back to his subject. 'He's remaining most awkward. Refusing to cooperate in any way.'

'He's still in Paris . . . ?' asked the Minister vaguely.

'If you remember, Minister, you agreed that we should keep him there for the time being. You also agreed that I should go over and see him. Try to persuade him to see reason.'

The Minister shook his head. 'That wretched file . . .'

'He has no passport. Very little money. He's extremely vulnerable. We could set something up there.' Seeing the look on the Minister's face, Cuthbertson added, 'I'm not thinking of anything violent, Minister. Perhaps just tipping off the gendarmes?'

The Minister shook his head again. 'It could backfire. Get us in even deeper.' He paused for a moment, then said, 'I don't think you quite understand, Cuthbertson, things are changing fast. With Winston at the helm . . .'

'Are you suggesting, Minister,' said Cuthbertson, with unconcealed disdain, 'that we abandon our brief? That we allow Manning to come to England?'

The Minister took a long time to answer. He stared at his blotter, then across at Cuthbertson. This, of course, was where he and Cuthbertson were so different. Cuthbertson, with his damned idealism, had no idea what common sense meant.

'There could be difficulties either way,' said the Minister cautiously. 'But with this attack on the Western Front, Winston in Number 10 . . .'

The Minister, Cuthbertson decided, was a spent force. He had lost his way. Tomorrow he would lose his Ministry.

'You have kept Manning out of the country kicking his heels in Paris a fortnight, Minister,' said Cuthbertson. 'That's going to take quite a bit of explaining.'

The Minister saw the point and it added to his anxieties.

'Nevertheless . . .' he began, when Cuthbertson interrupted.

'From now on, Minister, everyone will be concentrating on the fighting. A lot of issues that have worried the country in the past will now be relegated if not actually forgotten.'

'You're thinking of the plight of the Jews, Cuthbertson?' said the Minister, slightly accusingly.

Cuthbertson nodded. 'Manning's information is still an embarrassment to those of our persuasion, his detention in Paris still something to be explained, but his asset and nuisance values to the new Government will be considerably less than they would have been to the old.'

'In that case,' said the Minister, 'perhaps he should come over. Give everything a good airing.'

'I meant, Minister,' said Cuthbertson, 'that he may soon become irrelevant to everyone but us.'

The Minister said nothing.

'May I ask,' said Cuthbertson, with unusual forthrightness, 'whether you've given up all hope of a negotiated peace with Germany?'

The Minister thought for a long time. At last he said, 'I have a feeling that with Winston in Number 10 the subject will never again be discussed. Personal feelings will have to be subjugated to the total war effort.' Suddenly he got up, went to the window and said, 'Let's see what the battle of France brings. It might be better to keep Manning in Paris just a few more days and discuss the whole thing again when the dust has settled.'

Cuthbertson said, 'Yes, Minister,' and went out.

They were sitting in Sinclair's flat, Cuthbertson drinking, Sinclair trying to be temperate.

'One hell of a week, Ross,' said Cuthbertson, leaning right back in the chair, his feet on the table. The glass that hadn't left his hand all evening was now at a precarious angle. 'The Tories turning on their leader, Keyes all dressed up like a commissionaire blasting the War Cabinet, Amery putting the finger on Chamberlain and echoing Cromwell's words to the Rump. Then in a matter of hours, Chamberlain going and Churchill walking into Number 10.' He turned his head and looked at the younger man. 'Where does that leave us, eh? And the Minister on the slippery slope and knowing it.'

'Rumour has it,' said Sinclair, 'that he's staying in the Cabinet. It looks as if Winston isn't making the clean sweep everyone expected.'

'If he doesn't today he will tomorrow,' said Cuthbertson curtly.

There was a long pause. Cuthbertson filled his glass.

'How's your man in Paris?' asked Sinclair after a while.

Cuthbertson dropped his feet to the carpet and struggled into a standing position. He held on to a chair for support and glared down at Sinclair. 'To put it mildly, a bloody nuisance. I wish the bugger was dead.'

Sinclair tilted his head and said, 'Tut-tut.'

'Don't think I don't like him,' said Cuthbertson. 'In fact there's something very endearing about him. He believes in his cause, that's endearing, but he's so damned naïve. Anyone who thinks they can defy their own government is either stupid or mad.' He lowered his voice. 'If we had any sense we'd just send someone over there, bump the blighter off and take his blasted file and burn it!'

Sinclair shook his head. 'We don't do things that way.'

'Why do we bloody English always believe we invented fair play,' said Cuthbertson angrily. 'We've done things all over the world that are no better than the Nazis are supposed to be doing in Poland. Go to Africa, India, Ireland where they know us. They'll tell you how dirty our hands are!'

'Manning's an individual, we don't do the dirty on individuals, only groups,' said Sinclair.

'We lack trained government assassins!' said Cuthbertson, collapsing back into the chair and thrusting his feet up on to the table again. 'That's our trouble. We've got them in battalions, brigades and divisions, but not where they'd be most useful, as individuals.' He paused for a moment, then said, 'And the bloody Minister doesn't help. As far as peace is concerned, he's forgotten the meaning of the word.'

'Let Manning come over,' said Sinclair. 'He can't do any harm now the war's got going properly. And without support from the top, you can't keep him in France for ever. You might as well accept the situation.'

'It may sound funny to you,' said Cuthbertson bitterly, 'and to most others now, but I still believe in peace. And if that information of Manning's gets out, it will put the kibosh on peace for years.'

'So what are you going to do?'

Cuthbertson filled his glass, shut his eyes and said, 'Have one more go. Rebuild his confidence. Restore his faith in us. Get him back where he belongs, on our side.'

'You're mad,' said Sinclair.

Cuthbertson opened his eyes, and stared at Sinclair as if he had just seen a vision. 'Don't you understand, Ross, at heart he is one of us. All I have to do is hold up a mirror. Show him himself!'

Simon had bought the inevitable newspaper. He was reading it as he went up the stairs. In the hallway there were an unusual number of muddy footmarks. As he put his key in the lock, he knew exactly what he was going to find. He was right. The sight of the ransacked rooms sickened him. In the bedroom, the intruders had been busy. His few clothes lay on the floor, the bed had been taken apart, and the suitcase lay upon the jumble of blankets and sheets, its lid ripped open.

He poured himself a drink and began tidying. The doorbell rang. It was Cuthbertson. Simon let him in. Cuthbertson seemed surprised at the mess.

'Was it the French police you sent or some other set of thugs?' asked Simon, with cold, accusing anger.

Cuthbertson found a glass, indicated the bottle and said, 'May I?' Simon nodded. Cuthbertson sipped his drink, knelt and began putting books back in the bookcase.

'Are you trying to say this was nothing to do with you?' asked Simon.

'I hope our methods aren't as crude as this,' said Cuthbertson, still on his knees. 'However, with things as they are, if the gendarmes did raid you, you can't blame them.'

'Don't they know the flat belongs to their Allies?'

Cuthbertson said nothing. Suddenly Simon unbuttoned his jacket and took the Abwehr file from the lining. He laid it on the couch by Cuthbertson's face. Cuthbertson looked at the file, then up at Simon.

'Does that mean you're giving in, old man?' he asked, smiling.

'No, just that I'd like to air the matter.'

Cuthbertson got up and looked at the room. It still might have suffered an earthquake.

'The responsibility of keeping it is too great, is that it?'

'I've pretty well memorised the facts,' said Simon, 'even though they're in German. One thing my second-rate public school did for us, made us learn reams of Macaulay and Tennyson by heart. Amazing how that helps with SS statistics.'

'I never expected you to throw in the towel like this,' said Cuthbertson, refilling his glass. 'Just because the gendarmes, or the Deuxième Bureau, or the Gestapo, or maybe your own Abwehr friends pay you a visit.'

'There's been a change of government in England,' said Simon. 'Churchill's now Prime Minister.'

'Ah,' said Cuthbertson, 'and you think that may have changed our approach, is that it?'

'Churchill's no appeaser.'

Cuthbertson indicated the chair and the couch, picked a cushion off the floor and said, 'If we are to have this airing, do let's sit like civilised beings.' They sat. 'You'd be surprised, Manning,' said Cuthbertson, the glass in his hand, his legs crossed, the toes of his well-polished black shoes pointing towards Simon, 'how little things change in the warrens of Whitehall, even when the big white chiefs change. We may put a brief in the filing cabinet for a while, but we never forget it. It's our training, you know. Our upbringing. Briefs are very important. The oxygen of government. They represent time, money, thought, discussion and ultimately power. They are never discarded.'

'The Dutch have asked for an armistice,' said Simon, 'and the Germans seem to be doing pretty well between the Meuse and Sedan.'

Cuthbertson scratched his chin. 'Ah, so now you think that events will change our approach?'

'Why have you come back?' asked Simon after a while.

Cuthbertson looked surprised. 'Because you're in my charge, my responsibility. I can't just leave you to rot in Paris.' After a moment he added, 'Anyway, I have a new brief that should get us out of this quite ridiculous impasse.'

Simon waited.

Cuthbertson indicated the flat. 'After this intrusion, it's quite evident that you can't keep that file. Oh, you can carry it about with you, hide it in your jacket, but anyone can follow you, knock you on the head and take it. You can leave it in the Gare du Nord left luggage, buy a tin box and bury it in the Bois de Boulogne, but none of that will help in the end. You see, the

Germans will be here within three weeks, and you'll have to get out.'

Simon sat upright. 'The Germans in Paris within three weeks!'

Cuthbertson nodded. 'Things are far worse than the communiqués lead you to believe. The Germans have done something neither side achieved in the last war. They've broken through. In a few days they'll have cut the Allies in two. In a fortnight the British'll have no soldiers and no equipment. The French, the relics of an army without morale or weapons. It'll be the end of the war on land. With Churchill at Number 10, we shall hang on and fight from our little island, all quite uselessly. Eventually the U-boats will starve us out if the Luftwaffe hasn't obliterated us.'

'Christ!' said Simon, quite forgetting his situation and getting up. 'I must get back to England and join up!'

Cuthbertson laughed. 'A stupid waste. There's enough cannon fodder over there already. Besides, I warned you what might happen if you did come back.' He paused for a moment, then added, 'We would also be most concerned to whom you spoke and what you said.'

Simon remained silent. Cuthbertson refilled his glass.

'Events are pointing only one way. We touched on it the other evening. The peace offensive. With the disasters of the battlefronts, the peace offensive is becoming more vital each day.' Cuthbertson looked into Simon's eyes. 'We, that is HMG, want you in Europe as a link between the Generals' conspiracy in Germany and the British Government.'

Simon stared in astonishment. 'I can't do anything.'

'You've done a great deal already. You've brought a very important file out of Germany. All we want you to do is carry on where you left off. You know K. He evidently trusts you. You've also met the Generalmajor. You're *persona grata*, that's important.'

'I'm not getting mixed up in this any more,' said Simon vehemently. 'I've had enough.'

'You can't get out, old man,' said Cuthbertson quietly. 'You're in it up to your neck. K baptised you when he took you to his office.' He saw the look on Simon's face and added, 'It's like a family, it envelopes you. Once you're in, it doesn't matter on which side, you never get out.'

'It's not my way,' said Simon.

'You speak French and German. You'll stay here till things get too hot, then live in Switzerland. Rather nice.'

Simon paced the room and Cuthbertson watched him.

'You haven't any choice, old man. You've got to get in someone's good books to survive. You might as well make it ours.'

'I thought I was an Abwehr agent?' said Simon sarcastically.

'Fate has given you a role,' said Cuthbertson, ignoring the remark, 'a much more important role than tramping the barrack squares of Aldershot as a second lieutenant and ending up in a POW camp.'

Simon said nothing, just stood staring into space. Cuthbertson got up, put his hand out and touched Simon on the sleeve.

'Think about it. Sleep on it. You'll find it very logical and farsighted. You have a real part to play in this conflict.' He opened his case and took out a revolver and a small cardboard box. He put both on the couch. 'You may feel better with this. I'm afraid it's not as good as the German Luger, but if you're found with it, it won't be an embarrassment. It's standard British Army issue and can make a horrid mess of anyone if they're near enough.' He indicated the box. 'Fifteen rounds should be enough.'

Simon picked up the revolver. It was a Smith and Wesson .38. He stared at Cuthbertson and began to laugh. Cuthbertson didn't see the joke.

'Peace! Brotherhood! That's what you've been preaching!'

'It's for you, not me,' said Cuthbertson. 'I'm in no danger.'

Cuthbertson moved towards the door. 'Count me out,' said Simon, and offered the revolver. Cuthbertson didn't give the weapon a glance but said, 'Sleep on it.'

'I'm not a man of action,' said Simon, and Cuthbertson stopped.

'You think being an academic stops you from being anything else?' he asked. 'You think brains are a hindrance?'

Simon remembered the file on the couch.

'Redundant,' said Cuthbertson, 'overtaken by events. But if you still want it to get to the PM, why not put a little faith in someone for a change, and trust our despised "usual channels"?'

Simon hesitated.

'You'll be far safer without it,' said Cuthbertson, 'but you can let me know in the morning. There's no hurry.'

From the window, Simon watched Cuthbertson get into the embassy Hillman and drive away. Then he put the file back in the lining of his jacket, the revolver in his pocket and went down to the concierge. She had seen no stranger all day.

He slept fully dressed, the file and revolver under his pillow. He awoke in the night after a bizarre dream, got up, put on the light and stared at himself in the mirror. His hair had grown and he now looked like a mad golliwog rather than a starved beanpole. He got back into bed and tried to remember the sequence of barrows around Stonehenge, and the numbering of the sarsens and bluestones. He slept for an hour after dawn, got up, shaved, had breakfast and went back to the embassy.

The First Secretary received him with warmth. It was evident that Cuthbertson had already paved the way for this visit. The moment he had been ushered into the chair he was given an envelope containing 20,000 francs.

'How long's this meant to last?' asked Simon innocently.

'We just want you to be comfortable,' said the First Secretary. 'Enjoy life.'

'While I have the chance?'

The First Secretary looked puzzled.

'In case you haven't read the papers or listened to the wireless, the Germans seem to be on the move pretty damned fast!'

'My dear fellow,' said the First Secretary, 'do you remember your OTC days and the danger of being enfiladed in a salient? The thing that every commander does his best to avoid? That's what the Hun's got himself into — a long, thin, excessively vulnerable salient.'

'You sound as if we've let them through deliberately?'

'I'm not actually saying that,' said the First Secretary, 'but I wouldn't want to be in the Huns' shoes, I can tell you. Not when the BEF and the French start counter-attacking from the north, and the French from the south. Then it'll be the Huns' turn to be cut off.'

Simon stared at the First Secretary. Obviously he wasn't Cuthbertson's complete confidant. He was getting up to go when the First Secretary opened the drawer of his desk, and handed Simon his American passport.

'You must have papers,' said the First Secretary with perfect seriousness. 'You can't go on existing here without. Not with things the way they are.'

'What about my own passport?' asked Simon.

The First Secretary indicated the one now in Simon's hands. 'Cuthbertson said a neutral one would be more useful for the moment.'

'Does Cuthbertson run everything?' asked Simon sarcastically.

'One other thing,' said the First Secretary, ignoring the question. 'Letters to your mother. They're not getting through. You really ought not to waste the time and energy writing them.'

From the door Simon said, 'Bonfires in the Quai d'Orsay. The French are burning papers. Have you started yet?'

The First Secretary shook his head. 'If ever we do, I'll get you to help.'

# CHAPTER 8

Canaris came back from OKW headquarters in the Bendler-strasse and went straight into Oster's office. The Colonel was standing, staring at the wall map. One group of flags encompassed Dunkirk, another stood along the line of the Somme. Oster offered his chief a chair. Canaris sat and stared up at the map.

'Makes one quite schizophrenic,' said Oster, indicating the flags. 'You warn the British and French of "Case Yellow", you try your hardest to get rid of the Corporal, then you see your own panzers racing through the old Western Front battlefields, you read Guderian's report and feel proud. You can't help it, Herr Admiral, it's there in the breast however hard you try.'

'It's not surprising, Hans,' said Canaris, smiling. 'After all, we are Germans.'

'You feel it, Herr Admiral.'

It wasn't a question. After a while Canaris said, 'In the Bendlerstrasse they're almost dancing in the offices. It is quite infectious.'

'Good for Hitler,' said Oster quietly.

Canaris nodded. 'The only breath of criticism is for his order to hold back the panzers on the line of the Aa. A few weeks ago they were calling him mad for starting, now they're calling him mad for stopping.'

'Do you think he deliberately halted XIX Army Corps to give the British a chance? Save them from complete humiliation?'

Canaris shook his head and laughed. 'He got cold feet, that's all. He was frightened of a counter-attack. Thought his luck might run out. Besides, he could smell the salt sea air. That would put him off his strategy. Hitler knows nothing of the sea.'

'That's all very well,' said Oster, sitting down behind his desk, 'but if the British do get their army back, and the French ask for an armistice, where does that put us?'

'This side of a no man's land called the Channel,' said Canaris lightly.

'It could be crossed. A plan exists. The Kriegsmarine drew it up six months ago.'

'Roosevelt won't let England fall,' said Canaris with considerable assurance.

'You sound almost optimistic, Herr Admiral.'

'Churchill's main strategic effort now will be to get America in the war. He's a friend of Roosevelt. In the meantime he'll hold on in England, and with their command of the sea there'll be stalemate.' Canaris paused for a moment, then said, 'We've got to remind the British that in spite of the victories, we still exist. Hitler will be removed.'

'Colonelgeneral Halder seems to have left us,' said Oster gloomily.

'Others will join,' said Canaris, 'particularly when events in the east get known. The Wehrmacht won't stand for what the SS are doing. And the stalemate will help us. Hitler only

44

thrives while the army's going forward.'

For a while they were silent, then Oster said, 'Perhaps you're being a little too sanguine, Herr Admiral. Churchill for Chamberlain could have more effect on British attitudes than we bargained for.'

Canaris shook his head. 'He'll stiffen their morale, make them hold out against Hitler. But we mustn't be put off by Churchill. He's anti-Nazi, not anti-German. He's also a great romantic. He'll want to save the Poles and Jews. He still sees himself the chivalrous knight in shining armour, and particularly where Europe is concerned.'

'You're assuming the British Government have received the information,' said Oster quietly.

'They must have.'

'We don't know for certain.'

'A man comes over from London three times to see Manning. Manning goes to the embassy every day.' Canaris shook his head. 'They must know the information, even if Manning still has the dossier.' He paused, then said, 'Generalmajor Weber wanted a firm assurance that the Englishman, and the dossier if he still has it, cannot possibly fall into the hands of our own advancing Wehrmacht. I have just given him that assurance.'

Oster nodded and picked up the phone.

Sinclair was at his desk when the phone rang and a man who said he was from Military Intelligence asked if they had anyone connected with the FO called Manning. Sinclair said, No, not so far as he knew, when suddenly he remembered.

'Manning ... Simon Manning?'

'That's him,' said the voice at the other end. 'What do you know of the blighter?'

'Very little. He was in Paris a couple of weeks ago. We had some correspondence.'

'Ever met him?'

'Never.'

'Know anyone who has?'

There was a long pause, then Sinclair said, 'Manning has nothing to do with the FO.'

The voice asked whether Sinclair was free for the next

half-hour. When Sinclair said he was, the voice said he was on the way.

The man, stocky, with a small moustache and carrying a green pork-pie hat in his hand, introduced himself as Hill. He wasted no time.

'This fellow Manning. You've had correspondence with him but he's nothing to do with you, is that it?'

Sinclair said it was, and asked what it was all about.

'Oh, just routine,' said Hill vaguely, 'quite routine. What was the correspondence about?'

Sinclair thought for a while, then said, 'Not sure I remember.'

Hill took out his pipe and sucked it.

'Phone me in half an hour,' he said, giving an extension number, 'when you've had a chance to chat with someone.'

He got up, and brushed the seat of the chair as if his trousers had soiled it. Sinclair opened the door. Hill left with a faint smile that Sinclair didn't really like.

The moment he was alone, Sinclair rang Cuthbertson. They met in the park. Sinclair was very agitated.

'Steady, Ross, steady,' said Cuthbertson, 'it can't be all that bad.'

'MI are on to your chap Manning.'

Cuthbertson whistled. Sinclair reported his meeting with Hill.

'What did you tell this man?' asked Cuthbertson.

'Just that we had some correspondence with Manning.'

Cuthbertson stared at Sinclair. 'Why tell him anything? Why say you've ever heard of the wretched man? Manning's nothing to do with the FO.'

'This chap took me by surprise. Asked if we had anyone of that name. I remembered that report.'

Cuthbertson's stare changed to compassion. 'It's nasty, but it's not the end. It'll sort itself out.'

'I've got to ring back.'

They walked on, Cuthbertson scratching his ear as he thought. At last he said, 'Tell him that this fellow called in at the embassy, left a note on something or other. You must have some bumf in the files you could dish up. After that you've no idea where he went.'

'That won't wash, he's bound to make inquiries.'

'There's a war on over there,' said Cuthbertson. 'Things are getting rough. MI have their hands full. They can't do anything. They'll lose their agents and France won't exist in a fortnight.'

Sinclair looked doubtful.

'It's all you can do,' said Cuthbertson. 'That, and pray.'

Not even the weather could brighten the last days of May for Simon Manning. His inactivity was debilitating. Avidly he listened to the worsening news and felt guilty he was not part of events. He cursed Cuthbertson and Canaris, fretted and bought every newspaper.

Only a day or two ago, the names had been those of Flanders fields. A drum-roll Simon had grown up with and been told would never be forgotten. Lille, Ypres, Menin and Armentières. Now the names were much closer. Amiens, Abbeville and the Somme. At night he switched from counting archaeological sheep to his father's old sepia photos in the cake tin. He saw endless belts of barbed wire, tanks like lozenges floundering in the mud, solid-tyred London buses with their sides boarded up, dugouts, puttees, splintered trees and duckboards. In the language of his childhood there had been no horror. Just a play to be listened to and wondered at. Now it was all very real and very close.

He hurried to the embassy. The restaurants and cafés were as full as ever. The rich, beautiful and elegant still abounded. There were generals and staff officers looking worried but important, but there were almost no private soldiers. Every poilu had been raced to the disintegrating fronts between the sea and Switzerland. It was different for the British. They were trying to get back to England. Running away, the French said. Simon was conscious of the smears. He was conscious too that Cuthbertson was right. Soon we wouldn't have an army, soon Paris must fall. The exodus had already begun. In spite of the surface normality, the feeling of impending doom was everywhere.

Outside the embassy, a tubby little man was struggling with a bulging Revelation suitcase, while trying to keep a thin summer overcoat draped over his shoulder.

'Nothing going from the Gare du Nord,' said the man, staring at Simon with eyes that blinked behind thick lenses and thin frames, and beneath a forehead glistening with sweat.

'You're an optimist,' said Simon. 'The lines have been cut for days.'

'They said try the Gare St Lazare,' said the man, indicating the embassy, 'for Havre or Cherbourg, or Montparnasse for one of the Brittany ports.'

The man looked so helpless and harassed that Simon changed his direction. He put his fingers through the straps of the case and walked beside the man. Soon he had the whole weight. As they crossed the Boulevard Haussmann, the man seemed to be in less of a hurry and offered Simon a drink. They sat in the sunshine, the suitcase between them. The man said his name was Hopkins. He lived in Birmingham and represented a firm of pump manufacturers, amongst whose clients were the French Ministry of Defence. Indeed, Hopkins' pumps kept the Maginot Line dry. Simon was unable to be so forthcoming, but he too was in Paris on business, he too would like to get back to England.

'With luck,' said Hopkins, mopping his brow with an already sodden handkerchief, 'in twenty-four hours I should be seeing the white cliffs.'

'Not from Cherbourg you won't!' said Simon.

Hopkins gave a feeble, self-conscious laugh. 'What about you?' he asked, levelling his glasses and digging them into the right part of his nose.

'There are difficulties,' said Simon, and left it at that.

'You can't stay here!' said Hopkins.

Simon said nothing. He was about to ask the man to take a message to his mother when Hopkins got up and said he must find a lavatory. Simon jerked his thumb towards the interior of the café. Hopkins said, 'Keep an eye on the case for me, old chap, will you?' Then, indicating the chair he was vacating, he added, 'There's a paper there if you want to see it.' With that he struggled through the packed tables and into the café.

Simon picked up the paper. On the wicker seat was a British passport. It was old, worn and shiny. The gold printing and crest had toned to a pale greenish-grey. But it was the top insert that caught his eye and froze him. The blue ink had faded but it was still perfectly legible. 'Mr S.I. Manning' stared up at him. He picked up the passport and opened it. The photo was his, the details were his, there were visas and immigration stamps much as he remembered them, but it was not his passport. There was no entry for Germany in April '39, but there was one for France via Calais in April '40. There was also an identity card, a wad of dollars and a railway ticket.

He stared at the door of the café. There was no sign of Hopkins. He put the passport into his inner pocket, and a handful of coins in the saucer. He gave Hopkins another three minutes to reappear but knew he wouldn't. Hopkins' work was done.

The garçon collected the money, and Simon picked up the newspaper and moved slowly away. He had just started to quicken his pace when the garçon called out that he had left his case. He turned, and the expanded suitcase was pushed towards him. He put out a hand, yanked up the case and staggered with it down the boulevard. He took the first street to the left, put the case down and tried the catches. It was unlocked. Inside were tightly-tied bundles of old newspaper and a hastily scrawled note apologising for the weight but wishing him good luck. He shut the case, left it close to the wall, and went back to his flat and packed his own meagre possessions.

A train was due out at six, and already the platform was crowded. The train arrived at seven and instantly filled. Simon eventually managed to get a place in the corridor. Most of those travelling were civilian, British and French, but there were a few soldiers. There were rumours and speculation. This would be the last train out; the crews had refused to take any more; in the morning they would be dive-bombed; the Germans were already roaming the Normandy countryside as far as Rouen in captured French and British uniforms, blowing bridges and derailing trains.

They left at eight-thirty, and travelled all night, stopping it seemed every few miles. As the hours wore on, bottles intended for England were opened. In the end, a journey that should have taken five hours took nearly fifteen. At the Gare Maritime they gave the blue-smocked engine crew their remaining francs, then made for the barriers.

The docks at Cherbourg presented an extraordinary sight. Just landed were rows of new lorries, 25-pounder field guns and cruiser tanks, some without guns. Other rows of dusty lorries and their weary occupants were awaiting embarkation. At the same time as bringing new fighting troops over to add a token force to the crumbling French, the British were evacuating the thousands that had been strewn across Brittany and Normandy on the lines of communication.

Simon had the Abwehr file in the case he had bought to replace the old one ripped apart. He had taken the calculated risk that in the chaos of evacuation no one would search him. That if they did he could explain. Military and civilians were separated. The military line moved quickly. A scan of their paybooks and they were through, moving towards the destroyer with steam up. The civilians moved more slowly. The French authorities ignored them; the British didn't. They looked at his passport and asked for his identity card. They noticed his Calais entry date and asked his business. He gave the story he had prepared. An archaeological exchange. He was asked to wait in the corner of the hut with three others. He was questioned by two civilians and repeated his story. They checked him against a list. One of the civilians said, 'You came over on 21 April?'

Simon nodded.

'How?'

'On the cross-Channel packet.'

The man slowly shook his head. 'Think again.'

Simon felt numb but managed to look puzzled. 'I'm afraid I don't understand.'

'It was too foggy,' said the man with a smile. 'Only one leave-boat ran that day. There was no packet, not on the 21st.'

Simon swore. So much for Abwehr efficiency. If it *was* the Abwehr.

They marched him to another hut, where the window was whitewashed and day-and-night illumination was provided by a single electric bulb hanging from the cobwebs of the ceiling. They searched him and found the revolver, the American passport and dollars, and the file. They sat him on a hard chair and left him alone with two Military Police. Tall and ominous-looking, their revolver lanyards prominently displayed, the two MPs stared implacably ahead. He asked a few questions but got no answers, and decided it was part of the softening-up process.

After an hour the civilian who had first asked the questions returned with a major. They invited him to make a statement, pointing out that a complete confession would save everyone a great deal of trouble, as they already had enough evidence to shoot him ten times over. Deciding that life was more important than home, Simon told them to ring a certain Mr Cuthbertson at the Cabinet Office. This was obviously a most unusual request, and it upset them. He was taken out while they discussed the matter.

They brought him back, said they couldn't get through, and told him to start his statement. He told them to try the British Embassy in Paris. This time they went out and left him with the MPs. For the first time in his life, Simon prayed for the health and well-being of a First Secretary. After an hour, during which he was given a mug of tea and a sandwich, the civilian stuck his head round the door.

'There's a car waiting outside. You'd better get going. So far as we're concerned, you've never been here.'

They gave him back his possessions, and an MP took him out to an old Citroën.

'We don't have the proper trials over here, sir,' said the MP as he opened the car door. 'There isn't the time. If they aren't satisfied they rustle up a firing squad and march you out to the warehouse. You've been lucky, sir, firing squads here are mostly C3 men, not very good marksmen. Not like at home. Have a good journey, sir.'

The MP saluted. Simon raised his hand in reply, then sank back in the old leather seat and shut his eyes.

# CHAPTER 9

The First Secretary jumped up from a crowded desk and held out his hand.

'My dear fellow, how nice to see you back.' He looked at Simon as a tailor might inspect the fit of a new suit. 'You look damned tired. I imagine it was a hell of a journey. Mind you, you were lucky to even get to Cherbourg with the Hun strafing the trains.'

Simon dropped into the chair. 'I suppose I owe you my thanks. British Military Police don't make the best company.'

The First Secretary went back to his desk. 'There's no question of thanks, we're all in this together. Your real bit of luck was that the telephone was still working and I happened to know the fellow who took you in. They gave you back your things, I hope? Everything intact?'

Simon nodded.

'I'd love to see that passport,' said the First Secretary, actually getting up and walking round to save Simon the effort. Simon handed the passport over. The First Secretary took it to the desk lamp and examined it.

'Damned clever piece of work,' he said at last. 'Wish we did them as well.'

'But not clever enough,' said Simon.

'Oh, don't blame the passport,' said the First Secretary. 'You were caught by an old trick, that's all.' He turned to the Calais entry stamp and held the passport up for Simon to see. 'Is this the one?'

Simon nodded.

'Fog, did they say?'

'Yes.'

The First Secretary smiled. 'They didn't know anything about the weather on the 21st. We're not that efficient, you know. They took a chance on it to ruffle you, and you fell.'

Simon closed his eyes and put his head into his hands.

'Cuthbertson was very upset when he heard,' said the First

Secretary. 'But there again we were lucky. I managed to get a telephone line to Whitehall. Imagine how long it would have taken if we'd had to put it all in cipher. As it was, he was able to hush everything up. So the fact that you had been picked up at Cherbourg with a forged passport supplied by the Abwehr never got through to Military Intelligence in London.'

Simon looked up. 'It might have been better if it had. It was a damned close thing!'

The First Secretary shook his head. 'It would have been horrid for you, old chap, if London had found out. I'm sure Cuthbertson told you of the difficulties. MI get this bee in their bonnet that everyone's a spy. They'd have shipped you back to the UK just for the hell of it. Being a civilian it would have been Wandsworth or Pentonville and the jolly old rope. No beefy guardsmen lined up with rifles in the Tower for you.' He stopped, made a grimace and added, 'All terribly barbaric!'

'Things were nasty at Cherbourg,' repeated Simon. 'It was bloody close.'

The First Secretary shook his head.

'Not as close as all that. Not as close as it would have been in London.' He paused for a moment then said, 'Although with a revolver in your pocket, German documents in your baggage, a second passport — American — in your jacket and a fistful of dollars, they must have thought you pretty fishy.'

'They did,' said Simon dryly. 'Very fishy.'

The First Secretary glanced at his watch. 'As long as you now realise, old man, that you're safest staying close to me?'

Simon shrugged.

'In that case,' said the First Secretary, 'let's go out and have a drink.'

As they walked down the steps of the embassy, the First Secretary took Simon's arm and said, 'Keep this under your hat, old chap, but there's talk of the French Government pulling out. Tours could be the next capital. You see the Hun is over the Somme and going hard. If it is to be Tours, we may have to take you with us.'

At three in the morning, Simon was woken by a furious ringing of the bell and hammering on the door. He called out and the First Secretary answered. Even at that hour the First Secretary appeared shaved and elegant. His only concession to the early hour was a pair of spats and an overcoat with a fur collar.

'As our dear friend Herrick said, "Come let us go while we are in our prime".'

Simon stood gazing stupidly at the man.

'We're going, old fellow, leaving Gay Paree behind!'

'Tours?' asked Simon, struggling to awaken.

'For the Ambassador and one or two others, yes. For you and me, no. It's simply a case of getting out of France as fast as possible. So into your clothes, *vite!*'

Simon dressed, repacked his case and they ran down the stairs to the Hillman. As they drove up the Avenue de Malakoff, Simon asked where they were going.

'I've taken things into my own hands,' said the First Secretary. 'Can't get through to London, and anyway there wouldn't be anyone there now if I could. Not at this hour. There's a destroyer leaving Havre at noon. Got some of our confidential stuff on it.' He jerked his thumb towards the rear seats. 'There's a bit more there.'

'England?' said Simon in astonishment. 'You mean I'm going to England?'

'You're not supposed to,' said the First Secretary, snuggling his chin into the fur of his collar, 'and heaven knows what Cuthbertson will say when he finds out, but what else could I do?' He turned his head. There was genuine bewilderment in his face. 'I couldn't leave you in Paris. The Ambassador wouldn't have wanted to take you to Tours. No orders from London. Can't send you to Switzerland on my own. What's a chap to do?'

Simon leaned back in his seat and laughed. The First Secretary watched him.

'I hope to God Cuthbertson'll take it like that,' he said, 'but at least you'll come over with me' — he put his hand in his left pocket — 'on your proper passport. So there shouldn't be any problems. No fear of the MI boys getting their fingers on you this time.'

'Isn't Havre a bit dicey?' asked Simon when he had his breath back. 'If the Germans are over the Somme, there's not all that far to go.'

The First Secretary shook his head. 'I checked. The 51st

54

Highlanders are falling back to cover Rouen. We'll pass through them, then the road'll be clear.'

North of Magny-en-Vexin, just after dawn, they ran into the refugees. They were trying to thread their way through half a dozen carts when an officer of the Armée de l'Air spotted the English car with the Union Jack on the bonnet and the quite evidently English driver. He shouted to them and the First Secretary braked.

'Are you going to England?' called the officer.

'Hoping to, old fellow,' said the First Secretary.

'Take me,' shouted the officer, running towards the car. 'You are going to need good pilots soon.'

The First Secretary looked the officer up and down, then indicated the back. 'Hop in.'

As the Frenchman was getting in, Simon got out. 'You're French,' he said, 'you'll be more useful in the front.' Simon got in the back, the Frenchman in front. The First Secretary let in the clutch.

Obergefreiter Walter Haak was conscious only in bouts. He had lost a lot of blood from a thigh wound. His Armoured Reconnaissance Battalion had been acting as advance guard to the 7th Panzer Division with orders to cut the main Paris-Rouen road. After the race from Germany to the sea it had looked easy enough. The French and British holding the line of the Somme were already demoralised from the earlier fighting and were in no state to resist a determined attack.

Once the tanks had punched their way out of the bridgehead, the nine armoured cars of his company had found the going easy. It was hot, the dust and the refugees were a nuisance, but other than scattered small-arms fire that pinged on the armoured plate they might have been on a Sunday drive. It was when they had come down a lane out of the trees, and were in sight of the road they had been sent to cut, that they ran into trouble. A troop of French 20mm anti-tank guns. Haak's vehicle and two others had caught fire. The remaining cars had withdrawn, leaving Haak and his gunner, Ott, the sole survivors. They had crawled into the ditch and lain there until the French had gone.

Their present resting place was a barn a hundred metres east

of the road. They were without food, had very little ammunition and no contact with the rest of the company. They had
managed to get the MG34 out of the burning car, and this now
rested on the straw-baled parapet. Haak was lying on his back,
his eyes closed. Ott was crouched beside the MG34, staring
with tired, bloodshot eyes at the empty road. Suddenly he
grabbed the Obergefreiter's shoulder and pointed. 'A car!'

In spite of the pain he knew any move would cause him,
Haak struggled to roll over. Ott passed him the glasses. Even
to Haak's dimmed brain, a French officer was clearly visible
beside the driver. Had there been any doubt, a Union Jack
fluttered on the bonnet. Haak nodded. Ott cocked the machine
gun, and Haak himself held out the belt-feed.

The First Secretary had just said, 'I hope after all this the
bloody Navy is there!'; Simon had nodded, and the French
officer had smiled a little sadly, for he was leaving his country,
when Ott squeezed the trigger. Thirty 7.9mm bullets were
aimed at the black Hillman. The majority ripped into their
target.

Simon felt the car shudder, watched holes appear in the
bonnet then climb lazily up and across the windscreen. He
flung himself down on the floor, and as the car careered across
the road he was conscious of the high-pitched, quick chatter of
the machine-gun above the sickening smack of the bullets and
the muffled, choked cry that came from the front. The drop
into the ditch was almost graceful, and as the car ended up,
poised delicately on roof and side, the last of the fifty-round
belt-feed hit the still spinning wheels.

Simon realised that he was lying face upwards, his feet above
his head, staring through a shattered window at a bright
morning sky. He felt no pain, just an ache. He tried to
remember all that had happened, but was conscious only of a
steady drip. Petrol from the fractured tank was seeping down
the rear seat and falling on to the inverted roof. Vapour filled
the car. He struggled up and tried to open the door above him.
It was jammed. The other door was deep in the ditch. He
twisted around in the confined space. Where the Frenchman
had been the door was open. He wriggled upwards and realised
he was pushing something soft. The Frenchman's uniformed

back lay sprawled across the overcoat-covered remains of the First Secretary. Simon reached down and tried to drag the two men apart, but they were wedged against the windscreen. He saw the first flicker of fire, pushed with the strength of panic against bodies and steering wheel, and landed on the grass as the car exploded.

He was lying dazed and sickened, his right leg twisted under him, when he saw, in the light of the flames, a man in the black beret and uniform of the panzers standing over him. In his right hand the man carried a machine-gun, from the barrel of which hung a tripod. Simon was quite certain that this was Götterdämmerung, that he was about to join the First Secretary and the Frenchman, when Ott grabbed his arm and dragged him from the searing heat.

Taking all the weight on his left leg, Simon fumbled for his American passport. The young German was not greatly impressed. He searched Simon, pocketed the Smith and Wesson, and at gunpoint steered him back to the barn and the Obergefreiter. Haak, however, was only semi-conscious and answered none of Ott's questions. It was evident that this tiny isolated unit was not geared to taking prisoners.

Simon sat on the straw and massaged his knee. It was an oppressive atmosphere. The only sound was the little Obergefreiter's breathing, rasping and erratic. Ott sat staring, the MG34 across his lap, his finger on the trigger. Simon explained that he was a neutral, but without effect. He asked what they intended doing with him and got no answer. He was slipping into despair when he had an idea. 'A few weeks ago I was in Berlin,' he said, smiling, 'in the Tirpitz Ufer, talking to your Admiral Canaris of OKW.'

Ott didn't speak but he looked sufficiently interested for Simon to feel encouraged.

'The Admiral expected great things of you.' Simon glanced towards the door of the barn. 'It looks as if you've succeeded handsomely.'

Ott's grasp on the machine-gun visibly relaxed.

'When you get back, the Führer will have you all to Berchtesgaden. Ever been to Berchtesgaden?'

Ott shook his head.

'It's a wonderful place,' said Simon. 'You'll find it very

exciting. You'll have lunch and a film show, and come away with the Iron Cross.' Simon pointed at Ott's left breast. 'The Führer can be very generous.'

Ott had no idea what to make of this American who spoke such excellent German and actually seemed to be on visiting terms with the great. He wished the Obergefreiter could hear, but the Obergefreiter was quite evidently hearing nothing. Just before noon, Ott put down his machine-gun and passed his canteen over. Simon reckoned that he should at least see the sunset.

In a moment of clarity, Obergefreiter Haak struggled into a sitting position and asked if there had been any firing. Being told no, he ordered Ott to go back up the lane and find the advanced dressing-station. Ott said the rest of the company must have withdrawn hours ago. To emphasise their isolation, he peeled back Haak's blood-soaked tunic and trousers and checked the field dressing himself. Haak repeated the order.

'What about the American, Herr Obergefreiter?' asked Ott, indicating Simon. Haak stared at Simon and seemed not to understand. Ott repeated the question. Haak muttered something about looking after the American himself. Ott stood for a moment undecided. Haak moved his head, indicating that Ott should go. With one more glance at Simon, Ott left the barn.

Haak lay with one hand resting on his pistol holster, the other on his chest. With glazed, bloodshot eyes, he stared straight upwards. Simon spoke and the German mumbled through froth-covered lips, then closed his eyes. When he was certain the Obergefreiter had slipped back into unconsciousness, Simon thanked his Maker for his luck, got up and limped away.

At first, with life and freedom, Simon forgot how exhausted he was. He would liked to have skipped and run, but his knee was too painful. Even had he been able to run he soon realised he would not have done so. The Obergefreiter might have regained consciousness, or any of his comrades tucked into nearby ditches might have found a quickly moving target irresistible. So Simon hobbled sedately.

It was sight of the burned-out, upside-down Hillman that removed the last vestige of euphoria. In the still air, he caught the first whiff of that peculiar, pungent scent that is the compound of burned metal, wood, paint, leather and flesh. He circled wide, intending to pass the wreck, when he found himself approaching it across the scorched grass where he had flung himself a few hours earlier.

Sheets of charred and half-charred paper lay scattered about. Automatically he collected them. He had no intention of looking in through the open, twisted door, but found himself doing so. At the bottom, a massive black jelly only betrayed its human origins by the bones of a hand that crowned it like a garnish. He retched and turned away. Steeling himself, he returned to the blackened shell and peered in through the melted window of the rear door. He couldn't identify his case, but amidst the pile of blackness at the bottom were more sheets of charred paper. He collected what he could and made a heap. When a farmer came along with a water-cart, he borrowed a match and set the heap on fire. With the farmer watching he stirred the sheets to make sure every piece burned, and saw both English and German type. When he had destroyed all he could, he got up on the cart.

As they rumbled their way between the poplars, he thought of the First Secretary. He forgot all the obstacles the man had put in his way since he had first arrived in Paris, all the chicanery with Cuthbertson, and remembered only an eccentric, blinkered Englishman. He even shed a tear which he wiped away with a dirty, smoky finger. Then he remembered, with a pang of anxiety, that the remains of his real passport must still be somewhere on the First Secretary's body.

# CHAPTER 10

Sinclair turned his back to the bar and said, 'Thought you'd like to know, old chap, I'm joining up.'

Cuthbertson gave a sardonic laugh. 'Too late, Ross! The war's over! Everyone knows that. Even the PM, although he won't admit it. That visit of his to Tours yesterday must have been pretty sobering. Weygand wanting an armistice, the PM's pal Reynaud talking about a separate peace, the Germans polishing their jackboots for the march down the Champs-Elysées, our last division surrendering at St Valery. Before the week's out, the only British troops left in Europe will be prisoners.'

Sinclair shook his head. 'This war is going on. For a very long time.'

'And where are you going to fight it, for God's sake?' said Cuthbertson.

'Defend this place first, I suppose,' said Sinclair, a little doubtfully. 'Then with Italy in, there'll be Abyssinia, North Africa ...'

Cuthbertson shook his head once more. 'Easy to talk, Ross, until the bombers come. Look how they went through France!'

'We've got the Channel. The Navy's intact, so is Fighter Command.'

Outside in the street Cuthbertson said, 'When are you off?'

'Three days, just tidying up.'

Cuthbertson smothered his feelings, and they shook hands and parted.

Cuthbertson picked up the phone to inquire whether the Minister was in the House or his office, then changed his mind. The Minister was now irrelevant, almost a liability. Anyway, the note he wanted Sinclair to dispatch was his affair and no one else's.

He put down his pen and stared at the window. His attitude to the war hadn't changed. Events had overtaken him, that was all. He still firmly believed that British-German cooperation was the best safeguard for Europe. With that settled, he turned to Manning. Manning had been the bearer of admittedly damaging evidence against Germany, but in the context of Russian communism and imperialism, that was a minor matter. Now, as Sinclair had said, it was a case of tidying up. And the only loose and dangerous end was Manning.

The message was short, just two sentences. Cuthbertson put it in an unaddressed envelope and took it straight to Sinclair at the Foreign Office.

'How long to get to Germany?'

Sinclair shook his head.

'The very last thing I shall ask of you, Ross,' said Cuthbertson, 'the very last.'

After a long time Sinclair said, 'Three days, maybe four to the Vatican, then a couple of days for our man to find the contact . . .'

Cuthbertson shook his head. 'Too long. It must be in Germany in forty-eight hours.'

'Maybe you should try MI6?'

'They work with the Abwehr,' said Cuthbertson angrily.

Sinclair stared at the envelope.

'I won't ask what's in it,' he said after a while. 'But we are sending some stuff to Stockholm tonight. An air courier. It could, I suppose, find its way to the German Embassy.'

Cuthbertson took out his pen and wrote 'To the Reich Sicherheitspolizie' on the envelope, then gave it to Sinclair.

'Put it in another envelope, Ross, addressed to whoever you address these things to, and send it on its way.'

He stayed on the watercart until they reached a farm, where he spent thirty-six hours sleeping and resting his knee. No one had any idea where the dreaded panzers might have reached and rumours abounded, but it was quite evident that both the farmer and his wife wanted Simon away as quickly as possible. He was given a stout walking stick, an old haversack containing a loaf, butter, cheese and cider, and sent on his way.

He set off westwards. On the Atlantic coast, ships would be leaving for England right up to the last moment. He seemed the only person in France. Before and behind, the road was empty. There was no German, no straggling poilu, no plodding refugee. It was so eerie he felt the goose-pimples on his back. He reminded himself that a defeated army could be as stupidly vicious as a victorious one. It was as likely that a French machine-gun would suddenly splutter from the trees ahead as that one of those formidable grey panzers would suddenly rake him from behind.

In this fearful mood he rounded the bend in the road to witness an extraordinary sight. Stationary, half hidden by the trees, was a magnificent Sedanca-de-ville. Standing by the open driver's door, berating the occupants, was a woman, dark haired and Junoesque. As Simon approached she ceased her harangue, and turning towards him demanded to know, in the voice of one used to being obeyed, whether there were any Germans between here and the Seine. Simon did not reply at once but stood staring, taking in every detail of the bizarre sight.

The car, sweeping and sumptuous, sat low on its springs. Somewhere under the long bonnet was a Bugatti engine. Simon knew enough to realise that it was special, but not enough to know how special. In fact he was looking at a very rare vehicle. A type 57 Bugatti with Sedanca-de-ville coachwork. However, he was not only impressed with the vehicle, which in England would have cost all of £1,500, but with the contents. The interior was crammed with trunks, some closed and bound, some so full that they were unable to be closed, forcing furs, silks, linens and cottons to press flat against the glass of the windows. In the midst of this vast, hastily packed wardrobe sat two young women, one in the back, one in the front, both dressed in white, both pretty, both crying. Simon began to laugh. The woman, surprised, repeated her question. Simon started to reply in French when the woman interrupted in English.

'Can you drive, Monsieur?' she cried, then pointing down the road added piteously, 'My driver was commandeered by the Military.'

Although the Sedanca-de-ville was enticing, Simon hesitated. It was late. Soon the short May night would set in. It was foolish to drive in the dark. On foot or hitching he had been unobtrusive. Driving this car would be like ringing a leper bell. Nor had he any wish to risk his life for the sake of a woman's fineries. He stared at the trunks, and was about to suggest that she threw them out when the woman suddenly pointed at the girls and cried, 'You cannot leave two such innocents to the Boche!'

Simon looked at the sky. 'It will be dark in half an hour. It would be madness to drive in the dark.'

'Ten kilometres, Monsieur!' cried the woman. 'Just ten kilometres, no more. There I have friends where we can stay the night.'

When the woman went down on her knees, held his hand and repeated her words, Simon shrugged. Instantly he was thrust into the driving seat, to be wedged between one of those innocents and the velvet-upholstered door. As they pulled back on to the road, the woman asked his name.

'Simon. Simon Manning.'

'We shall call you Simon,' cried the woman, 'won't we, girls?'

The girl next to him, who had a mole on her cheek, nodded. The girl in the back said, 'Yes.'

'And you, Madame?' asked Simon.

'Corbasson. Madame Corbasson.'

The interior of the Sedanca-de-ville was as scented as a perfumery, but Simon revelled in it. As he went up through the gears and felt the big engine pulling so readily, he marvelled that there was this small, enclosed cell of femininity amidst the desolation of war. He forgot that he had ever thought of demanding that the wardrobe be jettisoned, and joyously filled his lungs with the pomandered air. Then suddenly he became conscious of his own filthy state, and glanced at the girl next to him. If she noticed, she showed no sign. Nor did either of the others. He could only conclude that they were all too happy at being saved from the rapacious Boche.

'My friend the General would have driven me,' announced Madame Corbasson in her husky voice. 'But he had to go back with the army.'

Simon nodded. Two sentences and he came close to knowing her whole story. That is what war did.

'So when your chauffeur was taken, you were left with your wardrobe and your two maids?' he said with more sarcasm than sympathy.

The woman sighed and nodded. 'If it hadn't been for my

dear Lucienne and Marie, I don't know what I should have done!'

Lucienne and Marie giggled.

'And where is your friend the General now?' inquired Simon.

'With the new armies beyond the Seine,' said Madame proudly. 'He is setting up his headquarters in a château near Brionne.'

They soon discovered that there were Germans between them and the Seine. A whole village of them. Tanks and trucks lined the street. They were stopped and surrounded. In the back, Lucienne began to whimper; in the front, Madame swore. An officer opened the door, flashed a torch inside and ordered them out. The officer demanded Simon's papers.

'You are an American, Herr Cotton,' he said without looking up. Lucienne drew in her breath even before Simon had said that he was. The officer swung the beam of his torch on to Lucienne's face. The girl began to cry.

'Why is she acting like this?' asked the officer.

'They've heard stories,' explained Simon, looking round at the silhouetted soldiers. 'They're worried about your men.'

The officer laid his torch on the bonnet of the car, took a field notebook from his pocket and carefully wrote down the details of Simon's passport. Then he handed it back, got in the car, flashed his torch all round the interior and had one of the trunks brought out and opened. The layers of petticoats brought a roar of laughter. The officer smiled, and had the trunk replaced.

Simon explained that they were making for a house, now no more than six kilometres away. There they could spend the night. The officer shook his head. They were civilians in a war zone. They came under the orders of the Wehrmacht. They were to get off the road at once.

Madame enfolded her girls, protested violently, but to no effect. They were taken to the attic bedroom of a large house, which had been looted two days ago by Algerian Tirailleurs and this afternoon by Pomeranians. It stank from both visits, and to add to the discomfort Wehrmacht boots clattered on the floor below. A Feldwebel brought blankets and a dixie of soup, and took a fancy to Madame. It needed all Simon's insistence and his watch to get him back downstairs. The moment he had gone, Madame whispered her thanks.

'A hazard of war,' said Simon. 'The men are supposed to be killed, the women taken off. It's traditional.'

'It's not so much for myself that I am worried, as for my maids,' explained Madame.

Simon said he understood.

'Why did you tell us your name was Simon Manning,' asked Madame suddenly, 'when your passport says "Cotton"?'

'A long story,' said Simon, 'so long it would take days to tell.'

'You're English, not American. They are your enemies too.'

Simon agreed that they were.

The women dragged a mattress to the window. Simon lay in the remains of a chair. The two girls soon fell asleep, but Madame talked until well into the night. She was shocked but not daunted by her sudden change of circumstances. She said she had no children, but seemed more motherly than many who had. Already he felt more secure. The protector protected. An earth goddess, Simon decided. The prototype of that ancient woman who had inspired the Neolithic temple builders of the Mediterranean. Exhausted, and with that pleasant thought, he fell asleep.

They awoke to find the German unit had moved on, no follow-up troops had yet arrived to take their place, and the birds were singing. They breakfasted from Madame's hamper, then headed westwards. Well before the river they discovered that the crossings at Vernon and Les Andelys were in enemy hands. They kept off the main roads and bumped down the side roads, hoping to avoid the panzers and find a bridge still held by the French. There was no sign of war.

As they approached the village of St Ouen, in the loop of the river, Simon braked. If there were Germans, this was where they might be expected. If there were French, as reported, no one wanted to provoke a burst from a Hotchkiss. They drove slowly past the houses, all shuttered and silent. The road straightened and ahead lay the bridge. Where the parapet began a crowd was drawn up on both sides of the road. Almost all of those in the front were women. When they saw the car, some raised their hands, a doubtful almost furtive gesture, half of surrender, half of welcome. Simon slowed. Ancient and stone-built, the bridge seemed intact. '*Vite!*' cried Madame. Simon pushed the accelerator to the floor. The Bugatti leapt forward just as the crowd, realising it was not the panzers, moved into the roadway.

Simon braked hard. Madame shouted for Simon to go on, but the crowd were all around them. There was a moment of calm while the people of St Ouen stared at the strange sight in their midst. They had awaited the Boche with apprehension, now they inspected the Sedanca with surprise and at first amusement. But the amusement soon gave way to envy, disgust and hatred. For many, the luxurious vehicle, its contents and occupants epitomised all the inequalities of the Republic. Simon whispered, 'For God's sake, whose side are they on?' and put the car into reverse, but there was no way back. A woman called out that an officers' brothel was being moved. Another that it must be Daladier's mistress. Madame called them fools and shouted at them to get out of the way. The fury burst.

The doors of the Sedanca-de-ville were wrenched open, and Simon, Madame and the screaming girls dragged out to shrieks of 'Whore!' and 'Pimp!' An old crone, black of hair, dress and eyes, climbed into the back of the car and emerged with a long silk nightdress. She draped it against her own skinny body and performed an obscene pirouette upon the roadway. Inspired by the old crone, the rest of the women proceeded to loot the interior of the vehicle with a speed and ferocity that could not have been equalled since the days of the Revolution. Lucienne and Marie fled across the bridge.

Madame fought to preserve her possessions. Simon struggled to get her to safety. Dresses, blouses, skirts, négligés, petticoats, furs, silks, stockings and shoes were displayed, torn and trampled on, spat upon and hung like trophies from the balustrade of the bridge. Scent bottles were emptied on to the roadway. The hamper was ripped open, and delicacies like aspic de crevettes and pâté de Faisan were handed to children like ice-creams. The car seemed to infuriate the mob as much as the contents. The interior was vandalised, children sent in to urinate and tyres slashed in an orgy of knife thrusts. In a final act of frenzy, the vehicle was turned on to its side and set on fire.

Grasping Madame's hand, Simon dragged her over the bridge. They were abused, laughed at and pelted with rubbish, but only the children bothered to follow them, and they gave up at the last of the houses. On the hill overlooking the rooftops, the two terrified girls waited.

Madame stood staring down at the village, '*Salauds*!' she whispered in the midst of her anger. Simon told her she was lucky to have got away with her life, but she was not impressed. Her own salvation in no way compensated for the loss of all her personal possessions and her friend the General's car. When she dwelt on the irony of the General being only twenty kilometres away in his headquarters, Simon had to disillusion her. Even if he got to his château, there could be no army for her General to command.

They had started walking when a truck backed down the road. Two French sappers offered them a lift. Gratefully they climbed into the back. The sappers told them that the women of the village had prevented them blowing up the bridge. They told the story philosophically, almost with humour, pointing out that the Germans had crossed the river anyway. Now the sappers were returning to their billets where their CO was already arranging a surrender. They asked where Madame and the girls were going. Madame said Brionne. They asked Simon, and he said Cherbourg or St Nazaire. They put them all down at a crossroads. When the truck drove away it was exactly noon.

# CHAPTER 11

In spite of his demotion, the Minister still occupied the same office and desk. Churchill had set the pattern by staying at the Admiralty even after taking over the Premiership. The idea was to reduce disruption during the critical days. When Cuthbertson asked on the phone whether the Minister was in, he knew exactly where to find him.

In their two meetings since the Cabinet changes, the Minister had detected a shift in Cuthbertson's manner. Cuthbertson quite evidently graded his Ministers, and the Minister of Local Government was not in the top grade.

'Sit down, Cuthbertson,' said the Minister, trying to show firmness, and Cuthbertson sat. 'What exactly is it?'

'We've had some news from France, Minister,' said Cuthbertson with undisguised excitement, 'that may interest you. Manning, the fellow with that Abwehr file, was killed three days ago.'

'Killed?' said the Minister, his voice rising. 'Manning killed?'

'Yes, Minister. He was in a car with the First Secretary. The First Secretary told someone at the embassy that he was going to pick Manning up at the flat. They were trying to get to Havre and ran into an ambush. The whole thing went up in smoke. Two bodies were found. It all ties up.'

After a long silence, the Minister said, 'I believe you said Manning was unmarried?'

'Correct, Minister. His next of kin is a widowed mother living in the north, somewhere near Durham.'

'What is she being told?'

Cuthbertson smiled contemptuously. 'Nothing, Minister, for she knows nothing. Manning has no chance to correspond with anyone.'

'So she still thinks her son is an internee in Germany?'

'Presumably.'

'There must come a time,' said the Minister, 'when she begins to wonder. Manning must have written to her via the Red Cross.'

Cuthbertson shrugged. 'If she writes to the FO she won't get anywhere. There are no papers on Manning. The only other person who knew about him, the First Secretary, is dead. Manning's exploits are completely untraceable.'

'There's your friend in the FO?' said the Minister.

Cuthbertson smiled. 'He won't say anything. Besides, he's joining the Navy.'

They sat for a minute in silence, then the Minister said, 'I don't know about you, Cuthbertson, but I find the whole affair leaves a bitter taste.'

'That's a personal matter, Minister,' said Cuthbertson cooly, 'but I am quite sure that when you agreed that Manning should be kept in Paris for the time being you thought it was the right thing to do.'

'Times have changed, Cuthbertson,' said the Minister. 'We should have foreseen that.'

'I don't think we can get all emotional about one single person,' said Cuthbertson, 'and Manning did die in the best possible way. Working for peace.'

'The Americans have a phrase for it. Chasing rainbows,' said the Minister. 'Perhaps we've all been doing it?'

'You're a politician,' said Cuthbertson, almost with contempt. 'I don't think it's possible for a politician to be interested in the individual.'

The Minister sat upright in his chair. 'If I'd said that at the General Election, I'd have been torn limb from limb! Disowned by my own party!'

Cuthbertson shrugged. 'Nevertheless, it's true, as I'm sure you've found out.' He got up and added cheerfully, 'At least, Minister, it's nice to have everything tidied up.'

The Minister closed his eyes. God damn the man, he always saw everything too simply. Cuthbertson was at the door when the Minister remembered that everything hadn't been tidied up.

'That file? The details of the camps and death squads?'

'Probably with him in the car, Minister. There were charred papers about. But it doesn't really matter. If anyone does find it, or bits of it, it's more likely to be the Germans than anyone else. In a way it is their property. Of course, we wouldn't want any harm to come to the Generals, but knowing K he'll get there first and clear it up.'

The Minister nodded and hoped Cuthbertson was right.


Hopkins had to be careful. Carrying that heavy suitcase in Paris had left him breathless, and hurrying out of the back of the brasserie in the Boulevard Haussmann had given him severe palpitations. He had had to rest in a doorway much too near the brasserie for comfort when he should have been in the Métro miles away.

He was ordered to Le Bourget, and climbed into a tiny overloaded Fieseler Storch to be told he was going to Berlin to see Canaris. He took out his bottle of smelling salts and sniffed. For the rest of that bumpy journey he was either being sick or struggling not to be. He was driven to the Tirpitz Ufer in a state of considerable physical distress, but found the energy to climb the stairs. Once in Canaris's office he sank gratefully into the leather chair.

Canaris ordered him a black coffee, apologised for having flown him half across Europe, then questioned him about the Englishman.

'You were with him for a while. Did you notice whether he had a ring on his finger? A distinctive tie-pin?'

Hopkins shook his head. 'I don't think he had either.'

His own memory confirmed, Canaris opened the drawer of his desk and took out a charred object whose outline still showed it to have been a passport. When he opened it, the centre of some of the pages was still legible.

'Manning's passport. Not the one you gave him, his real one.'

Hopkins held the blackened relic. It had an extraordinary feel that dried his fingers. It also had a strange smell. He felt sick again.

'Where was it found?' he asked.

'On the remains of a body in an English car in France. There was another body with it. The question is, is one of them Manning's?' Canaris again opened the drawer of his desk, took out an envelope and handed it to Hopkins. 'Fortunately the Gestapo are as thorough as the rest of us. Here is Manning's dental sheet. It may be all of him you are able to recognise.'

Hopkins stared at the envelope and passport.

'What happened?'

'That's what a lot of people would like to know, including no doubt the British. Manning left Paris with an Englishman from their embassy, presumably for Le Havre. Their car was machine-gunned and caught fire. Locals found the remains of two persons and buried them. The question is, in spite of the evidence of the passport, is one of them Manning?'

'It would look pretty conclusive,' said Hopkins.

'All the circumstantial evidence is that Manning is dead,' said Canaris. 'Two bodies were found, only two left Paris in that car. It's all very neat, but it seems that someone may have survived.'

Hopkins took out his handkerchief and wiped his forehead. It looked as if he might be going back to France soon, and the thought didn't please him.

'You know that?' he asked.

Canaris got up. 'A section under the command of an Obergefreiter Haak of the Armoured Reconnaissance Battalion of the 7th Panzer Division probably destroyed the car. It seems, however, that a survivor was, for a short time, a prisoner. Who he was — indeed, whether he ever existed — I don't know. That's what I want you to find out.'

Hopkins took off his glasses, wiped them and said, 'Surely the panzer boys must know?'

The Admiral shook his head. 'The Obergefreiter was already badly wounded when the sole survivor of his car, a certain Oberschütze Ott, machine-gunned the vehicle. When he was picked up, Haak was delirious. His statement about Ott with a civilian might be no more than the result of that delirium. On the other hand it might not.'

'And Oberschütze Ott?'

'Killed trying to find the rest of the company.' Canaris paused, then said, 'He did, however, have an English revolver on him. Of course, he may have acquired it anywhere.' He opened the door. 'A nice little mystery for you, Hopkins. Oh, and I've arranged for an army dentist to meet you. Don't tell him much. Just use his expertise. And check for charred paper.'

Hopkins struggled to his feet. 'To tell you the truth, Admiral, I could do with a bath and a bit of sleep. Hela hasn't seen me . . . oh, it must be a month now.'

The Admiral shook his head. 'Your daughter's fine and doing excellently at school. She sends her love. As for the bath, have it in France when you've had a look at the body.'

Hopkins hesitated, realised it was useless to argue, and moved slowly and wearily towards the door.

'If it is his body, Admiral, I'll say a prayer for both of us. You see, I left the poor bugger to pay for the drinks.'

Canaris smiled and watched the man go out into the corridor and down the stairs.

While his men brewed up, Sergeant Cornford stood at the roadside and phlegmatically surveyed his tiny command. One lance-corporal, one sapper, two drivers, three privates, one three-ton Thorneycroft truck and a very dicey bren carrier. The personnel all exhausted, the two vehicles badly in need of maintenance.

They had started as part of 'Holtforce', hurriedly organised from line of communication troops to protect the flank of the retreating BEF. Their brigade had been sent to plug the gaps south-east of Arras, and had immediately been bumped by Guderian's XIX Panzer Army Corps. They had been overrun, and the survivors told to make their way back to the Channel as best they could. Under cover of darkness Cornford had set off with the remains of the carrier platoon, but finding all directions but south barred had turned deep into France. They had lost their second carrier to a French anti-tank gun, but had acquired an RE three-tonner and driver. They had crossed the Somme with the tag-end of the French 7th Army, and now, like Simon, were hoping to reach Cherbourg or one of the Brittany ports. It was the long way round, but the only way. Indeed, in spite of their weariness, Cornford felt satisfied, even optimistic. Not a man lost and he was once again on the right side of the lines.

'OK, start up!' he shouted, and climbed up into the front of the Thorneycroft. For four kilometres they took the main road, then came to a crossroads where the signpost had been removed. They had slowed down to ask the way when Cornford spotted a man and three women sitting in the dappled shade of a tree.

Simon heard the clatter of the carrier, looked up and saw the Thorneycroft. With its six wheels, open front, camouflage and netting he had no difficulty in recognising it. He had seen others like it in England before the war. If he had had any doubts, the driver's battledress dispelled them. He jumped up and waved.

Cornford leaned across the driver and shouted, 'Les Alleymen . . . Les Boche?' then pointed ahead and to right and left trying to convey the rest of his question.

They stood in a circle, the NCOs and Simon watching Madame draw a map in the dust, the rest eyeing the two girls.

'You say Jerry is across the river?' said Cornford, in his slow West Country voice.

Simon nodded. The sergeant turned to the lance-corporal..

'Don't see all that much of a problem, Acker. We want the sea, Cherbourg or St Nazaire, the lady wants this Brionne place. It doesn't look all that far out. And if her general is there . . . ?'

'How can he be?' said Simon curtly. 'Everything's collapsed!'

There was a pause. Cornford scratched his ear.

'We can have a go,' he said at last. 'Try and get them there and have a look, so long as we can get the petrol.'

Lance-Corporal 'Acker' Church, a weaselly little man with a pencil moustache, looked first at Madame, then at the two girls and made a typical gesture. The men sniggered.

'And you bloody well behave yourselves!' shouted Cornford, and provoked an unintelligible murmer. 'That's settled, then,' he said. He turned and addressed Madame. 'Marm, please accept the hospitality of the 5th Wessex.' He held out his arm and escorted her to the back of the Thorneycroft, where eager, grasping hands lifted her and the girls into the back.

Simon was about to follow when Church pointed his rifle and said, 'What about 'im, Sarge? Behind the lines in France in civvies? Fishy, I'd call it.'

Taken aback, a pleasant afternoon suddenly ruined by this reminder of war, the sergeant stopped, looked Simon up and down and eventually asked for his paybook. Simon reluctantly produced his passport.

'This is American, sir,' said the sergeant, with a lift of his eyebrows. 'I thought you were English?'

'I am.'

'Then why have you got an American passport?'

'If I were to tell you,' said Simon wearily, 'I doubt if you'd believe me.'

'Try, sir,' said the sergeant sarcastically.

'To get out of Germany.'

There was a long pause.

'Fifth Columnist or deserter, Sarge,' said Church, thrusting the muzzle of his rifle nearer Simon's stomach.

Bewildered, the sergeant called up to Madame: 'What do you know of this man, Marm?'

'Saved us all from the Boche,' said Madame staunchly. 'Without him we wouldn't be here.'

'Knows all about 'er General's HQ,' said Church.

The sergeant gave the tricky matter five more seconds, then said, 'Take him up with you, Acker, keep an eye on him, and we'll hand him to the first MPs we see. It's their business, not ours.' Then to Simon he said, 'Sorry about this, sir, but I'm sure you understand, you can't be too careful, not these days.'

The Thorneycroft had stopped many times, but this halt was different. Everything loose went plunging forward. Simon picked himself off the floor and looked out through the open back. 'Nipper' Cole in the carrier had avoided running into them by six inches. Now, wiping his boyish face with a sweat rag, he was grinning up at the girls as they rearranged their dresses. Simon recognised the boulangerie. For the last three hours they had been driving in a circle. He turned back to the shadow of the canopy. Three of his fellow occupants were searching the blankets for their cards, and Church was searching for his Lee-Enfield.

Cornford came round from the front and tapped on the tailboard. He had done this each time the carrier had shed its track and they had stamped on the floor and shouted. He had done it when the carrier's engine had overheated and refugees had blocked the road. But this time was different. Cornford was accompanied by a dapper French colonel with a Charlie Chaplin moustache, whose pistol was drawn, and four armed soldiers, who like the colonel looked anything but Allies. With an air of infinite weariness, Cornford addressed Madame.

'If you wouldn't mind, Marm, just telling the colonel here exactly who the general is that we've been trying to find?'

Madame leaned over the tailboard, fixed the colonel with her most formidable glare and said, 'General Jean Laigle. He was to set up his headquarters here in Brionne.'

'Your papers, Madame!' demanded the colonel, holding out his hand.

Surprised, Madame handed over her papers. While the colonel examined them, she explained. 'My husband, Major of the Reserve Artillery Claude Corbasson, is in the Maginot Line. General Laigle is my friend. It was he who told me to come to Brionne.'

The colonel was not impressed. 'According to your papers, Madame, your home is near Bernay, less than thirty kilometres away. You would be well advised to get there as quickly as possible.'

'But *my* General!' cried Madame, 'he is expecting me!'

The colonel pulled himself to his full inadequate height. All day he had been vainly trying to put order into chaos. He was tired and his temper was short. He had been warned about Fifth Columnists and Germans in captured French and British uniforms. He had been about to sit down to eat when he had been told of the Englishmen driving about the town asking for French headquarters. He stared at Madame and was reminded of everything that was wrong with the Third Republic from Premier Reynaud's meddling mistress, the Countess Hélène de Portes, to the aged, reactionary generals he had to take orders from. With an icy, un-Gallic calm he said, 'General Laigle is not here. He was relieved of his command last week.'

Madame gave a cry of disbelief and shock, and collapsed into the arms of her girls. The men were ordered out of the lorry and were marched to the gendarmerie at gunpoint.

They spent three hours in a filthy cell, a bucket in the corner and a charge of desertion on their heads. They decided that if they weren't shot by the French they would die of dysentery. Then, in the evening, the colonel reappeared and ordered their release. They were reunited with the carrier and Thorneycroft and escorted to the Place to await a British officer. Across the street, outside a café, were Madame and the girls. The men were about to cross to the café when the British subaltern arrived. Still in his teens, he was far more concerned with getting his own three lorries out of the shambles and back to a port than in rounding up stragglers. Nevertheless, he produced a map and held an O Group exactly as he had been trained.

The Germans held bridgeheads over the Seine, the French were crumbling, the British were both evacuating and returning. It was a messy situation and his orders were to direct all British stragglers to Cherbourg. Although the sergeant hadn't a map he gave Cornford a map reference where he could refuel, and told him to get going.

'The French ladies, sir?' said Cornford, pointing across the Place. 'We'll have to see them on their way first.'

The officer looked worried.

'French ladies?' he said, following the sergeant's outstretched arm. 'Do you mean, Sergeant, that you've been carrying French civilians in WD vehicles?'

The sergeant shrugged. 'Picked them up sir, at their last gasp.' Then he pointed at Simon. 'Ask him, sir, he seems to be in charge of them.'

For the first time the officer became conscious of Simon.

'Who are you?' he asked curtly.

'Simon Manning,' said Simon, 'an Englishman with an American passport.'

'Says he's been in Germany, sir,' said the sergeant. 'We were going to hand him over to the MPs but there aren't any about.'

The officer glanced at his watch. This was no moment to linger. Simon explained that he had been attached to the embassy, and it sounded weak.

'You say you're English?' said the officer, scanning Simon's clothes. 'Who won the last Cup Final?'

'Portsmouth.'

'Who did they beat?'

'Wolverhampton . . . four-one or four-two.'

'Who is Funf?'

Simon looked puzzled.

'Funf?' he repeated, frowning.

'When were you last in England?'

'April '39.'

'Richmal Crompton?' snapped out the officer.

'William . . . Ginger.'

The officer smiled. 'School?'

'Rushden. 240 boys; fees, £150 per annum. Present headmaster, "Piggy" Mason.'

The officer held out his hand. 'We used to play them. St John's, Croftside. Glad to meet you.'

Simon shook his hand. It was good to have left the ranks of the Fifth Column.

'The French ladies, sir?' inquired the sergeant.

The officer took off his tin hat, scratched his head and said, 'I'd rather not know, Sergeant, but for God's sake don't hang around long.' He looked around the Place. 'The French are getting pretty jumpy. It could be damned unhealthy.'

There were rapid salutes, and the officer went back to his lorries. Sergeant Cornford's little army watched them move off, then the sergeant turned to Simon. 'Where exactly is Bernay, sir?'

'Not far. West of here.'

The sergeant looked up at the sky. 'On the way to Cherbourg?'

'Pretty well.'

The women were crossing the street.

'From the look of 'er, she's probably got a very nice little billet, Sarge,' said Church. 'We could have one night there. It is sort of on the way.'

After a while, the sergeant nodded. 'We ought to try and get them home. It's the least we can do.'


Heydrich's adjutant burst into his Chief's office in the Prinz-Albrecht-Strasse block in a state of considerable excitement. SS-Sturmbannführer Krüger, the SD representative in the Stockholm embassy, was on the phone with the most extraordinary information. The adjutant thought that Heydrich ought to hear it himself. When Heydrich had listened to the story, written the message verbatim on his pad and had it repeated twice, he was equally astonished.

The information seemed clear enough. It might well be true; that Heydrich would find out. But why had it been sent? On the face of it, it seemed incredible.

'Does Krüger drink?' asked Heydrich.

The adjutant shook his head:

'Not especially, Herr Obergruppenführer.'

'Does he have hallucinations, walk in his sleep, dream?'

'That I don't know, Herr Obergruppenführer.'

'Tell me,' said Heydrich, staring up into the face of his adjutant, 'why do the English deliberately tell me that their own agent, Manning, is now in Paris, posing as an American under the name Cotton, and that he has full knowledge of the activities of the Einsatzgruppen in Poland?'

The adjutant shrugged. 'That is exactly why I thought you ought to speak with Krüger yourself, Herr Obergruppenführer.'

Heydrich buried his head in his hands. 'Do you think it's a plot?'

'A plot, Herr Obergruppenführer?'

'Yes, you fool, a plot!' shouted Heydrich. 'Manning is reported posing as an American. England is to be lulled back into appeasement. It is part of the American plan to destroy the British Empire. But supposing the English want us to arrest Manning to anger the Americans . . . ?'

'But he isn't an American,' said the adjutant slowly.

'Of course he's not!' snapped Heydrich. He paused, then added, 'The Abwehr are in it somewhere. But why provoke us further?'

'If the Englishman really has this knowledge,' said the adjutant, 'it could be awkward.'

Awkward was not the word. Disastrous was better. But Heydrich didn't bother to put his adjutant right. All that mattered was finding the man.

'Circulate Manning's photo and description to every unit of the Sicherheitspolizie and SD moving into France,' he said, 'also to the French police as we occupy each region. If Manning is alive in Paris, I want him!'

'Yes, Herr Obergruppenführer.'

The adjutant saluted and went towards the door. There he stopped. 'The information from Krüger is that Manning is posing as an American.'

Heydrich looked up from his desk and nodded.

'There was a report of an American being questioned by the

Wehrmacht in the battle zone . . .'

'Then check it, Helmut!' said Heydrich, smiling. 'Check it!'

The salute was repeated and the door closed. Three minutes later the adjutant was back.

'The name of the American questioned *was* Cotton, Herr Obergruppenführer. Just east of the Seine, a week ago.'

Heydrich jumped to his feet. 'Find the Wehrmacht officer who checked Cotton. Get every detail. How the Englishman was travelling. Whether he was alone, with anyone. Exactly what happened to him.'

'Yes, Herr Obergruppenführer.'

The adjutant saluted and hurried from the office.


# CHAPTER 12


Major Karl Ludecke had much to be proud of. Barely eight months after receiving the Iron Cross, First Class, from the hands of the Führer himself, he had been awarded the clasp. Stukageschwader 2 'Immelmann', of which his Gruppe was part, had in the last month blasted a way for the panzers with a skill, precision and daring that had made the world hold its breath. Karl Ludecke's decision, taken four years ago, to fly the Sturzkampfflugzeug rather than the more glamorous fighter had been fully vindicated. Yet for all this, as he stared down at the bespectacled Oberst behind the desk, Major Ludecke had a struggle to keep his temper.

'But Herr Oberst, we've sat here for nearly a week doing absolutely nothing!'

The Oberst shook his head. 'That's not true, Karl. You've been putting six new pilots through their paces. Acclimatising them to the Staffels, to your Gruppe. That's not doing absolutely nothing. It's doing a very great deal.'

'Herr Oberst,' said Ludecke in despair, 'all that could have waited.' He pointed towards the south-east. 'All the fighting is through the Weygand Line, in the Marne-Meuse gap. That's where the French armies of the Maginot Line will be destroyed. And if we're not there, then we should be attacking the English still fleeing towards Cherbourg and the Atlantic ports.'

The Oberst smiled at the impressive young officer standing before him. 'Tell me, Karl, how many missions have you flown in the last month?'

Ludecke thought for a moment. '85.'

The Oberst nodded. 'I understand your disappointment, but you needed a rest. The attack on the so-called Weygand Line is proceeding according to plan. The panzers are already through. As for the Normandy and Brittany ports, the English are finding the evacuation a very costly affair. As at Dunkirk, they're leaving all their equipment behind.'

Ludecke smiled. It was good news indeed, but it highlighted his own enforced idleness.

'Nevertheless, Herr Oberst . . .' he began, when the Oberst cut him short.

'Have you ever destroyed a tank?'

Ludecke shook his head. 'No, Herr Oberst, at least, not that I have proof of.'

The Oberst got up, walked to the window and stared out at the flying field.

'There's one more battle to be fought here in Normandy. The French are building an army west of the Seine. There is talk of a Brittany redoubt that even the English would return to help defend. The French still have armoured forces in the area, including the massive Char B. Thirty-five tons against our latest Panzerkampfwagen III's twenty-five tons and mounting a 75-millimetre cannon! These forces are now moving north. You and your Stukas may have destroyed everything from bridges to ammunition dumps, but never tanks.' He turned, glared at Ludecke and said, 'All I await is the operational readiness of your Gruppe and the first precise observation report.'

Major Ludecke sprang to attention. 'My Gruppe is ready, Herr Oberst.'

'Good! Then this afternoon should be your chance to open a new chapter in aerial warfare. Aeroplane versus tank!'

Ludecke saluted and left the hut. His step upon the firm spring grass was sprightlier than it had been a few minutes earlier, and his head was held higher. He felt sufficiently excited to make a detour towards a group of his new pilots clambering over the burned-out wreckage of an Armée de l'Air Potez 54, one of seven that littered the airfield.

The pilots, who had watched him enter the Oberst's office, crowded round, seeking news of their first sortie. Ludecke pointed to the nearest.

'What's the closest you have put a bomb to the target, Felix?'

The man thought for a moment, then said, 'Five metres, Herr Major, at the Training Unit.'

Ludecke shook his head. 'No good,' he said. 'When we go up this afternoon, it must be within *one* metre or the French tanks will simply blow their horns at us!'


A high-winged monoplane, at first sight like a British Lysander but with slightly swept-back wings, appeared from the east. Ignoring the ill-aimed, erratic bursts of anti-aircraft fire that sprouted from the otherwise unblemished sky, then hung like black puff-balls above the town, it began to circle. Cornford recognised the plane as a Henschel 126 reconnaissance aircraft, and knew exactly what was to happen. He had seen it before at Doullens.

He shouted for Cole to start the carrier, grabbed the women, thrust them into the Thorneycroft, then leapt in himself. They took the streets with the least traffic, the direction was unimportant. Two miles out of Brionne they came face to face with a column of French Char Bs. The 35-ton monsters, in their brown and green camouflage, their squat 75-millimetre guns pointing lethargically downwards, and only their drivers visible through the hatches, filled the road.

Cornford shouted, the driver braked, but the Chars kept grinding towards them. To turn back to a town that was about to be divebombed was folly. In the face of the oncoming tanks, it was also difficult. On this narrow road only the carrier could turn quickly. The only other way was the field on the left. Cornford pointed, the driver pushed the accelerator to the floor and they crashed through a scrubby hedge, Cole swinging the carrier after them.

'Under those trees!' shouted Cornford. 'Until this bloody lot's passed!'

At 3,000 metres, Ludecke led his two Staffels of twenty-six Stukas south-westwards. He was conscious that he was about to launch one of the last air attacks of the war. With the French defeated and Paris wide open, it would simply be a case of making peace with the English.

Inspired with the majesty of the moment, his head was as light as it had been on his first operation. He was whistling as he searched the roads for the tank column. With the Armée de l'Air destroyed, the remains of the RAF back in England and their own escort of Bfl09Es 4,000 metres above them, Ludecke could concentrate all his efforts on the ground. His only worry now was that the long evening shadows might mask the enemy.

After fifty minutes he turned north. The tank column should now lie ahead. Approaching from the rear he would have all the advantages of surprise. From 3,000 metres, each field might have been etched with a mapping pen. The road still had width, and a convoy of vehicles would not be difficult to see. Ludecke saw them, ahead and to port. At this distance it was difficult to distinguish tanks from trucks, but the constituent elements of the convoy were large. Below him he was sure lay his armoured column.

Ludecke tilted the Stuka and saw the road and convoy slowly disappear beneath the leading edge of his starboard wing. Then, levelling the machine, he continued to watch his prey through the target-viewing window between his feet. At a hand signal the two Staffels swung into echelon formation. Each pilot ran through the cockpit drill before the dive. Pitch controls, superchargers and throttles were set, radiator flaps closed, siren screamers armed.

Ludecke was exactly astern of the ground column and the sun was level with his wing-tip when he lowered his air brakes and the single 500-kilogramme bomb on its cradle. Then he half rolled, and turning with his ailerons began his near vertical dive. Sky changed to land. The Jumo's note altered, the plane began to shudder, and from the small generator on his starboard spat came the unmistakable wail of the 'Jericho trombone'. With that dreaded signature tune, the Stuka attack began.

They lay in the shallow ditch by the hedge, cheeks pressed into the damp grass, embracing the hard earth. The hideous scream as the first plane dropped from the evening sky was as chilling as a supernatural visitation. From this horizontal position, Simon saw the machine dive to within 500 feet of the ground, release the single, black bomb that had nestled between the undercarriage like a snatched lamb, pull out less than fifty feet above the tank turrets, and climb back into the darkening blue. He also saw and registered the dark green camouflage on the fuselage; the pale blue-green beneath the wings; the white band by the tail; the letter 'L' upon that white band; the white outlines of the great black crosses; and the bomb wobbling on its original course until it disappeared behind a Char to throw up a dirty brown cloud that reached the tree-tops.

Ludecke's bomb, as might be expected from a Stuka pilot with a clasp to his Iron Cross, First Class, was well placed. It burst so close to the third Char B in the convoy that it tossed the tank sideways, ripped off the exhaust system, tore the steel plate of the engine grating like the lid of a sardine tin, and twisted the huge driving sprocket so that the track jammed and the tank's own momentum snapped it. With that Char B immobilised, the remaining Stukas hurled themselves at the pent-up column.

The planes screeched, the earth shook, the tanks jinked, revved and roared as they tried to evade the bombs, deploy, and elevate their machine-guns to meet the onslaught. Under the Thorneycroft the girls screamed. Cole crawled from the ditch, set up the bren, fired half a magazine before Ludecke himself spotted him. A Stuka was directed in, dropping two fifty-kilogramme bombs that riddled the Thorneycroft and appeared to end the heroic resistance of Nipper Cole. But miraculously the carrier driver picked himself up, staggered back and would have repeated his act had not Cornford dragged him back into the ditch. When two of the Chars crashed through the hedge towards them, Church leapt up and tried to wave them away. With their hatches shut, the crews never even saw him.

'If the Stukas don't get us, those bastards will!' he screamed, before he too was dragged back into the ditch.

The two Chars clattered slowly across the field, the fresh grass mercilessly crushed beneath the great steel plates of their tracks, the dark earth ripped like rind each time they turned. With their huge slab sides towering above the skyline; their two, stubby, wicked-looking cannons; their twin machine-guns; their squat turrets with the evil eye slit below the crown of the commander's hatch, they were like wounded Stegosauri seeking shelter from a pack of angry Pterodactyls. Simon wondered how it was that with such monsters on the Allied side the panzers had got so far. As the tanks emerged from each dark eruption, they seemed impervious to anything man could throw against them. Behind their sixty millimetres of armoured plate, the crews must be laughing.

With one tank disabled, half a dozen lorries burning, the field pitted and a dozen cows killed, Ludecke's Staffelkapitän lined up to add his single 500-kilogramme bomb to the chaos. He had begun his dive when he noticed the two Chars moving across the field. A slight easing of the rudder bar pedal, a check on the red diving lines painted on the side window, and the target was realigned. The bomb landed ahead of the Char nearest to the carrier, and by the ditch. When the smoke and dust cleared, the carrier lay overturned and on fire and part of the ditch had been obliterated, but the Char was jinking away unscathed.

For the survivors of Sergeant Cornford's little band there was silence. The Char moved silently away from them, the carrier burned without the usual crackle of fire, the penultimate Stuka was diving without the usual scream of a banshee. On the lip of the crater, three grotesque khaki bundles were being inspected silently by Cornford and Cole. Marie, the girl with the mole on her cheek, apparently disfigured by no more than a trickle of blood from her temple, had her head cradled by a silently weeping Madame.

Major Karl Ludecke cut the engine, slid back the cockpit canopy, gave the thumbs-up sign to his Staffelkapitän drawing up next to him, then clambered out on to the wing. They walked back to the dispersal hut and made their reports. As they came out, Ludecke said, 'The last battle, Willie, the curtain is about to fall on Armageddon. By the autumn we shall have forgotten there ever was a war.'

The Staffelkapitän laughed, and broke into a run. 'The Bollinger '32, Herr Major! The six crates left by the Armée de l'Air. A crate for each tank we've put out of action.'

Ludecke beat him to the mess door by three clear metres.

# CHAPTER 13

As he stared through the vibrating window six inches from his face and looked down upon the darkening landscape, Hopkins decided that he would never get used to his job or the little Fieseler Storch that in the last three days had almost become his own private aircraft. The moment he had climbed in and the pilot had turned and said, 'With our extra fuel we're well over our 1,320 kilos, so don't get worried if the take-off seems a bit long,' all the butterflies in his stomach had started flapping again. He remembered the pulped messes he had just seen that only a few days ago had been two healthy men, and realised with horror what blazing petrol could do.

The take-off had been long. For a plane capable of landing in a football field, they seemed to run the length of France before crawling into the sky. Now, with less than an hour to go, he sat tensed in his cramped seat, his attaché case clutched firmly on his lap, wondering why he was doing what he was doing and suffering as he was suffering. The answer was, there was never a way out. Even in the aeroplane he was locked in.

When he again climbed the stairs in the Tirpitz Ufer, helping himself up with the aid of the banisters, Canaris was waiting. Hopkins managed to collapse into the chair before answering the first question. Yes, he had met the army dentist and thank God the man had been present.

'And was either of the bodies Manning's?' asked Canaris.

Hopkins mopped his brow, took off his spectacles and wiped

them as well. 'Not according to the dental evidence, Admiral, and that's the only evidence there was.'

'The dentist was quite certain? And you checked?'

'The dentist was certain, and I did check to the best of my ability.'

'So your compatriot is still alive?'

'It would seem so,' said Hopkins, without much enthusiasm.

'The burned papers?' asked Canaris.

'There were still some in the grass and in the ditch. The rest must have blown away. I collected what I could and gave them to your man as instructed. On one bit you could still see the type. It was German.'

Canaris took Hopkins to the door. At the door he said, 'You've done very well. My clerk has a cheque for you. Take Hela out for the afternoon. Have a jolly time and forget everything.'

Hopkins thanked the Admiral and went to the clerk's office. When Hopkins had gone, Canaris asked Oster to come in.

'Hopkins has just got back,' said Canaris. 'The dentist's report is negative. That means Manning is alive. If he is, where is he?'

'And the dossier, Herr Admiral?' asked Oster.

'We'll know more of that when the back-room boys have had a look at the paper.'

'A lot of English are still making for Cherbourg and the Atlantic ports,' said Oster.

'And there you think goes our man?'

'Where else?'

Oster went to the map and swept his hand towards Brittany and the west. 'There is nowhere else. Not if he was north of Paris.'

'We must know for certain,' said Canaris. 'Manning can't be allowed the freedom of Europe.'

'British Military Intelligence?' asked Oster.

Canaris nodded. 'But be discreet, Hans, very discreet.'

Oster saluted and left the room.

They took a tram-ride and ended in the Tiergarten at the zoo. They walked a long way before leaning over the railings and throwing crumbs to the ducks. It was a warm afternoon but a gentle breeze kept the temperature from soaring. Nevertheless, Hopkins was sweating as he knew he would. As Hela laughed at the antics of a duck and her darting duckling, Hopkins was conscious that the armpits of his jacket were wet and stained, and that he should have changed his shirt.

He glanced at Hela and hoped she didn't notice. He knew he was no fit company for a schoolgirl of nine, even if he was her father. As always, he was amazed and thankful that she had been spared almost all his physical characteristics. She had never looked like him at any time of her life. It wasn't that he was actually ugly, he was nothing. A man you passed and left alone. When he dressed, stared at his food-stained, crumpled suit, or looked at himself in the mirror, he always thought of an ageing myopic dumpling. A mercenary. Never as anything better. He had no illusions, and Hela's pleasure at seeing him always surprised him.

She asked where he had been and he told her away on business. She didn't question it for her father travelled a lot. He asked her if there was anything she needed and she said, 'No'. He asked whether everything was all right, and she said, 'Of course'. Although she was standing next to him, he felt miles away. It saddened him that he could seldom tell her a truth, that always there was this gulf of deceit between them. Not only was his work secret, but their very existence was too precarious for confidences. When your mother had been partly Jewish, your father half English and you lived in Nazi Germany, you were exceedingly vulnerable. You needed a fairy godmother to survive, and Canaris filled that role. That was why Hopkins could never get out of the trap.

'You're so like your mother.'

The girl gave an embarrassed laugh. Her father said that every time they met now.

'She was a very beautiful woman.'

That was another puzzle. Why had she ever married him? Perhaps it had been the hope of getting out of Germany. Going to Ireland or England. More and more now he thought that was the reason. With time he could find no other. But he was already involved with the Abwehr at the time of their marriage. When Canaris took over in 1934, his commitment became complete.

In the evening he bought Hela the best ersatz cream cake he could find and took her back to her aunt.

# CHAPTER 14

It was in the evening of Friday, 28 June that an old furniture van delivered the survivors of the Stuka attack — Madame, her maid Lucienne, Simon and five British soldiers — at the door of a stone farmhouse, one and a half kilometres from the village of Notre-Dame de Grâce and eight kilometres from Bernay. They were welcomed by the sole occupant, an elderly lady in black, Major Corbasson's formidable mother.

For a fortnight they had sheltered in the stark, whitewashed rooms of the nuns of Saint Geneviève. There, those with wounds had been nursed, and there they had heard of the fall of Paris, Pétain's request for an armistice, and the departure of the last ship for England. There too they had first learned the meaning of the word 'occupation'. A three-hour, devious, bone-shaking journey to the shallow plateau between the valleys of the Charentonne and the Orbiquet had brought them to the undistinguished village and the house that was to be their next lodgings. While the two women again embraced the comforts of home, the men exchanged one set of whitewash for another. Their new shelter was the cellar. Dark and damp, and with a broken ladder, it had one asset. It was cool in the summer heat.

They were fifty kilometres from the Channel in a region swarming with Germans. They needed food and medical supplies, and knew they couldn't stay long. To move they needed clothes, papers, transport and eventually a boat. They discussed the matter *ad nauseam*, but without any conclusions. In the afternoon of their third day, after the food had been passed down, Madame opened the door of the kitchen, lifted the trap and shouted. She was in a state of great excitement.

Flooded with daylight, her pale green eyes shining, her cheeks high and rosy and the dimple in her chin exuding joy, she looked like an archangel. As she came down the ladder, Cornford assisting her with firm hands round her waist, she announced that she had just seen Madame Lochard, the undertaker's wife, and had the most wonderful news.

'Madame Lochard has a brother,' cried Madame, looking round at the grey faces illuminated only by trap and grating, 'an old soldier from the Marne. He works on the quay at Dieppe unloading the fishing boats.' Her face beamed with excitement.

'He is in Notre-Dame for the funeral of their cousin. Tomorrow, before he goes back, he will see Simon and the sergeant!'

She waited for the reaction.

'You mean this chap can get us a boat?' asked Cornford in disbelief.

'You discuss it tomorrow,' said Madame almost coyly, as a nurse might keep a treat secret from an inquisitive child.

'Surely the Germans don't let boats go out fishing?' said Simon.

Madame's demeanour changed. She flushed and raised her hands in a Gallic gesture indicating the stupidity of question and questioner.

'The Boche like fish, don't they? Just like everyone else! The restaurants of Rouen, Havre, Deauville, Dieppe, everywhere, depend on fish. The Boche are asking for their stuffed crab, their sole Normande, their lobster à la crème.' She smiled, leaned forward and said, 'In spite of the edict forbidding fishing, one or two boats do go out. Officially . . . unofficially. They take two soldiers, maybe three, but they go out!'

Simon and Cornford sought more information. Madame grew petulant and told them to wait until they saw Monsieur Varlin. It was beginning to look a little difficult.

'Where are we meeting this man?' asked Simon.

'In the Café des Voyageurs.'

'Why can't he come here?'

Madame shrugged. 'We thought it better he didn't.'

Simon glanced round the cellar. 'It's crazy going out.'

'There are no Boche in Notre-Dame!' retorted Madame contemptuously.

Cornford plucked at his tattered battledress. 'I can't go to the village in this.'

'Tonight you and Simon will have papers, and you, Sergeant, will have clothes. Everything is being taken care of.'

Simon looked at Cornford. Madame cried out, 'You want a boat, don't you?' Cornford nodded. Simon said, 'Of course,' and thanked her. She gave him a glance and went back upstairs. When the trap was again shut, Church leaned over and touched the sergeant's sleeve.

'You want to watch out, Sarge. Even if we get to Dieppe, it's not going to be a cakewalk. Jerry doesn't much like people escaping.'

'It's worth a go, Acker,' said Cole. 'Don't put the damper on it before we've even started.'

'This isn't a trip round Weymouth Bay, you know,' said Church.

Cornford told them to shut up.

In the evening they heard a tap above them and the trap door opened. Simon climbed the ladder and disappeared. Madame and her mother-in-law were in the kitchen. Two loaves, butter, eggs and a few slices of ham lay on the long scrubbed table. Soup simmered on the range. The mother-in-law handed Simon a mug of coffee.

'The Boche are taking everything,' said Madame with a sigh. 'It's as if they'd never seen food or wine in their whole lives. It's quite disgusting!'

Simon went to the open window. It was a beautiful June evening. Tiny green apples had replaced blossom on the trees. Hens scratched in the dirt. Every time he came up he felt the same excitement, but he knew enough about events to realise that any sense or safety of freedom was a dangerous illusion. Lucienne came in with a pail of milk. Quietly, so that her mother-in-law shouldn't hear, Madame said, 'There is a notice on the door of the Mairie. It's been there for days. Anyone harbouring British or French soldiers will be shot.'

Simon said nothing, just turned his head away. After a moment Madame laughed. 'Anyway, you're not the only ones! Tell him, Lucienne.'

'Madame Lochard,' said Lucienne shyly, staring at the

flagstones, 'has three Tommies in her embalming room.'

'All alive!' cried Madame gaily, then put her finger to her lips.

They stood together looking out at the orchard. Madame teasingly touched Simon's cheek with her finger and said, 'I'll miss you.' The old lady coughed.

'With the Armistice signed,' said Simon gently, 'the Major'll soon be home.'

There was a silence. After a while Madame gave Simon a quick glance and said, 'The Boche are looking for billets. They're concentrating troops for the invasion of England.'

Simon looked down at her and grinned. 'They haven't a hope! The Channel's not the Somme or the Seine. Remember, your old friend Napoleon thought about it once and gave it up!'

'It's not just the Boche who think that the war with England is nearly over,' said Madame quietly. 'Many French think your country will surrender in the next two weeks.'

Simon remembered Cuthbertson. There must be others like him in the Government. Perhaps many like him. He worried about the truth in Madame's words, but laughed.

He told Cornford the news that Britain was being written off and the Germans concentrating for an invasion. Presumably a near bloodless one.

'You realise, don't you, Sergeant, that even if we did get away we could have no country to go back to?'

Cornford shook his head. 'I can't see that, sir. No one in England would let Jerry in. It wouldn't be like here. It's true we'd be on our own unless the Yanks came over, but that might be a blessing. At least we wouldn't have Allies just packing up and running!' He paused for a moment, then said, 'You know, we were never actually beaten. The BEF was only caught because the Belgians gave way on one flank, the Froggies on the other.'

'I don't think they were actually caught,' said Simon. 'According to one of Madame's friends, the BBC said that something like 340,000 got out via Dunkirk.'

'That's what I mean,' said Cornford cheerfully. 'You can't get an army away if it's properly knackered.'

'That's if you can believe the BBC,' said Simon.

Cornford was astonished. 'If you can't believe *them*, who can you believe?'

Simon shrugged. He thought of telling Cornford about his meeting with Canaris and Cuthbertson but decided it would be unfair. They needed this faith, however vague and undefined it might be. Besides, Cornford would never have believed him. Instead, Simon said, 'The Germans are looking for billets. The Gestapo will be nosing about any day now. We must clear out, it's not fair on the women.'

Cornford grunted, lay back on the sacks, closed his eyes, and said, 'Looks like it's all up to the old fellow from Dieppe.'

To walk again under a blue sky within a few days of midsummer; suck in the pure air; smell the heat on the grass; assimilate the myriad of colours that make up an orchard in full sunlight; and see cows pressing into the shade, their tails and tongues beset by perpetual motion, was, after the incarceration in the cellar, a joyous novelty. While it lasted they forgot. Field grey in France was a bad dream. No German could possibly appear to destroy such a noontime peace. Simon might have been walking down to the North Tyne Valley, Cornford to a Wiltshire village. Then they saw the tattered red-and-white awning that proclaimed the Café des Voyageurs; the rickety table perched on the pavement visible from 300 yards; and the plump woman pointing them out to the bird-like man sitting beside her, and all the euphoria vanished.

'Christ Almighty!' said Cornford in an awed voice. 'They must be bloody mad sitting out there like that!'

They weren't mad. It was simply that Monsieur Varlin, Madame Lochard's brother, liked the sun on his back. It soothed his wounds from the Marne. So Madame, Simon and Cornford settled at the pavement table to discover that they were not only exceedingly obvious but that they would have to shout, as the old man was deaf.

It took half an hour to reach the possibilities of a boat, and it was soon apparent that there were several difficult and profound problems. They ranged from the fact that very few boats actually went out, and those that did were carefully watched, to the Boche themselves. Nevertheless, old Varlin was not wholly unoptimistic.

Simon translated for Cornford. Cornford was for going back at once to the relative safety of the cellar when a black Citroën, followed by a green truck, roared down the road and halted outside the café. An Oberleutnant stuck his head out of the Citroën and asked if the champagne was good. That was the signal for a dozen soldiers to leap out of the truck and go into a well-drilled charade.

Six of the truck party, steel-helmeted and armed, took up positions either side of the café. Six others, wearing the more informal forage caps, dragged out a table, added it to the empty one already on the pavement, sat down and called for two bottles of champagne. A uniformed photographer, two cameras slung round his neck, moved in and began directing his subjects, both military and civilian. It was evident that these were not just pictures intended to show the world how the happy, conquering Wehrmacht relaxed, but to show the cordiality between conquerors and conquered. Happy, smiling French were as essential to the production as happy, smiling Germans.

Swiftly changing the poses, the photographer clicked his Leica, the two Englishmen said a dozen silent 'Cheeses', and the coarse, sweaty field-grey cloth engulfed them. In the midst of this precarious maelstrom, one man sat apparently unconcerned. Old Varlin, isolated by deafness, sipped his cider and sucked his pipe as if the Boche were still the other side of the Marne. It was not until Cornford's anxious bewildered face began rewarding the Germans' sense of fun that old Varlin suddenly leapt to his feet.

'My Captain!' he cried, indicating Cornford, then pointing to his own ear. 'He is as deaf as me and he is also dumb. He has been like that since he was a baby!'

A soldier cried out that this was a village of idiots, picked up Cornford's glass of cider and emptied the remains over the sergeant's head. Laughing, they climbed back into their vehicles and left as suddenly as they had arrived. When the truck at last disappeared down the long straight road, Cornford lowered his head into his hand and said, 'Oh, my God.' Old Varlin put an arm round the sergeant's shoulders, spat ferociously upon the pavement and said, 'You come to Dieppe, my friend. We'll get you a boat.'

They still didn't know how he would get a boat, but at that moment Dieppe seemed the only step in any direction.


# CHAPTER 15


Hill phoned Sinclair's number and was told that he had joined up. He got his flat number and tried that. Sinclair was there. They arranged to meet in a pub in the Strand. Sinclair walked in in his RNVR sub-lieutenant's uniform. Hill bought him a pink gin and said gruffly, 'How's your old friend Manning these days?'

Sinclair shrugged and said he hadn't the faintest idea. He'd never set eyes on Manning and had no idea where he was.

'Remember telling me,' said Hill, taking his pipe out of his mouth and surveying the bowl, 'that he had brought some papers to the embassy in Paris? Information on French steel production, projected figures for '40, '41?'

Sinclair went cold inside but nodded.

'Two very odd things have happened,' said Hill. 'K is making inquiries about him again. Wants to know if he's in England. Now K doesn't make inquiries without excellent reason.'

Hill stopped, sucked his pipe and ran a finger across his moustache.

'Look,' said Sinclair, 'I'm in the Navy now. I'm nothing to do with the FO any more. Try someone else.'

Hill shrugged. 'Who else is there to try? No one else there knows anything about Manning except you.'

'Next time try Cuthbertson, Cabinet Office,' said Sinclair sharply.

Hill nodded, took the extension number, repeated the name and said, 'One of our chaps who was at Cherbourg covering the evacuation remembers a fellow called Manning arriving there with a dicey British passport. They gave him a bit of a going-over, and surprise, surprise, do you know what they found?'

Sinclair shook his head.

'A second passport, American, in the name of Cotton, a Smith and Wesson — which shows he wasn't much of an agent — and a file of documents in German. Just as they are going to take him to pieces, he starts dropping top names and tells them to ring your fellows in Paris. The next minute there's a call from London, from damned near the summit, telling them to drop Mr Manning forthwith and get him back to the embassy on a red carpet.' He stopped, stared at Sinclair and said, 'Now don't you think those two events together are pretty damned odd?'

Sinclair had to agree that they were, and was thankful that he was due to report to Portsmouth in the morning. Two minutes after Hill had left the pub, Sinclair rang Cuthbertson.


When Cuthbertson came in, the Minister pointed to a chair.

'This may be a bit of a shock, Minister,' said Cuthbertson carefully, 'but it is just possible that we were wrong about Manning.'

The Minister raised an eyebrow and said, 'How do you mean, "wrong", Cuthbertson?'

'MI are interested,' said Cuthbertson. 'They have contacts with the Abwehr. The Abwehr want to know whether Manning is in England.'

'You said he died in that car,' said the Minister accusingly.

Cuthbertson scratched his ear. 'That was our information, Minister. And as I said at the time, it was a most reliable source.'

'Obviously not reliable enough,' said the Minister dryly.

'The point is, Minister,' said Cuthbertson, 'do the Abwehr know of the car incident? Or are they just asking us out of concern for the file?'

The Minister got up from the desk and walked to the window. 'I might as well tell you, Cuthbertson, that none of this is a complete surprise to me. You told me Manning came out of Germany on an American passport under the name of Richard Cotton. One of the US Counsellors here had a query from their people in Berlin about an American called Richard Cotton. It seems he was stopped by the German military in

France, allowed to go, but as a matter of routine his passport details were sent back. The query reached the German Foreign Ministry.'

'When did that happen?' asked Cuthbertson quickly.

There was a pause, then the Minister said, 'After the car was shot up.'

'You said nothing!' said Cuthbertson.

The Minister shook his head. 'It didn't have to be Manning. An American passport could have been very useful during recent events.'

'No, Minister,' said Cuthbertson, 'it doesn't have to be Manning, but if the car he was in got burned up, and if the bodies were unrecognisable, then it's very difficult to explain what his American passport is doing unsinged.'

The Minister remained silent.

'Where did all this happen?' asked Cuthbertson. 'Perhaps we can make some discreet inquiries from this end.'

'East of the Seine, south of Vernon.'

'If he did survive,' said Cuthbertson, 'what on earth happened to him? There's no record of him coming back with the last of the BEF, although we're still checking. And if later he got put in the bag, then the Abwehr would know and wouldn't be asking questions.'

They sat in silence until the Minister said, 'After all the fighting and chaos there must be thousands missing over there.'

'Nevertheless, Minister,' said Cuthbertson, 'I'm sure you would agree we must know for an absolute fact whether Manning is dead or alive. Things must be settled!'

The Minister agreed but wasn't sure how to go about it.

Madame had felt the hostility. In the village they whispered whenever they saw her. She had never actually heard what they were whispering, and when she stood in the queue at the baker's and caught everyone's eye they smiled as they always had, but she knew they were whispering about her. When Lucienne burst into the kitchen, wide-eyed with excitement, there was another blow.

'The English have attacked our fleet in Oran, Madame,' cried the girl. 'The *Bretagne*, *Provence* and *Dunkerque* have all blown up! Hundreds are dead!'

'The English have attacked the French?' cried Madame in utter disbelief.

'Yes, Madame.'

'Nonsense, girl,' said Madame. 'The English would *never* attack the French. We're on the same side.'

'It's on the wireless,' said Lucienne. 'In the village they now hate the English as much as the Germans!'

'It's Boche propaganda!' cried Madame. 'They're driving a wedge between the Allies.'

'Madame,' said Lucienne, fighting her tears, 'we're no longer allies. We have signed an armistice. Why should the Germans say that the English have attacked us if they haven't? And you know perfectly well British bombers are already attacking France. We watched the searchlights and the guns shooting at one last night.'

'You stupid girl!' cried Madame. 'They're attacking the Germans in France, not the French.'

'Their bombs fall on us, Madame. In Le Havre, houses are destroyed and people killed every night.'

Madame buried her face in her hands. She couldn't understand the war any more. When it started it had seemed straightforward. Now there was neither direction nor logic. She kept the news of Oran from the Englishmen, but Simon and Cornford both sensed the hostility from the girl. In the evening Madame told them. When it was nearly dark the two men went out into the orchard.

'We find a man who works in the docks, has access to boats,' said Cornford bitterly. 'We get him lined up, go to that bloody café and the bloody Navy bugger everything up!'

Simon shrugged. 'The Navy probably had a reason. Anyway, old Varlin wasn't exactly a certainty.'

Cornford indicated the house. 'We're dependent on the French for survival. You saw the way the girl looked at us.'

Simon was searching for some non-existent source of hope when he felt a sharp sting on his right knee. He thought nothing of it, for the air was full of gnats and he had long forgotten the sprain where he had leapt from the car. They went back into the house.

Their reception by the women remained chilly. They said goodnight and went down into the cellar. In spite of the cool of that place in the night, Simon's knee irritated enough for him to take the blanket away. By the following afternoon, the limb was hot and swollen, the skin stretched tight and shining. Madame inspected the inflamed area, pronounced it vital that the poison should not reach the groin, and ordered him up from the cellar and into her bed. Oran seemed to have been forgotten.

That night Madame slept across the passage with Lucienne. Simon had the great ancestral bed with its four heavy wooden posts and carved headboard to himself. But for the pounding in his leg it would have been something to savour. In the morning he had a fever. Madame and Lucienne dosed him with aspirin and applied cold poultices. With the blinds drawn he slept fitfully. In the afternoon, in the midst of an enormous sweat, he was suddenly conscious of shadows at the foot of the bed. When his eyes focused and his mind cleared a little, he saw a German officer. Next to the officer was Madame. Simon heard Madame say, 'This is my cousin who has a fever. I couldn't possibly move him.' The officer grunted and they both left the room.

In the evening, when Madame spoon-fed him, she whispered, 'Don't be frightened, but we have a colonel now billeted upon us!'

Feebly Simon nodded. Had he been well the news would have terrified him. As it was he was too ill to care.

'Although he is a Boche,' said Madame, 'he is very much a gentleman, for which we must all be grateful.'

Simon smiled, letting the wide mattress enfold him.

'The colonel even offered to send their own doctor to you,' said Madame, 'but I told him you were past the worst.' Then she laid her cool fingers upon his forehead, wiped the sweat from his body and changed him into another of Major Corbasson's night-shirts.

Whichever way he lay, however well he tucked his blanket and greatcoat around, Lance-Corporal Church couldn't get to sleep. He should have been used to the boxes and straw that cushioned him from the stone floor, but tonight they were rock hard. So he lay with his hands behind his head staring at the tiny rectangular grating that let in their air supply, meagre

98

daylight and nightglow, and brooded.

He tried to thrust the hopelessness of the situation away by thinking of his wife; the terraced house they shared with her parents; his daughter; the yard where the bath hung and the privy was; the vegetable patch with the rhubarb growing through the broken bucket; the Lord Nelson; and Woolworth's on a Saturday afternoon. But it was no good. Reality was the cellar. The smell of old food compounded itself with stale male sweat, fleas and the slow, deep, unsynchronised breathing of the others who shared his refuge.

There was another reality, however, a very enticing one. As the night wore on it even overcame the bodies in the cellar and the German officer upstairs. Lucienne's slim legs. When she had sat in the cellar in the evenings, Church had found it impossible to take his eyes from them. Now he remembered every detail of ankle, shin and knee, and in particular that mysterious hidden area in the darkness between the folds of her skirt. He remembered the way she had smiled at him and looked down when she had seen him smiling at her. He remembered that Manning was upstairs in a decent bed, away from the smell of dried sweat, feet and bad breath. Manning was near the smell of women.

He sat up and looked around the cellar. The deep breathing went on unchecked, so did the crickets beyond the grating. He swung his feet on to the floor, pulled on his trousers, did up his shirt, threw his greatcoat over his shoulders, picked up his boots and went up the ladder as silently and stealthily as if he was crawling under a belt of enemy wire. When he lifted the trap it creaked but the sergeant, though immediatley beneath, didn't move. Church lifted himself into the cupboard, gently lowered the trap behind him and opened the door into the kitchen.

For a long time he stood at the window staring at the still night countryside, at the dark silhouettes of the apple trees, and upwards into the sky itself. Then he put on his boots and went out into the garden.

Lucienne had the room at the back, and with the warm night her window was open. Church climbed on to the lean-to and levered himself in over the sill. He saw the shape on the bed and moved quickly towards it. He clapped a hand over the

99

sleeping girl's mouth and whispered, 'Don't worry, it's me, Acker. I only want a chat.' Lucienne awoke, bit the hand and screamed. Church shouted, 'You stupid bitch! I said it was me, Acker!' and struggled to quieten her, but in the darkness she slipped from the bed. He managed to stop her from undoing the bolt, but not from hammering on the door. When he heard Madame on the landing, and a moment later deep guttural German, he let the girl go and ran back to the window. A German stood in the garden, his rifle pointing upwards.

Church swore, and turned from the window.

'See what you've done, you silly little bugger!' he shouted at the girl, then went to the door and slid the bolt. When he saw Oberst Brauer, his greatcoat over his pale blue pyjamas and a Luger in his hand, he slowly raised his arms and said, 'Don't shoot! It's a fair cop!'

At some time in the night, Simon heard the commotion. He had no idea what it was or where it came from. At another time, also in the night, Madame came into his room with a candle. She was crying as she mopped his chest and changed his nightshirt, but she said nothing.

Simon awoke late in the morning. From the patterns of light coming through the edges of the blinds, he knew that the sun was high. He felt clear, sensible and at peace. The throbbing in his leg had ceased, his body was no longer consumed by that burning heat. Cornford, in shabby suit and ubiquitous beret, crept into the bedroom.

'You're looking better,' said Cornford, easing open the corner of the blind and letting more light into the room. 'Just to tell you we're off. It's too hot here. They've found us a barn. See you in a couple of days.'

'The German?' said Simon, wondering if the officer he had seen was a figment of his delirium.

Cornford nodded, said they were bloody lucky not to be all in the bag, and recounted Church's exploits.

'Mind you, Madame really pulled a fast one. Pretended she'd never seen Acker in her life and that the bugger had broken into the house to get some grub!'

'And Church?' asked Simon faintly.

The sergeant shrugged. 'So far as I know, didn't say a bloody word. Let's hope it stays that way.' Cornford stuck out a great hand. Feebly, Simon took it.

'We're going by bus. It's not far, about ten miles. I hope to God we haven't got to speak.'

'You'll be all right. Give them my love.'

Cornford winked. 'See you in a couple of days. Look after Madame for us.'

He touched his beret and walked out of the room. Simon realised that once again he was on his own.

He had fallen asleep with his head between her breasts, her arms clasped around him and a sense of such utter peace he could remember no moment like it. Now he lay with his eyes open, listening. Although the moon was obscured, there was enough light to make out the footposts of the bed, the pattern of the wallpaper and the frame of the painting opposite. The mattress seemed the softest thing he had ever lain on; the quilt, the coolest, most fragrant cover that had ever enfolded him. After all his privations he was, for a moment, contented. Then he heard the Oberst cross the landing and remembered Church on his way to prison camp, the rest of the men in a barn and the hopelessness of his own position.

He turned on his side. Madame lay quiet, her black hair on the pillow. He looked at the crucifix on the wall above their heads and tried to touch it. Madame opened her eyes and saw him.

'Sorry about Acker Church,' said Simon.

'It was being in the cellar,' said Madame sleepily. 'It's not a good place for men.'

Simon smiled and went back to sleep.

# CHAPTER 16

Heydrich pushed the mass of papers away and got up. He was in danger of being snowed under. If he wasn't careful he would never leave his desk again, except perhaps to attend one of the Führer's conferences or one of Himmler's SS Knights' evenings. He needed to get back to something animate. To flesh and blood.

It was their own success, the success of the RSHA and the Reich itself that threatened to overwhelm them. Within ten months, half a million square miles of new territory and a hundred million new souls had been added to the Third Reich. Heydrich's responsibility for security was now enormous. It meant giving up much of his cherished sport and working all the hours of summer daylight. But when he felt smothered, as he did now, he needed to concentrate on just one item. Today it was Manning's file.

Canaris had reported Manning killed in France on 10 June, but Heydrich now knew that to be nonsense. Not only had the Gestapo checked the bodies in the car and reported that Abwehr agents had been there before them, but he had received the Cotton information. Whether the Englishman had been subsequently killed in the fighting, whether he was still in Europe or had got back to England were now the only matters for conjecture. Heydrich went back to his desk, scanned the last few entries in the file, then looked up at his adjutant.

'He is not amongst the prisoners of war?'

'No, Herr Obergruppenführer.'

'And the last of the English soldiers in France have been rounded up?'

'They are still finding a few, Herr Obergruppenführer.'

Heydrich handed back the file. 'If he has got back to England, we have no way of knowing. Unless, of course, our friends the Abwehr tell us.'

The adjutant laughed.

'You've circulated his photo and description to every Inspector of the Sicherheitspolizie and the SD in France?' snapped

Heydrich. 'Also to the French police both sides of the Armistice Line?'

'Yes, Herr Obergruppenführer.'

'You're trailing Abwehr agents going to France?'

'Yes, Herr Obergruppenführer.'

'Then we can only wait, Helmut, and hope for a break. With everything going our way, it shouldn't be long.'

The adjutant saluted and left the room.

In the evening, while Heydrich had a long conversation with his superior, Himmler, and assured the Reichsführer-SS that Manning was the key to the destruction of Canaris and the absorption of the Abwehr in to Himmler's SS empire, a few hundred metres away in the Tirpitz Ufer the little Admiral was poring over a desk covered with photos and magazines. When an Unteroffizier escorted Hopkins in, Hopkins stopped, stared at the mass of photos and stroked his chin.

'Looks like you've been on holiday, Admiral?'

Canaris ignored the joke, came round to the front of the desk and handed Hopkins a copy of *Der Angriff*. Hopkins took the paper, studied it, then handed it back, puzzled.

'The photo . . .' said Canaris, indicating.

Hopkins moved his glasses with one hand to make sure he wasn't missing anything, and held the paper with the other.

'Your soldiers enjoying themselves.'

Canaris indicated the photos on his desk. Most were in black and white, a few in colour.

'A magazine is about to be launched in Paris called *Signal*. Our photographers have been busy all over Occupied France.' He picked up a handful of pictures. 'As you can see, we have the Wehrmacht visiting the Madeleine, the Place de la Concorde, the Opéra, outside Maxim's, in the Métro, at the Grand Palais, even on the beach at Deauville. All to show the French and the world how well we all get on!'

Hopkins shrugged. 'It wasn't my war.'

'Pictures were also taken in some of the villages. This one, for instance. The original of the one in *Der Angriff*.'

Canaris handed Hopkins the photo and watched his face. Unlike the photo in the newspaper, this one was clear, the detail good.

'That man,' said Canaris, indicating with the tip of his pen. 'Ever seen that face before?'

Hopkins mopped his temples, looking longingly at the chair and said nothing. Canaris took the photo back and selected two more, one in colour.

'Taken at the same time and in the same place. Of course, the beret is strange, the clothes are baggy, there's a shadow across the eyes. But the jaw, the mouth, those thin cheeks . . .'

'The Café des Voyageurs,' said Hopkins quietly, reading the words on the awning. 'Where is it?'

From beneath the pile of newspapers, Canaris produced a map.

'In the village of Notre-Dame de Grâce, eight kilometres north-east of Bernay in Normandy.'

'And I suppose you want me to go there?' asked Hopkins without relish.

Canaris indicated the chair. Hopkins dropped into the leather gratefully. Canaris stared down at the photos.

'Whatever happens, your movements mustn't stir up a hornet's nest. The Gestapo have already been round the car and the bodies.'

'May I ask, Admiral,' said Hopkins, beginning to sweat under the heat of the desk lamp, 'why the Gestapo are interested?'

Canaris looked up and shook his head. Hopkins wasn't surprised. It was worth trying. It would have made the job and the man more interesting, but no doubt the less he knew the better. More often than not it was like that.

'I'm going to make you a soldier,' said Canaris with the trace of a smile. 'You can't go running about northern France any more as a civilian. Soldiers aren't so obvious.' He paused, looked at Hopkins and added, 'It'll have to be something very unmilitary. Know anything about horses?'

Hopkins shook his head.

'Pity, you could have been in the Veterinary Corps.' He thought for a moment, then said, 'You travel with the violet Waffenfarben of an army chaplain!'

Hopkins closed his eyes and sighed. His soul was already disturbed enough. He was the one who needed the chaplain.

To be a fake one only added irony to his troubles.

104

'You'll have a driver,' said Canaris cheerfully, 'and to throw any hounds off the trail you'll go by sea to Cherbourg. You'll take the train to Bayeux, and the driver will pick you up there. As cover, I'll arrange to have you attached to one of the signal units of 6th Army. I take it you know a bit about the Bible?'

'I started life as a Catholic, Admiral, but I wouldn't wish to give a sermon.'

Canaris smiled. 'You'd be a fool if you got yourself into that position.'

After a moment, Hopkins said, 'And if I find this man, how do I tell you?'

'Through the OKW net. We must think of something apt and not too dramatic.'

In the end they agreed upon a piece of Isaiah: 'Fasten him as a nail in a sure place.'


Church was deeply worried, as the sweat on the palms of his hands and in the hollow of his spine revealed. Throughout his military career he had been instructed that should he be taken prisoner he must give nothing but name, rank and number. William Ronald Church, Acting Lance-Corporal, 2147569. Unfortunately the elderly Hauptmann interrogating him thought this information quite insufficient.

'You must understand, we have no real proof you are even a British soldier?'

As evidence, Church fingered his tattered battledress. The Hauptmann laughed. 'They're ten a penny. So are identity discs. You can buy them in the Paris flea market.' He pointed at Church's head. 'You've no cap, no regimental badge and you won't say what your regiment was. That makes it very difficult for me. Also, you were captured alone. Soldiers don't travel alone. Only officers.'

'I told you,' said Church, 'I travelled alone.'

'Sleeping in barns and outhouses, stealing your food, all on your own?' said the Hauptmann sarcastically. 'You must think I'm a child.'

'It's summer, it's warm.'

The Hauptmann shook his head. 'Even if you were amongst the very last of the English army to flee from the Brittany ports, you could not have survived in the occupied part of France as long as you have without companions or without help from the local population.'

'I was alone I tell you!' said Church stubbornly.

'And if you had been trying to leave from the Brittany ports, why come back into Normandy?' The Hauptmann got up from the table and went to the wall map. 'From St Nazaire to where you were captured, 350 kilometres. From Cherbourg to where you were captured, 200 kilometres. What am I to make of that?'

On his hard chair, Church shifted uncomfortably. The longer he was questioned by the Hauptmann and the longer the red-faced Feldwebel stared down at him to intimidate him, the more truculent he became. He looked up at the map and shrugged.

'We wish to send you to a prisoner-of-war camp,' said the Hauptmann with a smile. 'But you are making it so very, very difficult.'

'All I have to tell you,' said Church, 'is my name, rank and number. You've had it. But if you want, I'll repeat it.'

The Hauptmann opened his cigarette case and offered it. Church hesitated then accepted.

'You must understand,' said the Hauptmann, 'that the war is virtually over. The French and English armies have been destroyed. Your regiment is now just part of history. Telling me what it was will make no difference to future events but it will prove to me that your story is correct and that you are a British soldier. After that you'll go to your prison camp and there, no doubt, you will feel completely at home amongst many of your old friends!' He stopped for a moment, then said, 'Are you married?'

Church nodded.

'Excellent, excellent! Then your wife will be officially notified of your capture, and all her worries and uncertainties will be removed.'

Church drew hard on the cigarette. It gave him the first peace of the week.

'Just your regiment,' said the Hauptmann, his pencil poised.

'5th Wessex,' said Church flatly.

The Hauptmann smiled and carefully wrote it down.

# CHAPTER 17

In the evening, Oberst Brauer asked Madame to join him for a drink in the sitting room. She was surprised, and at first a little shocked. But when she thought about the invitation, she found it not all that unreasonable. After all, they did live in the same house. So after a little hesitation she accepted.

At first the Oberst was meticulously correct, bowing when she came in, offering her the better chair, sitting across the room from her and confining his conversation to concerts in Berlin and visits to Paris before the war. After two glasses of Dom Pérignon, however, he began to relax. Madame, glad to find him so civilised, also relaxed.

When the Oberst learned that she had not heard from her husband in spite of the armistice, he promised to make inquiries. When he confided that he had intended writing to his wife that evening but now felt too tired, Madame understood. When he sat back, glass in hand, smiling at her, she decided he bore a remarkable resemblance to her friend the General. When he suddenly moved his chair nearer hers and leaned across to refill her glass, she was not the least alarmed.

'I hope, Madame,' said the Oberst, 'that your cousin is recovering?'

Madame flushed and murmured that he was. Brauer dropped his eyes from her face to her lap, gently laid his hand on that ample lap and added confidentially, 'Despite my fifty years I'm not all that old-fashioned, you know. Nor am I unaware that in France these things are treated, shall we say . . . differently?'

Madame flushed again and smiled. Brauer, suddenly conscious of his hand, took it away, sat back in the chair and began talking about himself. Verdun 1916 had given him his great respect for the French. Now, because of age and wounds, he was on the Staff. Not that he was having a quiet war. Modern blitzkreig saw to that. But the war wouldn't last much longer. After the defeat of their armies in France the English were very near collapse. Another week of attacks by the Luftwaffe, and Churchill, the main obstacle to peace, would go. Then England would sue for an armistice. After that the occupation of England would be a simple matter. He slid a cigarette into his holder, lit it, smiled, and said, 'In a way, the occupation of England has already begun. The island of Guernsey was taken more than a fortnight ago without a shot being fired. Jersey surrendered the next day, also without resistance. It is a sign that the English are nearly ready to give in.'

Madame felt a little sad, but decided that for everyone's sake it was as well to get the fighting over as quickly as possible.

'You don't think then, Colonel,' she asked, 'that the English will fight for their own country?'

Brauer shrugged. 'It is just possible, for a very short time. But their position is quite hopeless, as they must know in spite of Churchill's propaganda.' He opened a second bottle, filled Madame's glass, scraped his chair a little nearer hers and said, very earnestly, 'However, if the Luftwaffe doesn't finish the matter with England, then the army certainly will.' He raised his glass. 'Now France has broken off diplomatic relations with England, here's to peace and cooperation between our two countries!'

Madame did not actually respond, but murmured and sipped her champagne. Suddenly the Oberst tapped her thigh and said, 'Although I shall be very sorry to leave your excellent house, believe me, Madame, in two, maybe three, weeks from now General Strauss's 9th Army, and in particular VIII Corps HQ in which I have the honour to serve, will be requisitioning billets not here in Normandy but in Sussex, England.'

In view of all that had happened in the last ten weeks, Madame had no reason to disbelieve him.

It was half-past eleven when Madame rose to leave. Oberst Brauer hurried to the door and opened it for her.

'A favour, Madame, if I may?- I have three more cases of Dom Pérignon arriving tomorrow. I would deem it an honour if I might have them delivered into your cellar?'

Madame smiled. 'Certainly, Colonel.'

'Then perhaps my servant might keep the key?'

Madame agreed.

'One other thing,' said the Oberst. 'Owing to the fortunes of war, we share the same house. I think we may be called friends. After the despicable action by the English fleet at Oran and now Dakar, we shall soon be allies. My first name is Albrecht . . .' and he gave a little bow.

Madame waited a moment, then said, 'And mine is Juliette.'

As Madame passed under the Oberst's outstretched arm that held open the door, he brought his heels together and said, 'Then thank you, Juliette, for making an old soldier's evening so pleasant.'

Madame gave a little curtsey, left the room and went across the hall to the kitchen, amazed at the changes life could bring.

Simon was sitting on the bed when the old lady came into the room without knocking. She stared at the great family bed and asked if he was better. He said he was.

'When are you going, Monsieur?' she asked, still staring at the bed.

'In the morning,' said Simon.

The old lady nodded. Simon saw the look of pain in her face.

'You will be better with your friends,' she said.

Simon agreed. He would like to have said something about her son coming home, but it would hardly have been tactful. The old lady shook her head and left the room. Madame came in a few minutes later and quickly closed the door behind her. She was flushed and breathing fast.

'I don't know what the Oberst knows or suspects,' she said, 'but he wants to keep his wine in the cellar and asked for the key!'

'That's not all that unreasonable for the occupying power,' said Simon. 'You and Lucienne cleared it out after the others left. If that's all he wants . . .'

'He believes the Luftwaffe will destroy the RAF in another week, then the occupation of England will begin. It will all be over in a fortnight.'

'He could be wrong,' said Simon. 'England's been written off before.'

Madame hesitated, then said, 'He asked again how you were.'

'Being friendly, no doubt,' said Simon, then seeing the look of worry on Madame's face, added gently, 'It's all right. I'm going in the morning.'

She sat on the bed and put his hand in hers.

'I would never have asked you to go, you know that, but it's too dangerous here.' She shut her eyes. 'If you stayed, the colonel would want to see you and talk to you. He has also asked Lucienne about you. You seem to be a source of great interest to him.' She blushed and added, 'He has a picture of the French . . . and you are my cousin.'

'He's jealous,' said Simon curtly.

Madame looked surprised.

'Of course he is!' said Simon. 'The conquering hero, far from home and Brunhilde, with a smashing billet and a beautiful woman, and the only thing in his way is a runt of a cousin who's supposed to be in your bed because he's ill!'

He had started speaking in jest but ended in anger. He leaned back against the headboard, put his hands behind his head and stared at her. She turned her head away sharply. 'He is a Boche.' He put his arms round her and she began to laugh. He placed a hand over her mouth to stop her making too much noise. He called her a 'brazen hussy', which he had to explain.

In the morning, when the Oberst had gone to his head-quarters, she walked with Simon to the bus. He asked her to be sure and let them know the moment she heard from Monsieur Varlin at Dieppe. She promised she would, but he realised she was embarrassed about something. As they stood waiting, she gave him her copy of *Madame Bovary*. He was putting it in his bag when he recognised the undertaker's wife, dressed in black, coming out of the church. Madame Lochard saw them and deliberately turned away. Simon asked Madame what was wrong. Madame administered the *coup de grâce*.

'Her nephew, Monsieur Varlin's son, was at Oran. He was killed when the English blew up the *Bretagne*.'

She said nothing about old Varlin himself, and Simon didn't ask. It was a tearful, hopeless parting.

In the late afternoon, the village gendarme arrived with two French plain-clothed men and hammered on the door. Madame protested, and they said they had information. She cursed the local busybodies and the three men swept past her into the house. Two of them had just gone upstairs when the

Oberst returned. When he understood what was happening, he ran up the stairs and confronted the plain-clothed men. After a brief discussion all the police left. When Brauer came down to the kitchen, he found the three women sitting sewing and his servant boiling a kettle for coffee.

'I told them,' said Brauer very firmly, 'that the only English soldier in this house was the one I arrested personally in the night. The one that broke in for food.'

Still shaking, Madame thanked him.

'No one likes police in their house,' said Brauer sympathetically, 'even if they are only doing their duty.' Then he bowed and asked Madame to join him again after supper.

Madame glanced at her mother-in-law, hesitated, then said she would. With the house now devoid of either Frenchmen or Englishmen and the three women thrown together on their own, Madame realised, with both shock and guilt, that she had actually begun to look forward to the comforting sound of the Oberst's car upon the gravel.

# CHAPTER 18

The barn was typically Norman. The low sides half timbered, the roof tall, sloping and massive. It belonged to a red-faced, surly farmer, Jacques Frenay, who seemed to tolerate their presence rather than welcome it. If he was a little anti-British he was violently anti-Boche, and that was why they were there. He and his wife brought them food, enough to keep alive, but other than that they kept a distance. When either did speak it was to exhort them not to go out and be seen by the Boche and not to smoke. When Simon arrived, he made the tenth.

The moment he had flung his case on the hay, Cornford was asking for news of the old man from Dieppe. Simon passed on Madame's parting remarks, adding that they were unlikely to hear from old Varlin again. Cornford's face sagged.

'Can't really blame him,' he said after a while. 'I'd feel the same if someone blew my kid up. And if Acker talks and we're stuck here . . .'

'I wouldn't worry too much about Acker,' said Simon. 'We've had that hazard ever since he was taken. They must have finished interrogating him days ago. He's safely in prison camp by now.'

Cornford was not reassured. 'But supposing Jerry knows and they're just waiting to get as many of us as they can? Two more are due in tonight. That'll make twelve.'

'Acker doesn't know we're here. And if he did tell them about Madame's, no one came.'

Simon glanced across the heaps of green hay at his new home. There were men playing the inevitable cards, Nipper Cole carving a piece of wood, one reading by a shaft of sunlight that came through a cracked tile, the rest lying bored and waiting.

'How far's the Seine?' asked Cornford after a while.

'Twenty kilometres, maybe twenty-five.'

'Frenay said barges used to go down every day.'

They discussed the prospects of getting a barge and found them gloomy. 'A hundred miles to the sea, counting twists in the river,' said Simon. 'Germans on both banks, their patrol craft in the river and their navy at the coast. Dieppe would have been difficult enough, this is ten times worse!'

Cornford sat on the hay and stared up at the ancient beams that held the roof. 'The logical conclusion of your attitude, Mr Manning, is to give ourselves up.'

'And a fine mess that would make for people like Madame and the Lochards,' said Simon.

'So we go for a barge on the Seine?'

'Or the way no one seems to have thought of. South through the Armistice Line.'

'Twelve of us?' said Cornford scornfully.

Simon grunted. It was a hell of a lot to try and move.

'We're fifteen miles from the Seine,' said Cornford. 'It flows into the English Channel. That's the way out, it bloody well must be!'

Simon asked about the farmer and how long they could stay.

'Funny bugger, Frenay,' said Cornford. 'You don't know what to make of him. Talks about priests doing something. All the local priests seem to know we're here.'

'Must be the confessional,' said Simon, and sat down in a shaft of sunlight. He desperately wanted to be alone, and took out the book Madame had given him. It was in French. He had been reading for a few minutes when Cornford said, 'Did she give you that?'

Simon nodded.

'Miss her?'

Simon nodded again.

'Are you married?' asked Cornford.

'No.'

Cornford grunted and looked closely at the book. That it was in French greatly surprised him. 'Does *that* take your mind off things?' he asked doubtfully. Simon said it helped. The sergeant scratched his chin. 'I suppose we've all got our own way out,' he said after a while, 'otherwise we'd be raving mad by now.' He indicated the figures on the straw. 'Suspended animation, that's what most of them have. They acquire it as soon as they get in the army. Have to. That's what sees them through. You see, they don't find this place all that different from Aldershot or Catterick.'

'And what about a senior NCO?' asked Simon, giving up hope of reading.

'Neither flesh nor fowl,' said the sergeant. 'A sort of half existence, like purgatory.'

'Don't worry,' said Simon, smiling, 'if we're going to scramble down to the Seine and pinch one of those barges without a peashooter between us, and then take the damned thing down the river, there won't be much time for suspended animation or purgatory.'

The sergeant thought for a moment. 'Perhaps that's the way to go,' he said, 'in one bloody big glorious bang!'

One of the two to arrive that night was an officer, a Major from the Highlanders captured at St Valery who had escaped on the march. His arrival was not received with rapture. Behind the curiosity there was hostility. For other ranks used to the rough and ready rule of an NCO to have a Major suddenly in their midst took a lot of readjustment.

The Major felt the resentment in the morning when he stood

in the middle of the barn and surveyed the ring of scarecrows Cornford prepared for his inspection. But a brisk pep-talk on their doggedness in not giving in, a reminder of all the Huns occupied in looking for them, and therefore unavailable for any attack on Britain, did something to soften the atmosphere. Time did the rest.

In private, with Cornford and Simon, the Major was less confident. The catchment area over which the British were being fed into the barn alarmed him as much as it did Cornford. Even without the logistics of keeping more than a dozen men alive in enemy-occupied territory, it must only be a matter of time before they were betrayed. Crisply the Major inquired what the plan was.

'It's a matter of getting a boat, sir,' explained Cornford. 'The river's only fifteen miles away, the sea fifty.' There he stopped. The Major realised there was no plan.

The Major had been sheltering with a plate-layer in the Caux Region beyond the Seine. The railwayman had contacts with bargees working the river. Cornford inquired eagerly whether the man was likely to come up with anything. The Major was non-committal. He liked the fellow but was worried about his communism.

'Let's hope he does come up with something sir,' said Cornford optimistically, pleased to be handing over his responsibility, 'but Mr Manning here' — he indicated Simon — 'reckons south through the Armistice Line the best bet.'

'Spain or Switzerland,' said Simon.

The Major seemed to notice Simon for the first time. He gave him a disdainful look and asked if he was in the RAF. Simon was considering his reply when Cornford did it for him. 'He's a spy sir. A British spy.'

The Major glared. 'You're a what?'

Simon smiled and said, 'Tweseldown OTC Camp, 1927, Major. You were an instructor. I was a cadet. We took up a defensive position in the scrub just south of the racecourse, looking out over Farnborough aerodrome. There was a Hawker Hector that picked up messages from a piece of wire we strung up for it.'

The Major stared at Simon, then said, 'What school?'

'Rushden.'

'And now you're in the Intelligence Corps?'

Simon shook his head. 'Paris embassy.'

The Major nodded. Simon picked up his book but thought not of Madame Bovary but of Madame Corbasson. He remembered a great deal, all with fondness and respect. This was no place for love and he tried to keep love out of it, but wasn't sure he had succeeded. He hoped the German Oberst was looking after her. Knowing Madame, Simon reckoned that he would be.

Late in the evening Frenay arrived and said he had *'deux blessés'*. He needed help to get them in the barn. They were sappers, heavily bandaged. They soon supplanted the Major as the immediate wonder. Simon went to the one with both hands incapacitated and held a mess-tin of coffee to his lips. He discovered that his name was Freeman. As the sapper struggled to sip, he also explained.

'63rd Chemical Warfare Company. Top secret, but we were all ready to contaminate Jerry. Only we got a direct hit from the Stukas. In army language there are three sorts of gas. Lethal, lachrymatory and irritant. We left the phosgene to the Froggies and carried the irritant. To you and me, mate, that's burning. Bloody mustard gas everywhere!'

Simon stared down at the man's arm, where the bandages ended and the shirt had been cut back. The drying blisters, of every shape and intermingling, reminded him of photos of the moon.

'We were lucky,' said the sapper, indicating his mate, 'we got patched up in a clinic.' Then he closed his eyes and thanked Simon for the drink. No word of pain and no whimper.

Simon went back to Cornford. 'Every escape route in northern France seems to end at this bloody barn.' He said wearily, 'How many more, for God's sake?'

'It's like a lifeboat,' said Cornford. 'Fourteen, and we're down to the bleeding gunnels!'

Canaris had given Hopkins an enlargement of each of the persons in the photos. Hopkins sat in the car off the main road, the photos spread on his lap. It was overcast and drizzling.

115

Nothing about Notre-Dame de Grâce endeared itself to him, and the longer he sat the more he disliked the long sprawling village. When after three-quarters of an hour no subject from any of the photos appeared, he told the driver to get out and stop an elderly woman who was scuttling along the road with her shopping. The woman was brought to the car and Hopkins showed her the group photo taken outside the café. After a long delay the woman reluctantly identified Madame Lochard, her brother Monsieur Varlin and Madame Corbasson. Hopkins thanked her, spun an Irish penny and drove to Madame Corbasson's.

Madame was greatly disconcerted by Hopkins' arrival. He was an odd-looking man at any time. Wehrmacht uniform added a sinister element to that oddity. From his cap and collar patches she recognised him to be an officer, but there was something strange about the jacket. There were no shoulder straps. Then she saw the gold crucifix hanging from a chain about his neck and deduced he was an army chaplain. She instantly thought of the Oberst and wondered when he would return. Hopkins saw she was flustered, laid his cap on the table, ran his handkerchief over his forehead and asked for a drink of water. When she returned with a bottle of *eau minéral* and a glass, he produced the enlargement of Manning.

'Have you ever seen this man, Madame?' he asked, putting his finger in to the collar of his uniform jacket and trying to loosen it. It was evident she had seen the man, although she denied it. So Hopkins produced the group photo, with herself included. Madame said nothing, just prayed inside. When Oberst Brauer's tall figure passed the window, Madame knew her prayers had been answered.

Brauer had been surprised to find the car parked outside the house he had come to look upon almost as his own. He feared that the quartermaster had decided that although he was an Oberst he must share his modest billet. Then he saw Madame's face change to joy and relief at his appearance and realised that once again he had entered upon an interrogation.

The Oberst gave the dumpy, unprepossessing chaplain a brief glance and decided he must be proselytising. He briskly introduced himself and asked if he could help. Hopkins, upset by the sudden appearance of the Oberst, struggled to stay composed. He realised he was fortunate to be dealing with a conventional officer, completely predictable, and that helped him enough to request a private meeting. The soldier in Brauer made him instantly agree. When Madame had gone, Hopkins put the enlargement on the table.

'Have you ever seen that man, Herr Oberst?' he asked.

'What's it all about, Padre?' asked Brauer curtly. 'This woman's had a pretty bad time.'

'Security,' said Hopkins, smiling beneath his glasses.

Brauer picked up the photo and took it to the window. A man of about thirty, clean-shaven and gaunt, stared out from the printing paper. After a while Brauer put the photo back on the table and shook his head. 'Not that I know of.'

Hopkins produced the second photo. The group one. Brauer took that to the window and gave it a much longer examination.

'May I ask who he is?'

'An Englishman,' said Hopkins. 'You'll have realised, Herr Oberst, that that is the local café, and the lady on the right of the group is the lady of this house.'

Brauer was greatly troubled. He remembered the visit of the police and the way he had packed them off. He wished to protect Madame but was aware of the extreme gravity of the allegation. He didn't think he was dealing with the Gestapo, for quite evidently the padre was not from the SS. However, when at last he spoke he did so with considerable caution.

'I can't say for certain whether I have seen that man or not. May I ask your authority?'

'Abwehr,' said Hopkins.

Brauer nodded gravely.

'What men have been in this house or visited it since you arrived, Herr Oberst?' asked Hopkins.

Brauer hesitated. Hopkins saw the hesitation and said, 'Perhaps it will help if I were to assure you that Madame will come to no harm. The matter's entirely in the hands of the Abwehr. None of the Reich police are involved, nor will they be unless security is broken.'

'The only male persons in this house since I have been here, other than my own servant, were an English soldier who broke in looking for food, and Madame's cousin.'

'What happened to this English soldier?' asked Hopkins, shifting uneasily inside his uniform.

'I myself took him prisoner,' said the Oberst proudly. 'He gave his name as Church. I have a note of his number upstairs.'

Hopkins pointed at the photo. Brauer shook his head.

'And Madame's cousin?' asked Hopkins.

'He was ill when we arrived. Indeed, he occupied her bed. He left for home the moment he was well enough. After two days.'

'Where is his home?' asked Hopkins.

Brauer smiled and glanced down at the gold crucifix on Hopkins' chest. 'You don't know the French, my dear padre. That's not the sort of question you address to a lady in this country. She is married. Her husband is a major of artillery.' He shrugged. 'Even if we are the conquerers, we must show gallantry and discretion in matters of the heart.'

'I am sure you're right, Herr Oberst,' said Hopkins genially. 'How many times did you see this cousin?'

'Twice. But it was always dark. The blinds were drawn; he had a fever.'

'Might he have been wounded?'

The Oberst shrugged. 'Possibly.'

'Could you find out for me where her cousin lives?'

Brauer puckered his lips and stared down at the photos. He was beginning to find everything most distasteful.

'I think you should ask her yourself,' he said at last. 'I'll stay if you insist, but I'd much rather not.'

Reluctantly Hopkins agreed. Brauer left the room. Madame returned and Hopkins asked her about her cousin. She was confused, and disinclined to talk. She looked towards the door hoping for Brauer's return, but he stayed upstairs. Hopkins, wilting under her scent, invited her to sit down.

'If the man who was in your house really was your cousin, then you have nothing to fear,' he said. 'If on the other hand he was, say, an Englishman, the sooner you tell me the truth the better it will be.' Then he added, with the smile that now appeared almost demented, 'Remember, there are others in the house I can question.'

Trapped, with Hopkins staring at her in that maniacal way, Madame's fear turned to anger. She leapt to her feet and with her fingers out like claws, made for the man's podgy face.

'You fat little Boche swine!' she screamed. 'France will live again!'

Hopkins struggled to clamp her hands, and they stood, clasped together, turning and swaying, Madame shrieking at him to leave her house.

'Your cousin's name, you stupid old whore!' shouted Hopkins, the sweat running down his temples and cheeks, his glasses askew. When Madame spat in his face, he contained himself sufficiently to repeat the question.

'Pierre Rossel!' Shouted Madame.

'Address?'

She gave one in the 20th Arrondissement. She was certain he didn't believe her, but he let her go, straightened his jacket, picked up his cap and stumbled out of the house.

Ten minutes later, Brauer went out without a word. The moment his car disappeared, Madame ran to a neighbour and phoned Paris. Fortunately her cousin was in. After a heated and difficult discussion, he agreed to corroborate her story.

That evening, Madame's visit to the Oberst was strained. Brauer opened his usual bottle of Dom Pérignon and chatted about the day, but it was obvious the events of the afternoon had upset him. It was some time before he alluded to the matter, but in the end he took her hand, ran his fingers gently over the soft skin above the knuckles and said, 'You must understand, Juliette, that the visit of my compatriot today has put me in a very difficult position. He is, as you know, looking for an Englishman. I have told him that the only persons I saw here in the house were the man we captured and the man you called your cousin. Whether your cousin and the Englishman are one and the same person, I don't know. Nor do I want to know. But if they are, then I suggest that for the peace of all of us, and in particular for your family and your prisoner-of-war husband, you tell him the truth.'

Madame stared at Brauer, not sure what to say.

'It may help,' said Brauer, 'if I tell you that the man was not a chaplain nor from the police. He's from the counter-espionage and sabotage service of the German High Command. The equivalent of your Deuxième Bureau. At the moment this is purely a military matter and it would benefit everyone if it stays that way.' With that he rose and opened the door.

Madame left with the briefest words of thanks.

Church was angry, fed up and frightened. When he had told the Hauptmann that he had been with the 5th Wessex, he believed that he had booked his ticket for the prisoner-of-war camp. Yet he was still in solitary confinement, in this filthy room in a semi-demolished wing of an old French barracks. But for the fact that they brought his food he would have thought that they had forgotten his existence. When one morning he was marched back to the Hauptmann's office by a Feldwebel and two men with fixed bayonets, he had a strong feeling that it was not for his railway warrant.

This time the Hauptmann did not point to the chair but to the wall map. He tapped the area between the Pas-de-Calais and Somme Departments and said, 'The 5th Wessex were destroyed in a battle fought between your "Holtforce" and Generalmajor Guderian's XIX Panzer Army Corps.'

Church nodded.

'And that happened south-east of Arras on 21 May, 200 kilometres from where you were captured, and more than two months *before* you were captured!'

Church stared at the map, shuffled his feet and said nothing.

'A lot must have happened in that time,' said the Hauptmann quietly. 'It might help you to know that in the area for which I am responsible we have captured fourteen Englishmen in the last two weeks. In every case they are in parties of two or more. As I told you, no ordinary soldier, no junior NCO escapes alone. So where are your travelling companions?'

When Church showed his disinclination to say more, he was curtly informed that his transfer to official Kriegsgefangener status was being delayed for administrative reasons and that his interim resting place would be Fresnes prison, Paris. He had never heard of it, but imagined that it was a dirtier version of the Scrubs.

Oberst Brauer had acquired a new car and new driver. The car was a 1939 three-litre Hotchkiss of sleek lines and a high touring speed. It had been hastily painted green, and the Oberst himself had signed it into the Wehrmacht. The new driver was Obergefreiter Walter Haak, late of the Armoured Reconnaissance Battalion of the 7th Panzer Division.

After the dangers and exertions of 'Case Yellow', Haak found the war easy. Had he been fully fit he would probably now be back with his old division, but the wound in his side hadn't healed. Sick leave or an instructorship had seemed the only other likely alternatives, but Haak was an eager soldier. Unable to return to the panzers, he had pleaded to be posted to any army unit likely to see action in the near future. The 8th Division north of Rouen, preparing for the invasion, was his first home. From there to VIII Corps, HQ was but a step up the Seine.

At Corps HQ Haak was something of an oddity. A young 'old soldier'. Amongst the orderlies, drivers, signalmen and cooks, no one else wore the panzer unit marksmanship shield or the dark red ribbon of the Iron Cross, Second Class, with its white and black flanking bars. To the real old soldiers of the headquarters, who had had their battle initiation in the trenches of the Western Front, Haak was also one of the élite, epitomising the new ways of warfare. Brauer had been delighted to snap up such an admirable man, and twenty-four hours after arriving at VIII Corps, Haak was introduced to the Hotchkiss.

Haak enjoyed driving for the Oberst. Although one of the old school who did everything by the book, Brauer was fair, and in his way thoughtful. Furthermore he had an excellent billet. Although Haak had only had his new job three days, already Madame was providing titbits and making him coffee.

Today it seemed to Haak that the Oberst was in a particularly good mood. Whether it was the prospect of driving to the coast with Madame, or the award of the War Merit Cross First Class now hanging on the Oberst's breast, its ribbon the exact obverse of his own Iron Cross, Haak couldn't be sure. He fancied a bit of each, for being no more than an Obergefreiter, Haak had no knowledge of the events of the last two weeks that had sent such excitement through the upper echelons of OKW and OKH.

A fortnight ago the Führer had issued his 'Directive No. 16,

121

Preparations for a Landing against England'. Brauer had read the signal that morning and was so much in sympathy with it he knew the opening words by heart.

As England, in spite of her hopeless military situation, still shows no willingness to come to terms, I have decided to prepare, and if necessary to carry out, a landing against her.

The aim of this operation is to eliminate the English motherland as a base from which the war against Germany can be continued, and if it should be necessary to occupy the country completely.

OKW had now allocated the thirteen divisions to land in the first wave, on a broad front between Ramsgate and the Isle of Wight. As General Strauss's 9th Army, of which VIII Corps were part, was to land on the left of the front, Brauer's words to Madame of little over a fortnight ago that his next billet would be in Sussex, England, looked certain to come true. All he had got wrong was the schedule. Now that they might have to fight, it would be August not July.

Brauer, of course, could tell none of this to Haak. Nevertheless, as they drove north and saw a Staffel of Bf109Es returning to their base at Beaumont-le-Roger, the Oberst pointed and shouted, 'It won't be long now, Haak, then we'll be finishing off their good work.'

Haak had never been to England. His only knowledge of the country was from books, newspapers, magazines and the cinema screen. For a fleeting second he saw himself peering through the commander's slit of a SdKfz 231 at the façade of Buckingham Palace or the walls of the Tower of London, then he remembered the weeping wound in his thigh. He turned, grinned and said, 'As long as you promise me you and I will be there, Herr Oberst?'

Brauer smiled and nodded.

It was a strange journey for Madame, sitting in the back of this French car next to her immaculate protector, the German colonel, and behind the cocky little Obergefreiter with his endearing grin, heading north towards the Côte Fleurie. Once the haunt of the Impressionists and the English, it was now very much under the heel of the Wehrmacht. She knew that it wasn't just a summer afternoon outing to the seaside, nor a joyride for her, nor a test of the touring capabilities of the Hotchkiss, nor even a celebration of the new decoration Albrecht wore so proudly upon his chest. The Oberst was on a tour of inspection. All the rumours were of the forthcoming fight with England. Already that coast, with its clear light and green gardens, was being whispered about as the 'invasion coast'. Her feelings, therefore, as she sat back in the Hotchkiss and the Oberst took her hand and laid it in his, were very ambivalent and very muddled.

It seemed to Madame as if the only uniform in the world was field grey. With three of the Wehrmacht now living in her house, the Oberst inviting her almost every evening to share his nightcap, and the gutteral sound of German all around her, the Englishman and even her husband and her friend the General seemed part of an earlier incarnation. Survival, Madame decided, was easier without memories.

At Deauville, while the Oberst was in conference, Madame took a discreet walk. She saw a barge moored close to the shore. A dozen Wehrmacht were disembarking a lorry down a precipitous ramp into the shallow water. When the Oberst reappeared and they drove to Honfleur, they passed another barge. Again the bow had been replaced by a ramp. The Oberst ordered Haak to stop and he and Madame walked a little way from the car and watched. An anti-tank gun was being manhandled on to the beach. The task was difficult and caused much hilarity. In their lifejackets the soldiers looked like Michelin men. When an officer slipped and fell into the water, the laughter carried to the car.

'Will you be going on one of those barges, Albrecht?' asked Madame quietly.

The Oberst shook his head. 'Those are for the assault troops, my dear. For Corps headquarters there'll be steamers.'

'What sort of steamers?' asked Madame.

Brauer laughed. 'It's far too soon to say! Hundreds of things have yet to be worked out. Who will be in the first echelon, who in the second? What are the priorities? Infantry? Engineers to clear the beach mines? Panzers to break through? Only after all that come the loading tables.'

She would have liked to ask more but felt it imprudent to do so. She would wait until the evening when they were sitting together. It was then that the Oberst most liked to talk.

They drove back to Notre-Dame de Grâce, the Oberst's gloved hand resting gently on her lower thigh, her hand on top of his. Haak, like the good soldier he was, stared straight ahead. That evening, sitting in the chair opposite the Oberst, Madame returned to the subject. She approached it carefully, asking how dangerous the crossing would be, but she need not have worried. After the tour of inspection the word 'Sealion', as the Führer himself called the operation in his order of the 16th, was engraved on the Oberst's heart.

'Depends on the English,' he said. 'If they fight hard, then it might be dangerous. If they're sensible and come to terms, as I believe they must, then not so dangerous.' He leaned forward, smiled and said, 'But don't worry, my dear, I'm an old soldier. I've learned to look after myself.'

Brauer had never said much about his duties, but several times Madame had heard the words 'movement control'.

'I take it, Albrecht,' she said carefully, 'for a long time you will be on this side, in France, sending barges to England?'

Brauer slapped his knees in delight and jumped to his feet. 'You think I'll eat, sleep and dream barges? That I'll be so busy with them, there'll be no time left for our little tête-à-têtes? Is that it?'

Madame smiled. Brauer suddenly looked very serious.

'It's true that for the next few weeks, barges will become to me what lorries have been,' he said. 'It's true too that I shall have to visit the ports. But that won't come between us.' He bent, kissed her on the cheek, then put his arm around her shoulder. 'The sea air'll do me good. It'll give me an enormous appetite.'

Madame blushed. Brauer had never seen her look more beautiful. It was a shame to have to go to England, even though the English tailors were the best in the world and he badly wanted a new tweed suit.

They lay in the big bed under the crucifix — the Oberst on his back snoring; Madame, her eyes wide open, watching the moonlight pouring through the window. The same moon would be throwing its cold silver light upon the prison camp where her husband was; upon the house in Bayonne where her friend the General had his home, and from whom she had also not heard; and upon the ancient tiles of the barn where Simon was.

In the last few months her life had been such a cavalcade that she needed to lie awake sometimes just to try and catch up with it. Loyalty and disloyalty touched only the periphery of her mind. She had to stay alive, keep her home, look after her aged mother-in-law and Lucienne. The methods she used seemed her concern and no one else's. And as Lucienne was always reminding her, life under the Germans wasn't all that bad. The Wehrmacht were always very correct. Everyone, and particularly the Oberst, seemed to show the greatest respect for French culture and traditions. According to the papers, French intellectuals were being invited to lecture in Germany, and many exhibitions of French painters were being arranged to tour the Reich. Indeed, taking it all in all, everyone was getting on with everyone exceedingly well, and if one of Albrecht's barges might somehow or other get Simon and his comrades back to England, it seemed right that it should do so. That one man, even if he was German, should be helping another, even if he was English, was the basis of her Christianity.

In the morning, therefore, Madame was surprised to find another source of hostility in Notre-Dame de Grâce. Her aged yet still formidable mother-in-law followed a silent, frosty breakfast with the accusing words, 'You have been for a motorcar ride with a Boche officer! The whole village saw you!'

'It was to see the barges, Maman!' cried Madame. 'To help the English soldiers!'

The old woman shook her head. 'Every evening you sit with the enemy and drink his wine.'

Madame raised her hands in a gesture of anger and frustration. 'Maman, that is nothing. Read the papers and the magazines. See what is happening in Paris!'

'Paris!' spat the old woman. 'Don't talk to me of Paris!'

'Lots of people welcomed the Germans,' cried Madame. 'If we're honest, in the end most of France. You've heard the stories! I myself saw how the women of St Ouen stopped the military from blowing up the bridges and so let the Germans over. Toasts were drunk in hundreds of Mairies to German officers. Many of our men were looting. It was the Germans who restored order!'

The old woman took up the kitchen knife and in spite of her arthritic hands swiftly sliced the single large tomato. 'Do you ever think of your husband languishing in a prisoner-of-war camp?'

'You know I do, Maman! I think of dear, sweet Claude in my prayers every morning and every evening.'

The old woman nodded. 'Good! That is as it should be.' Then she turned, gave Madame an icy stare and said, 'Tell me, Juliette, why was the Boche colonel not in his bed last night? Why were his sheets not crumpled this morning?'

Madame flew at the old woman, her hands out, her fingers clawing for that wrinkled old face.

'You foolish old idiot!' she screamed. 'We have to go on living, don't we? You! Lucienne! Me! We've got to survive! The colonel will see that whatever happens, whatever the Germans may do, we survive. He'll see that you have food. That when the winter comes we have fuel for the stove, that we are not looted and raped.'

'And when this one goes on the invasion of England, will another come into your bed to look after us all?'

Madame put her hands to her ears and screamed.

'Will you turn my son's house into a Boche brothel?' cried the old woman.

Madame stood, her hands clenched, shaking. 'We need Oberst Brauer!'

'He is a Boche!' spat the old woman.

'He is a human being!' cried Madame. 'A man! He's in a strange country far from home. He is polite and courteous. It may surprise you but he actually loves France. Before the war he often went to Paris. He loves our painters. He can talk for hours about Monet, Pissarro, Renoir, Vuillard. He may be a German but he is also a gentleman.'

The old woman ran the blade of the knife across her thumb.

'Don't forget your Aunt Veronique,' she said quietly. 'In the last war she lived with a Boche flier. After the Armistice, no one spoke to her for six years!'

Madame collapsed on to the hard bench that stood by the wall, covered her face with her hands and cried. The old woman gave her a look of infinite scorn, then went out to collect the eggs.

Pierre Rossel, Madame's cousin in the 20th Arrondissement, did his best but it was not enough. When Hopkins returned to Notre-Dame de Grâce, the Oberst was at his headquarters. This time Madame had nowhere to turn. She had expected the tubby little German to be furious at being sent on a wild goose chase and was surprised at his civility. He invited her to sit with him at the cloth-covered table and she sat. He told her he knew it was not her cousin who had been ill in her bed, but an Englishman called Simon Manning. They had wasted enough time. He must see Manning at once and get him out of France before the Gestapo found him.

Madame stared at Hopkins, not sure what to believe.

'I understand your wish to protect Manning,' said Hopkins. 'It's laudable but foolish. You are defying the occupying power and thereby endangering yourself, your house, your family and your husband, who I understand is a prisoner of war. And you are not helping the Englishman, you are making life more difficult for him.'

Madame still said nothing, just hoped. Hopkins put his hand on her arm. 'Trust me, Madame, we both want the same thing. To save him.'

Madame would have trusted him but for his eyes peering from behind the thick lenses. In the end, Hopkins decided to play a hunch. He took a scrap of paper from his pocket, scribbled an address and put the paper on the table.

'I'll come back tomorrow at the same time. If you want me before then, I'm at the Hotel Bristol. Tell Manning I've got to speak to him. I give you my word you won't be followed. If he has any doubts, or thinks it's a trick, remind him of a drink in the Boulevard Haussmann a few weeks ago.'

Hopkins got up and left. In the car he opened his collar and fondled the gold crucifix. He hoped he had done the right thing. At least there hadn't been another undignified struggle and he wasn't all covered in the woman's scent. It would add another twenty-four hours to the search, but maybe the Oberst would hurry her along. He felt sure she would tell the Oberst. He glanced at his watch, thought of Hela coming out of school and wondered if it was as hot in Berlin. Then he closed his eyes and tried to imagine what Manning had done to become so important to both the Abwehr and the Gestapo.

When the Oberst returned that evening he found Madame in a state of decline. When he questioned her, she broke down completely, told him of Hopkins' return visit and who her cousin really was. That night, in spite of Madame's comforting body, the Oberst slept badly. First thing in the morning he called upon the Abwehr agent, and only after speaking with him did he drive Madame to Frenay's farm. As he told her repeatedly, it was without doubt the most irregular act in the whole of his twenty-six years of military service.

# CHAPTER 19

Cuthbertson had a job recognising Sinclair in his uniform. He had been expecting the dark suit with its faint pinstripe, and was not prepared for the navy uniform with its single gold wavy ring on the cuff. It was a nasty shock.

'I admire your nobility, Ross,' he said, staring at the man, 'but regret you should have joined the herd.'

'Perhaps the herd is right for once?' said Sinclair.

Cuthbertson shook his head. 'The herd's never right.' Then he raised his glass and said, 'The uniform suits you splendidly. Nice of you to come all the way to town to see me.'

Sinclair smiled and said he had had one or two things to clear up. They talked in a desultory fashion, Cuthbertson staring across the bar at the bottles, conscious of the speed with which the war was taking them apart. After a long silence, Sinclair said, 'What's the latest of your fellow Manning?'

'Probably alive,' said Cuthbertson gloomily. 'Exactly where we haven't the faintest idea.' Then to change the subject he said, 'How's Pompey? How are the Wrens?'

'Pompey's better than I expected,' said Sinclair. 'It's good to be doing something at last.'

Cuthbertson shut his eyes.

'Right on the invasion front,' he said quietly. 'Rosyth would have been better, or Scapa.' Then he opened his eyes and said, 'I miss you, Ross, and worry. You don't see the reports now, only the stuff that gets in the papers and on the wireless. Yesterday they had another go at a Channel convoy. E boats and bombers in a joint attack. They got five ships and damaged another five. They also hit a destroyer. Last night they were laying mines all along the coast. The sea's getting to be the very devil.'

'Twenty-eight were shot down,' said Sinclair.

Cuthbertson shook his head. 'As the claims are checked, they get less and less. Eighteen or twenty is going to be nearer the mark. We lost seven. Even a constant ratio of two and a half to one won't win us this battle.'

'Now they're coming over land their losses will rise.'

'If Fighter Command can survive that long. So far this month they've lost nearly 200 fighters, of which with luck seventy might be repaired. What's much more ominous is that they're more than ninety pilots short, and the real battle hasn't started yet.'

'For God's sake, man!' cried Sinclair. 'You can't work in the Cabinet Office with that attitude. Not now. You'd have to be a schizophrenic.'

Cuthbertson smiled sadly and said that sometimes he was.


Simon caught the bus and they met in a bedroom of a small hotel in the Rue Clemenceau, Simon wearing his shabby, ill-fitting suit and several days' growth of beard, Hopkins in his almost equally ill-fitting padre's uniform. When Simon saw him he burst out laughing. Hopkins took off his cap, threw it on to the bed, unbuttoned his jacket and flopped down in a heap of field grey. He apologised for leaving Simon to pay for the drinks in Paris, and congratulated him on getting out of the car. Simon thanked him for the passport.

'My orders are to get you out of France as quickly as possible,' said Hopkins. 'I've papers, money and a rail ticket. I'm to escort you to the Spanish border. I hope it won't be too hot.'

'Not in that, for God's sake!' said Simon, pointing at the uniform.

Hopkins ignored the jibe. 'You'll have to be up early. We leave Rouen at ten to nine.' As if it was an afterthought he added, 'You're a lucky bugger.'

'It isn't as easy as that,' said Simon. 'How much do you know about my present circumstances?'

Hopkins shrugged. 'I told the Frenchwoman she wouldn't be followed. That promise was kept. So far as I know the Oberst who was billeted on her drove her, as I guessed he would.'

'Some women need a protector in peace and war,' said Simon, in defence.

'I wouldn't know,' said Hopkins, and ran the tips of his fingers through his damp, thinning hair. 'All I know is that you've caused enough trouble and the Admiral wants you out.' He put a hand into the pocket of his jacket and pulled out a bundle of papers, which he laid on the bed. 'This journey to Spain. You'd better learn your cover. You're George Duclos, a Frenchman returning to your home in the Pyrenees. There's a police authority for you to leave the occupied zone, a visa from the Vichy Government...'

Simon shook his head. 'You don't understand, I'm not alone.'

Hopkins looked surprised.

'There's a group of us,' said Simon. 'We've travelled together, helped one another. I couldn't just pick up your papers and ticket and leave them.'

Hopkins stared at Simon as if he were a half-wit. 'Listen, I don't know what you've been up to, or why the Admiral wants you out and in England, but I do know bloody well that the Gestapo are after you! That would be enough for me. If I heard that and had the chance to beat it, I'd beat it fast!'

'I know,' said Simon, grinning. 'It's mad, crazy, but it's all to do with this wretched war and "chums". You see, I'm experiencing a sense of comradeship never experienced before. I couldn't just leave them here. I'd never have a decent night's sleep again.'

Hopkins lay back on the bed. After a while he said, 'How many "chums"?'

'Quite a lot,' said Simon, 'far too many to get on the train to the Spanish border. Of course, it might be possible to go in small packets, say five at a time.'

'For God's sake, how many?'

'At the last count, sixteen.'

'Sixteen, here in France!' cried Hopkins. 'Sixteen British, all hiding?'

Simon nodded. 'And I hear there are quite a lot more dotted around.'

'What do they think they're going to do?' asked Hopkins in amazement.

'Escape,' said Simon, 'one way or the other. You wouldn't expect me to tell you the details, surely?'

'It's impossible,' said Hopkins, staring at his boots. 'Get them to give themselves up. As POWs they'll be all right.'

Simon shook his head. 'They don't much like the risk. If they were going to surrender, they should have done so a couple of months ago. There could be complications. There are stories of the SS not being all that nice to prisoners.'

'You can't give up the chance to get out of this mess for the sake of blokes you've only just met,' said Hopkins. 'I know I wouldn't.'

'Do you want to get out?' asked Simon.

Hopkins shook his head in hopeless despair. 'I don't know what I want. And if I did know, it would be impossible.'

'How did you get in?'

'Money,' said Hopkins, staring at the ceiling and fingering the gold crucifix. 'Maybe even money and sex. Sometimes I think it might have been a bit of both. It's difficult to know now. There were complications then, there are complications now. Life's nothing but bloody complications.'

'Tell your boss the Admiral,' said Simon, 'that I'd love to leave France, but I'd like to take my mates with me.'

Hopkins grimaced. 'What's the point? He'd only get all worked up. You wouldn't do yourself any good. If he wants something he usually gets it, that's my experience. And he wants *you* back in England, not the rest of your lot.'

'Why does he want me back in England?'

Hopkins went to the door, down the stairs, shouted for a Perrier water, then when he got it, came back into the room and sat on the bed.

'I haven't the faintest idea why he wants you back in England, only that he does.' He thought about it for a while, then said, 'Maybe if you were in England, when the invasion comes you might repay one good turn with another. It's the usual way in this game.'

Simon suddenly burst out laughing. 'I'm to go back to England as a sort of potential double agent?'

Hopkins shrugged. 'Listen, Manning, I've learned to know as little as possible in this bloody business. It's the best way to work. To stay alive.'

After a while Simon said, 'We need a boat. I imagine the Chief of the Abwehr can arrange pretty well what he likes?'

Hopkins got slowly up off the bed, put on his jacket, picked up his cap and went to the door.

'Did you arrange that raid on the flat?' asked Simon.

Hopkins shook his head. 'Not guilty. Ask your own people.'

'A fishing boat would do,' said Simon. 'We can crew it. Of course, I'm assuming that he'd rather do that than move sixteen of us to Madrid?'

Hopkins did up his jacket, threw on his cap, said, 'You're a fool, a bloody fool!' and left.


The adjutant laid the file on Heydrich's desk. 'You asked to see all reports of British stragglers still being rounded up, Herr Obergruppenführer. A few have recently been taken in small groups but one has been captured on his own.'

Heydrich stared at his adjutant. 'Is that so strange?'

'The interrogating officer thinks so. Until this incident the only English taken on their own were officers. This particular soldier, a very junior Unteroffizier, has travelled 200 kilometres and been free more than two months. His regiment was destroyed on 21 May near Arras.'

Heydrich smiled. 'A resourceful man. He deserves promotion.'

'He was captured near the town of Bernay, Herr Obergruppenführer.' The adjutant went to the map table. 'It's not all that far from the Seine.'

Heydrich went to the map to see for himself.

'Your imagination is leaping too far ahead, Helmut. An

English soldier is captured in Normandy on his own. We have an unsubstantiated report of an Abwehr agent being seen at Vernon, sixty kilometres away.' He tapped the map. 'It's not even a coincidence.' After a moment he added, 'What's the name of this agent?'

'Hurley, Herr Obergruppenführer. By birth he's half Irish, half English. He also goes under the name of Hopkins, posing as an engineer. He's a widower, his wife was German and they had one daughter. She lives in Berlin with an aunt but Admiral Canaris pays for everything. Piano lessons . . . painting lessons . . . dancing lessons . . .'

'Canaris does look after his agents,' said Heydrich sarcastically, 'and this pampered girl is a quarter Irish, a quarter English and half German . . .'

'A quarter German and a quarter Jewish, Herr Obergruppenführer.'

'Really?' said Heydrich, his eyes opening. 'A quarter Jewish?'

The adjutant said nothing. Heydrich went back to the map. He had had no intention of visiting France. Now, the winding valley of the Seine and names like Versailles, St Germain and Fontainebleau began to beckon. Everyone who was anyone in the Third Reich had been to Paris in the last few weeks except the head of RSHA. Photos were still appearing of the Führer's visit more than a month ago. With summer at its height, France the scene of preparations for 'Sealion', and a new Sicherheitspolizie commander to be visited and encouraged, a journey to Paris suddenly looked essential.

'Rumours,' said Heydrich bitterly, turning away from the map table, 'rumours, never facts. For heaven's sake, what is wrong with us?'

'It's the Wehrmacht, Herr Obergruppenführer. They obstruct us every time. They refuse to provide soldiers for searches, close areas, even stop us investigating.'

Heydrich moved to the window. 'Tell me more about the English Unteroffizier.'

'The interrogating officer is so doubtful about his story that he hasn't sent him to prison camp. He's in Fresnes prison in Paris.'

Heydrich went back to the map and ran his finger across the

whole width of France from the Pas-de-Calais to the Brittany peninsula.

'Your nose leads you there?' he asked after a while.

'I could be wrong, Herr Obergruppenführer,' said the adjutant diplomatically, 'but with Hurley also in the area . . .'

'Rumour.'

'The description fits, Herr Obergruppenführer. And it's a very unique description.'

Heydrich returned to his desk. 'What you mean, Helmut, is that you fancy a visit to Paris. To Montmartre and "Les Girls"?'

The adjutant grinned.

'Go and pack your bags,' said Heydrich quietly, 'and if we have the time we might even visit your solitary English Unteroffizier. And make sure someone keeps a very close eye on this daughter of our Mr Hurley. We may need her at any moment.'

The adjutant saluted and left the room.

# CHAPTER 20

The Major was away twenty-four hours. He came back in the night from the priest's house where he had met his shelterer from the Caux. The priest was trying to form a network for the onward passage of escapees. The problem was that as yet they had no outlet. Everyone was in the pipeline to nowhere. The Major found Cornford in the darkness and asked for Simon. Cornford said Simon was out. When Simon returned and groped his way towards his usual piece of hay, the Major's whisper was sharp.

'I would remind you, Manning, that as senior British officer, every man jack in this damned barn comes under my command, and that includes you! Now, would you mind telling me exactly what is going on?'

'You were away,' said Simon wearily, 'and I had a summons.' He closed his eyes. He seemed to have been living in hay all his life. 'What's your position?'

The Major ignored that question and pursued his own. 'What was this summons?'

'A contact. Probably our only real chance of getting away.'

There was a pause, then the Major said, 'You might have told Cornford instead of letting me sit here guessing. Good God, man, I've got to know who I command and what they're up to! You're out when I come back, you might be a damned Fifth Columnist selling us all down the river!'

'What chance have your people got of getting a boat?' asked Simon.

'None,' said the Major curtly. 'The coast's too well guarded. Swarming with Huns getting ready for their damned invasion. It's safer inland. Father B believes the only chance lies in making for the Armistice Line and Spain.' There was a pause, then the Major said, 'This contact of yours, is he another Intelligence wallah?'

'On the other side,' said Simon blandly.

The Major thought about that for a while then said, 'Sounds more like John Buchan to me than 1940.'

'It's simple really,' said Simon. 'The governments on both sides like to keep in touch.'

The Major nodded, took the empty pipe from his jacket pocket, sucked it and said, 'This contact of yours? What's he going to do?'

'I've asked him to get us a boat,' said Simon.

The Major sat upright. 'I hope to God you know what you're doing, Manning, and don't get us all put in the bag.'

Simon glanced round the barn. 'You said there were others? Any idea how many?'

'No numbers were mentioned,' said the Major, 'but there must be at least twenty spread around. Mostly twos and threes in attics, barns like ours, cellars, churches.' Suddenly the Major took the pipe out of his mouth and said, 'Why should the Huns give us a boat?'

Simon tried to see the Major's face in the darkness, but had to work by memory. He remembered it as strong and angular, denoting a man of integrity and courage but not necessarily of

135

imagination. Simon's story demanded a man of imagination. Like Cornford, this regular major would find it too difficult to believe the facts.

'A senior officer in OKW wants me out of this country and back in England.'

It sounded pretentious and the Major thought it sounded fishy, and said so.

'I've asked to take you with me,' said Simon. 'If you can find out how many others there are, we might as well try and take them too.'

In the darkness the Major shook his head. 'You're a rum fellow, Manning, damned rum. Glad I don't know too much of what goes on behind the scenes. Best not to know sometimes, eh?'

Simon agreed.


When Hopkins came out of the hotel, he was surprised to find a large black Mercedes drawn up at the bottom of the steps in place of his much more modest Renault. He stopped, moving his glasses slightly to have a better view of the vehicle, when three men in pinstriped suits approached from three points of the compass. Without any preliminaries the rear door of the Mercedes was opened and he was bundled in. They drove fast to a lane near the river, where he was bundled out with an equal lack of ceremony. With the tallest beside him, the other two men behind, they walked along the old towpath. Two snapshots passed casually across told him most of the story. In the first he and Hela were leaning on the iron railings in the Tiergarten feeding the ducks. In the second she was doing much the same thing with a stranger. Hopkins felt sick.

'What do you want?' he asked, closing his eyes and stumbling on the uneven ground.

'What are you doing in France?'

'Ask the Chief of the Abwehr,' said Hopkins.

'Surely you're fonder of your kid than that?' said the man, with the trace of a smile.

Hopkins felt the sweat running down inside his uniform. He glanced to his left towards the fields. There was a belt of trees a hundred yards away. No one was to be seen.

'No one's going to come running to help a Wehrmacht padre

here,' said the tall man. 'And we haven't much time so you'd better start talking, that is if you want to see your kid again.'

'Abwehr business,' mumbled Hopkins, sucking in the hot afternoon air with the noise of an asthmatic.

'Briefing a spy to go to England before the invasion, is that it?' asked the man sarcastically.

Hopkins said nothing. He was measuring the distance to the water. But he was a lousy swimmer and they'd shoot him before he had taken two strokes. He was considering, too, whether flinging himself into the river would in any way help Hela.

'Pretty young girl, your Hela, padre,' said the tall man. 'Enjoying a fine full life. All provided by the Reich, living in luxury, with the Admiral a sort of Dutch uncle. It would be such a pity to end it all!'

Through his steamed-up glasses, Hopkins looked up at the man beside him. If he could get his hands round the man's throat before they shot him, there would be at least some satisfaction in his last seconds.

'Where is she?' he asked hopelessly.

'Being looked after,' said the man, glancing down at Hopkins. 'Now, let's stop playing. Where's the Englishman — Manning?'

There was a long pause. They went on walking. After a while the man said, 'That's all we want to know, where's Manning? Tell us that, and sweet precious little Hela goes right back to her aunt and her piano lessons.'

Hopkins tried to think. He wanted to tear the man to pieces, but it wouldn't do much good even if he could achieve it. On the other hand he knew the Gestapo well enough to know that any appeal to humanity, decency or respect for the innocence of children would simply make them laugh.

'Manning,' he said vaguely. 'Can't say I remember anyone of that name.'

'I'm sure we can help you,' said the man, taking back the photos.

Hopkins saw Hela, her fingers mutilated where the nails had been torn out, her face suppurating from cigarette burns, and shuddered. He was only useful to them alive. If he was dead, Hela would be safe. He must give way to his instincts, leap at the man's throat and let them shoot him. He shut his eyes clenched his fists and stumbled along.

'We're trying to do this nice and sensibly, with the least harm to anyone, particularly your kid,' said the man, turning his head and smiling. 'And with her being Jewish, once she's in trouble things could get very nasty.'

Before the icy numbness could paralyse him, Hopkins leaped. But even as he moved, the man brought his knee up into Hopkins' crutch. Hopkins collapsed to.the ground screaming. The man kicked him and shouted, 'Jew's husband, where's Manning?' The other two came up and joined in the sport. Hopkins stared at them, a trapped creature, cowed and wounded. They hit him on the side of his head and his glasses flew off. He heard the crunch as they were stamped on, but all he saw was a pale blue wilderness with dark, moving shadows.

One of them went back to the car to get the girl taken to Gestapo headquarters.

'There's a radio in the car,' said the tall man to Hopkins. 'We'll be relayed to Berlin in three minutes. I'm sorry for your kid. I hope she'll forgive her flabby old dad when she's on the wheelbarrow run in Ravensbrück.' He paused, took the snapshot out again and said, 'On the other hand, as she's pretty, they might find something better for her.'

Hopkins saw nothing but understood.

'You bastard,' he whispered.

The man rubbed the palms of his hands on his chest like a satisfied butcher wipes his hands on his apron.

'As I said, it takes three minutes. It's not too late. We can still stop it.'

In the next thirty seconds, Hopkins told them all they wanted to know. When he finished, they left him on the ground and hurried back to the Mercedes.

Hopkins peered at the two bands of unfocused colours, green and pale blue, called out but no one answered. He searched the ground and found his glasses, but even as his fingers closed round them the shattered glass fell out. He got up, put one foot in front of the other and laboriously tried to retrace his steps. He became puzzled when the pale-blue colour band suddenly divided, and he realised he couldn't tell sky from river. He froze and waited. He called out again and heard children's voices. He shouted to them in French, asking them to guide him to the road. They shouted directions and he followed, not knowing they were in a skiff fishing. When he fell down the bank into the muddy water, they came close and laughed. When they saw no one was looking they beat him with their oars. He struggled to swim and held up the gold crucifix, but it made no difference. They called him 'Dirty Boche' and beat him even harder. When at last he rolled over and his face disappeared below the surface, they moored the boat and ran home to tell how they had tricked the German officer.

As the white-coated waiter moved away, Heydrich leaned forward in his gilded chair and grasped the edge of the table. Lunch in the restaurant of the Prince of Wales Hotel had been excellent. For wartime, the food and wine had been of the best, the service impeccable and the setting most pleasing. It should have been the crowning to a perfect day, and it would have been but for two things. The cold shoulder he had received from the many senior Wehrmacht officers also dining there, and the phone call. The Wehrmacht attitude angered him, but he could sweep it aside. The news his adjutant brought him from the phone was quite different.

'Surely,' he said, struggling to stop himself from shaking, 'it isn't beyond the capability of the Gestapo to pick up a nine-year-old girl from school!'

'She didn't come out the normal way, Herr Obergruppen-führer,' said the harassed adjutant. 'We had men waiting and a car.'

Heydrich put his napkin to his forehead. 'She came out the back way, I suppose?' he said with icy sarcasm. 'And no one thought of the back way?'

The adjutant gave a barely perceptible nod. 'A side entrance, Herr Obergruppenführer. The janitor took her to a car. A black BMW that belongs to Abwehr HQ. It was later seen outside the Admiral's home. Frau Canaris must have her.'

As the adjutant sat down to finish his coffee, Heydrich flung down the napkin and jumped to his feet. He glared down at his adjutant and shouted, 'I hope for all our sakes, Helmut, that your English Unteroffizier will serve us better!' Then he spun round on his heel and marched out of the restaurant.

The adjutant caught him up at the door of the big Mercedes.

Church could see very little from the back of the van as they bumped over the pavé. Even had he been able to see past the two SS and through the tarpaulin that hung down to the tailboard, it wouldn't have been all that helpful. His cell in Fresnes prison and its immediate environment were all he knew of Paris. Where they were taking him he had no idea. But like the day he had been marched back to the Hauptmann, he was fairly certain that it was not to collect a warrant to prison camp.

Yesterday two SS officers had swaggered into his cell and asked him much the same questions as the Hauptmann had asked him days before. He had been frightened, but anger at his treatment had kept him truculent. Now, in the darkness of the van, with the sunlight throwing a thin strip of blinding white across the jack-boots that guarded him, he wished he had been more cooperative. If he had answered just some of the questions, instead of this mystery tour with black uniforms he might be heading towards that prison camp escorted by field grey. In the last twenty-four hours he had come to look upon field grey with something approaching warmth.

When the van stopped and they pushed him out, he was in a wood of tall, evenly-planted poplars. The sun was still high. Its light came down through the branches in thin columns, so close to the vertical that they made him giddy to look up. When he looked down, he saw a ground covered in coarse stringy grass, across which brambles swarmed and a small blue flower struggled to survive. Two cars drew up beside the van and six more SS got out. In spite of the fear that paralysed him, Church felt a moment of pleasure. It was good to be out of doors. Suddenly he was conscious of the two officers in front of him. One he had seen yesterday. The other, strikingly handsome, with a long thin face, whose oak-leaf collar patches and convoluting silver epaulettes proclaimed his high rank, smiled. It was a chilling smile, and seemed to have nothing to do with pleasure. Church shivered.

Heydrich surveyed Church with evident disdain. He was not surprised that the English armies had been defeated, and like the Hauptmann interrogator he decided that this man could not

140

possibly have survived on his own for so long in Occupied France. He asked Church who his companions were, and when in reply Church shrugged he nodded to the Unterscharführer who had been Church's escort.

Church felt the blow on his back, but not the one on his side, for he was already on his way down. Another blow landed on the back of his neck as he tried to turn his head, and he was conscious of grass and earth in his mouth and tried to burrow into the ground. But there was nowhere to hide. All he could do was put his hands over his skull and pray. Suddenly, instead of beating him, they were laughing. He screamed at them, calling them 'Bastards!' and 'Swine!', then with his face contorted with pain and anger he tensed, awaiting the next blow. But no further blow came. Instead, two hands went under his armpits and hauled him to his feet.

Heydrich stood in front of him, his thin mouth curved into that same icy smile. A spade was shoved into Church's hand and he was told to dig. He spat and was hit again. Two SS men covered him with their rifles, while the Unterscharführer marked out the shape of a long rectangle with the heel of his boot. After another flurry of blows, Church started work.

He knew he was digging his own grave, and felt immensely foolish. He had only to tell them of Cornford and the others, and he would be back in the van and then surely on his way to prison camp. And why not? None of them had a chance of reaching England. For all he knew they had already been captured. But the stubbornness that had made him such a difficult soldier made him a difficult prisoner.

They told him to kneel and he knelt. He could hear the Unterscharführer breathing behind him and then felt the cold hard muzzle of a pistol pressed on to the nape of his neck. He knew his hair was standing on end.

'For the last time, your companions?' said Heydrich.

'I've told you,' said Church wearily, 'I was on my own.'

'Have you ever heard of an Englishman called Manning?'

Church started to laugh. Great gusts of wild, high-pitched, hysterical laughter. He was going to die not for Cornford or Nipper Cole, nor for any of the others, but for that sod Manning!

Heydrich moved a step nearer and stared at the apparition,

on its knees, its pants wet, its whole body shaking as it sobbed uncontrollably.

'Was Manning with you, you fool?' cried Heydrich, flicking Church's face with his stick. Then an SS man jumped out of one of the cars and ran towards them. Angrily Heydrich waved the man away.

'You are wanted on the wireless, Herr Obergruppenführer!' said the SS man. 'It's urgent!'

Heydrich swore, pointed at Church, said something to his adjutant and went to the car. From the corner of his eye, Church saw Heydrich sitting in the car, the microphone to his mouth. Just as the adjutant came towards the Englishman, Heydrich shouted. Instantly the two officers got back into the cars, and the cars raced away.

Still on his knees, Church turned. The Unterscharführer and the two men with rifles were staring at him. Uncertain what to do, the Unterscharführer raised his pistol. Church suddenly remembered his company commander's remark when he had been given his stripe: 'Underneath your awkwardness, Church, there's an element of leadership. Let's see you use it a bit.' Church got up, dusted the dirt from his tattered uniform, said, 'Bloody hell, let's go home!' and walked slowly back to the van. The Unterscharführer and the other two SS watched him. Then the Unterscharführer shrugged, put his Luger back in its holster, picked up the spade and followed. Church had just got inside the van, into the heat, when he fainted. When he came round, they were bumping over the pavé again, and the Unterscharführer was offering him his water bottle.

Simon sat on the bed and waited. Hopkins was more than two hours late. When he heard a car draw up outside, he got up and peered down through the net curtains. A man got out of the car wearing a fawn topcoat and trilby hat. It was not Hopkins. When the man went into the hotel, Simon went back to sitting on the bed. A minute later there was a knock on the door. Simon got up, went to the door and asked in French who it was. Canaris announced himself from the corridor. Simon opened the door. Canaris came into the room and made the motion of a salute with his heels. Simon shut the door.

'I apologise for the surprise,' said Canaris, 'but I suddenly

142

found myself in France.'

Simon nodded.

'Our friend Hopkins couldn't tell you I was coming because he didn't know.' Canaris looked round the room. 'Where is he?'

'No idea,' said Simon, 'he was supposed to be here two hours ago.'

Canaris smiled. 'As I am sure you have noticed, Hopkins doesn't enjoy the best of health. However, it is my observation that men with weak hearts often outlive those with strong ones.'

Simon agreed.

The Admiral took off his coat. It was a thin summer one to hide the uniform beneath.

'You are causing me a great deal of trouble, Herr Manning, but first things first. The dossier?'

'Burned.'

Canaris frowned. 'How much of the information reached the British Government?'

'A précis went to England.'

Canaris said, 'Good,' went to the window, stared out across the rooftops and said, 'There have been many changes in England since "Case Yellow". Attitudes have hardened.'

'We call it having our backs to the wall,' said Simon. 'It's a stupid trait, although sometimes it wins the last battle.'

The Admiral flushed. 'This isn't the moment for jokes,' he said curtly. 'Our task and duty remain the same. Every day makes it more, not less essential that we have an honourable peace with Great Britain after the removal of the Nazi hierarchy in Germany. If we fail, the destruction of the eastern races, particularly the Jews, will continue unabated. The SS are already at work in France, Belgium and Holland. The problem is to make your countrymen understand that there is still goodwill here, that in the generals we have the nucleus of a new government.' He stared at Simon, then said with great intensity, 'Hitler can still be got rid of. This war can still be stopped. Thousands, millions of lives can still be saved. Even now it is not too late. But England must understand and be prepared to support us.'

Simon said nothing, just stood watching the little Admiral.

'I need you in England,' said Canaris firmly. 'You must open their eyes to the realities in Germany. You must leave tonight.'

'My friends . . .' began Simon, when the Admiral interrupted.

'They must surrender to the military authorities. Any idea of them going with you is utter nonsense.'

They were still standing facing one another when the squeal of tyres came from the street beneath. The Admiral looked down from the window. Then he turned, faced Simon, said, 'You're like a honeypot to bees!', unlocked the door, dropped into a chair and motioned Simon to sit on the bed. Heavy boots pounded on the stairs and along the landing. When fists hammered on the door, Canaris raised his head, smiled and said, 'Come in!'

Heydrich burst into the room, his adjutant behind him. Two other SS blocked the door. When he saw Canaris, Heydrich stopped. His handsome face flushed, his eyes half closed, and very slowly the pistol went back into its holster. Canaris got up and held out his hand.

'My dear Reinhard, how nice to see you! And what an unexpected pleasure!'

Heydrich turned his head towards Simon.

'I don't know whether you two have met?' said Canaris affably. 'Herr Cotton . . . Obergruppenführer Reinhard Heydrich.'

Simon moved his head a fraction. Heydrich remained rigid.

'Herr Cotton is, as you know, an American citizen. Unfortunately he finds himself marooned in this second-rate hotel. He is hoping to return to the United States shortly.'

Heydrich stared at his adjutant, at the two SS by the door, at Simon, and finally back at the Admiral.

'May I know what you are doing here, Herr Admiral?' he asked.

'Herr Cotton is going back to America via England. I wanted to talk to him about his stay there.' Canaris paused for a moment, then added, 'As you know, Reinhard, the Abwehr is responsible for all information activities outside the Reich. England, of course, at the moment *is* outside the Reich.'

'The man is an Englishman,' said Heydrich, beads of sweat suddenly appearing on his forehead, 'an enemy of the Reich.'

144

Canaris put his hand on Heydrich's arm.

'Ask your men to wait downstairs,' he said quietly. 'Manning can go with them, as long as they don't touch him.'

Heydrich hesitated. Canaris repeated his request, and Heydrich eventually gave the order. Canaris nodded at Simon, who went out with the others.

Heydrich stood, hands on hips, staring at Canaris. 'Manning is an enemy! Anyone who helps him is also an enemy!'

Canaris sighed. 'Please don't be a bore, Reinhard, we've been through all that. Manning is needed in England. "Sealion" is almost upon us.'

Heydrich dismissed the Admiral's words with an impatient gesture of the hand and began pacing the tiny room. Canaris closed his eyes and waited.

'You may know,' said Heydrich, 'that Manning is leading a band of *franc-tireurs*. The penalty for that is death!'

'Don't be foolish, Reinhard,' said Canaris wearily. 'You know perfectly well he's not leading them and anyway they're nothing more than the flotsam of war. They're ready to surrender.'

'They won't have a chance!' cried Heydrich. 'I've demanded Wehrmacht support in their capture.' Coming close to Canaris he stared down into the Abwehr Chief's face: 'You help English soldiers escape and you plot against the Führer. You're a traitor, Herr Admiral!'

Canaris wiped his hand across his forehead. It still pained him that he was about to finally demolish a long friendship. If God was watching anyone on this war-torn continent, He would know that at least he had tried.

'You have just accused me, without a shred of proof, of plotting against the Führer. How do you think he would feel if he was to find out that the number two of the Reichsführer-SS, the chief assistant to our much-respected Heinrich Himmler, the man chosen to head the SS Security Department, to resettle the Jews first of Poland and then of the whole of Europe, was himself partly Jewish?'

The blood drained from Heydrich's face. He tried to speak but merely distorted those fine classical features.

'It's a lie!' he screamed at last, and took another step towards the Admiral. 'A foul, wicked lie!'

145

Canaris shook his head. 'I have a copy of your ancestry list.'

Heydrich grasped the bed head.

'The matter was cleared up years ago,' he said, shaking his head. 'Dr Gercke examined the list and wrote a memorandum. It was dated 22 June 1932.'

Canaris smiled. 'I've a copy of that too. I remember the conclusions well. "The attached ancestry list shows that Leutnant, Navy, Retired, Reinhard Heydrich is of German origin and free from any taint of Jewish or coloured blood." But as you know perfectly well, Reinhard, it all depends how you interpret that list. There is your grandmother's second husband, a very doubtful character. Indeed, there is your grandmother herself.'

Heydrich suddenly recovered his composure. 'You've nothing new! Where's the proof of your dirty lie?'

'In Switzerland, in a bank,' said Canaris, 'along with the ancestry lists of all the top members of the Party. Most of them make interesting reading. In your case, however, there are some very pertinent notes that did not appear in Dr Gercke's final report. You see,' he added, 'we in the Abwehr do our homework properly. That is why we are perfectly capable of looking after Manning on our own.'

Heydrich said nothing, just stared straight ahead.

'No one can help their ancestry, Reinhard,' said Canaris, patting Heydrich on the back, 'but I think you'll agree it would be better if the SD did not interfere in the plans I have for Manning?'

Heydrich neither spoke nor moved.

'Nor for any plans I may have for his comrades. Indeed, it may even be necessary to call upon your help. I'm sure that if I did, you'd be only too pleased to oblige?'

Heydrich threw his arm up in a Nazi salute, cried 'Heil Hitler!', turned and left the room.

Simon sat on the hard cane chair surveying the dirty tablecloth in front of him. Heydrich's adjutant and the two other SS sat by the door, their legs thrust out, making a jackboot chicane. When Heydrich appeared in the hall, they leapt to their feet. He made straight for the front door, indicating that they should follow him. His adjutant pointed at Simon. 'The Englishman,

Herr Obergruppenführer?'

'Leave him!' said Heydrich sharply.

'But, Herr Obergruppenführer . . .' began the adjutant, when Heydrich cut him short.

'*I said leave him!*'

Simon was watching them march out of the hotel, when the Admiral came down the stairs.

'You made me play my trump card, Herr Manning,' said the Admiral gravely. 'I pray to God you'll be worth it.'

Canaris had intended going to OKW HQ at Fontainebleau, but sitting in the car, taking stock of the position, he realised how generous the fates had been. Not only had they placed in his hands an Oberst who was mixed up with a Frenchwoman, but that Oberst had both barges and transport under his immediate command. The idea excited him so much that he shouted at his driver to go first to VIII Corps HQ.

Brauer, flattered to be visited by the Chief of the Abwehr, invited Canaris to walk on the lawn of the château, where they could be private. Striding along on the rich summer grass, Canaris explained that he had an agent he wished 'introduced' into England to report on the English coastal divisions prior to 'Sealion'. As cover he intended adding that agent to a number of escapees now sheltering in the area. Brauer had both barges and transport. With help from OKW, he could make all the necessary arrangements.

Brauer was not enthusiastic. He foresaw considerable difficulties.

'You have a spy, Herr Admiral, you want landed in England. That I understand. But all you need is a U-boat or a parachute. Why let the others go back? They should be prisoners of war.'

Canaris didn't want the question. He had no real answer. The idea of getting the men away under the noses of Heydrich's butchers appealed to him. There was also an element of old-fashioned chivalry in the act. But he could tell none of that to Brauer. He allowed Brauer to enumerate other, logistic problems and listened sympathetically. Eventually, very quietly, he mentioned the French lady. After her, he reminded the Oberst of Frau Brauer sitting at home, knitting and tending the flowers.

147

Brauer stared at the Abwehr Chief in disbelief. If his understanding was correct, the Admiral was actually blackmailing a fellow officer.

'I'm perfectly serious, Herr Oberst,' said Canaris, seeing Brauer's face, 'I must have my man and his comrades in England within the next three to four days. You have all the facilities I need. The future of Europe and the lives of many thousands are at stake. I would like to have been able to do this without any disagreeable complications, but you were unwilling. So . . .' and he shrugged.

Brauer took out a cigarette, slid it into his holder and lit it with a shaking hand.

'Think about it,' said Canaris, 'and telephone me this evening at Fontainebleau.'

Brauer saw Canaris back to his car in a daze, then went into the mess and drank half a bottle of brandy. He was not quite sober when late in the evening he picked up the phone, called the Admiral and agreed to quartermaster the project.

From OKW Headquarters, Canaris phoned Oster.

'Hans!' he said, when he heard the bluff Saxon voice at the other end. 'Fifty-three Wehrmacht uniforms, to include two officers and six Unteroffiziers, to be delivered, baled, to Oberst Albrecht Brauer at VIII Corps HQ immediately.'

'What arm of the service, Herr Admiral?' asked Oster.

Canaris thought for a moment, then said, 'Infantry, it's the simplest. I'll tell you everything when I see you.'

Oster understood.

Canaris flew back to Berlin from Le Bourget in a Ju52 full of OKW and OWH, amongst them Generalmajor Weber. The Abwehr Chief was unable to say much, but he did manage to reassure the Generalmajor that he need have no further concern over the dossier or the Englishman who had carried it. Weber seemed relieved, but it saddened Canaris that the aims of the conspiracy were, for the moment, so evidently subsidiary to the excitement of 'Sealion'.

# CHAPTER 21

Just after sunset, when a large part of the Wehrmacht in northern France were off duty, the three-litre Hotchkiss, with Haak at the wheel and with Oberst Brauer beside him, led a small convoy of two empty lorries up the lane towards the Frenays' farm. In a field a hundred metres from the farm, the Oberst halted the column, turned the vehicles, stopped the engines and told the drivers they could smoke.

It had been a fine day, and except for a little high cloud it was a fine evening. Haak lit a cigarette and sat on the grass. A piece of paper, caught in a bank of nettles ten metres away, stirred with the evening breeze. Haak saw the paper move and noticed two other sheets a few metres away. He got up and picked them up. They were printed on both sides and were identical. At the top of the first page was a drawing of an anxious Wehrmacht soldier reading a sign which read, '*Wir Fahren gegen England!*' Below were the words, 'A little phrase-book for invaders'. The text was in German, French and Dutch:

BEFORE THE INVASION

1. The sea is vast-cold-stormy.
2. How many more times must we practise disembarkation?
3. Do you think we shall ever reach England?
4. Shall we ever come back?
5. When will the next English raid be? Today, in the morning, at midday, in the afternoon, in the evening, during the night?
6. Why isn't the Führer coming with us?

The phrases went on down the page. More under the headings DURING THE INVASION and AFTER THE INVASION filled the back. Haak began laughing. The other three drivers went over to him. He handed them the other two sheets, and they began calling out the phrases.

'Where did you catch that lovely cold-lumbago-pleurisy-nervous breakdown?'

'The sea here smells of petrol!'

'Look how nicely our Hauptmann is burning!'

The Oberst, drawn by the laughter, walked over to where they stood. Haak slipped his copy into his pocket. The Oberst took another copy from one of the drivers, put on his glasses and began to read. Haak indicated the drawing of the German officer in bathing trunks, directing barefooted, goose-stepping soldiers into small rowing boats.

'Must have been dropped by the Tommies, Herr Oberst,' he said with a grin.

The Oberst took the remaining leaflet and thrust both into his breast pocket.

'If you find any more of this rubbish, Haak,' he said angrily, 'hand them straight to me. Is that understood?'

Haak saluted. 'Of course, Herr Oberst!'

Brauer stared at all four men in turn. 'We are here for a very important and delicate operation.' He tapped his breast pocket. 'If I catch anyone wasting time with one of these, they'll be on defaulters' parade tomorrow!' Then he turned and strode away.

When Brauer was out of earshot, Haak shook his head.

'The Herr Oberst's not usually like that,' he said. 'He's got a good sense of humour. If you ask me, it's all to do with tonight. Coming up here.' He indicated the darkened farm. 'Picking up whatever we are picking up and being told not to open our mouths.' He turned to one of the drivers. 'Ever had your lorry full and been told not to open your mouth?'

The driver shook his head.

'That's what I mean,' said Haak. 'It's damned unreasonable!'

Brauer glanced at his watch and ordered the drivers back into their cabs. Haak he kept beside him.

'It is Saturday night, Herr Oberst,' said Haak gently. 'The lads are wondering . . .'

'Special embarkation exercise!' snapped Brauer.

Haak grimaced. He had a friend in the 16th Army who had just finished a live ammunition exercise at the Le Touquet training school. Nearer home, in VIII Corps, the 620th Engineer Regiment had been posted to Dieppe to prepare for landing manoeuvres. Yesterday two battalions had joined them. But yesterday had been Friday. As a good soldier, Haak knew that so far as fighting was concerned weekends were no different from weekdays. But exercises were different. Friday was all right for exercises, but not Saturday. Tonight they should have been out drinking.

Brauer had always believed that the chain of command was sacrosanct. He also believed that some semblance of a chain of communications helped. He knew his answer to Haak had not satisfied the Obergefreiter but there had seemed little more he could say. Eventually he added one sentence.

'I'll tell you, Haak, in all my twenty-six years a soldier, I've never had a more extraordinary assignment.'

'The army's a funny place, Herr Oberst,' said Haak philosophically, and appeared satisfied.

In an atmosphere of incredulity, and reminiscent of the preparations for a fancy-dress dance, they had undone the bales of field-grey uniforms and tried to match sizes to figures and ranks to ranks. The Major was to wear the uniform of a major, Simon that of a Hauptmann, Cornford that of a Feldwebel, and the rest of the NCOs the rest of the Unteroffiziers' tunics.

They had changed and checked clothes and equipment. They had rifles, respirators, canteens, boots, belts, ammunition pouches, but no ammunition. They had lined up for the Major's inspection, and with Cornford he had gone down the grinning, self-conscious ranks. When it had seemed that the last joke must have been cracked, the Major had rapped out his orders.

'Tonight we are joining with two other groups and being taken to Le Havre, where we shall embark. Tomorrow, if the weather is fine, we shall cross the Channel to England.' There he paused to allow the ripple of reaction to die. Then he had gone on. 'We're now the 9th Company of the 1,072nd Infantry Regiment. Some of you have got the numerals on your shoulder-tabs. They may be Huns but they're damned good soldiers! If we want to save our skins, then it's our job to try and look like them. We may not like wearing this uniform' — he had pointed to the Nazi eagle emblem on Cornford's right breast — 'but for the next thirty-six hours we've bloody well got to grin and bear it! No one but Mr Manning is to speak. Is that understood?' He had glared round the cavern. No one had moved. 'Mr Manning is our interpreter and liaison with the Hun. Any questions?'

There had been a few questions, none particularly difficult.

They had lined up at the barn door when Cole went to Cornford and said, 'Just one thing, Sarge. Were we meant to chuck our identity discs away with our old clothes?'

The question took the sergeant by surprise. His hand automatically went inside his tunic. His identity discs still hung on the thick string around his neck.

'A lot of chaps have taken theirs off,' said Cole. 'They didn't seem to go with the Jerry uniforms.'

Cornford was going to ask the Major, but the Major had already led the first group out. Cornford looked at Cole and made a gesture of doubt. Cole took his identity discs off, kissed them and threw them into the hay. Others followed his example, but the sapper with the burned hands was still fumbling with his when they reached the lane.

In the late evening light they marched like ghosts, appearing to see nothing but the field grey of the man in front. It was too dark to see the pallor of their faces, but a hint of their condition came from the fit of their uniforms. Brauer and Haak directed them to the lorries. When the last had climbed aboard, the two Germans returned to the Hotchkiss. Slowly the convoy moved into the night.

When they reached the main road the Oberst took out a handkerchief, mopped his brow and said, 'Part one completed, Haak. All we have to do now is rendezvous with the other two, get them to Havre and hand them over to the Kriegsmarine.'

Haak shook his head. It was, as the Oberst had said, an extraordinary assignment. Never in his four years' service had the Obergefreiter seen such an odd collection of Wehrmacht infantry as were now contained in the two lorries that ground along behind him. If this was a sample of the first echelon to land upon the English coast, the Tommies would be laughing.

'Some could hardly walk, Herr Oberst!' said Haak, unable to contain his disbelief and astonishment any longer. 'And I swear some of them were bandaged!'

'You've never seen them, Haak,' said the Oberst firmly. 'Never!'

'No, Herr Oberst,' said Haak, glancing at Brauer.

'And if you ever say you have,' said Brauer ominously, 'if you even mention them, you'll spend the rest of your life in a penal battalion in Norway. You won't even see the sun for six months on end!'

Haak knew that as a good soldier he wouldn't ever mention them, but it would still take him a long time to forget them.

They drove north under a sky touched with thin streaks of cloud, between whose fingers the stars shone in muted clusters. They passed through darkened Rouen and turned to follow the Seine towards the sea. At each of the great bends the river appeared on their left, a dark, sleeping serpent cradled in its own winding hollow, silent and oblivious to anything that did not ruffle its surface. Outside Caudebec they met the other two lorries. From there to Le Havre there appeared to be no landscape, just a straight road barely perceptible in the glow from the masked headlights. Occasionally, tall, dark shadows showed that they were passing through a village.

Their arrival at Le Havre coincided with the tail-end of an air raid. By the time the Oberst had found the Bassin de l' Eure, and the four lorries had drawn up along the edge of the quay, the sky was quiet and the last British bomber had recrossed the English coast.

Brauer gave the order to de-bus and Simon tapped on the tail-boards. They had been told to be silent and they tried, but hobnailed boots on a stone quayside and cold night air are not conducive to stealth. They marched in broken step, halted, stood about for an hour while they were counted twice, then filed down a steep gangway into the bowels of a self-propelled barge that still carried the musty smell of its peacetime cargoes.

Simon and the Major were the last to board. As he was about to go down the gangway, Simon saw the Oberst coming towards him.

'I have been asked to wish you a safe journey,' said Brauer coldly. Simon asked the Oberst to take his greeting back. The Oberst saluted. Simon returned the salute, as correctly as he could, then turned and groped for the gangway handrail. As he did so, Haak flashed a torch.

'Good luck, sir. Even in that old tub it shouldn't be too rough out there, not with the sort of weather we've been having.' Then Haak came close to him, steadied the handrail, and as he did so thrust a sheet of paper into Simon's hand. The torchlight flickered across the Obergefreiter's face and the panzer marksmanship shield on the left breast. Simon drew in his breath and was about to speak when Haak took a step back and saluted. Simon hastily returned the salute, then with a rigid spine, in the sort of stance to be expected from a Hauptmann of infantry, he made his way down the gangway.

They left the Bassin de L'Eure half an hour before sunrise. Simon as the only German linguist, shared the wheelhouse with an Oberleutnant and rating of the Kriegsmarine; the Major remained in the hold with the others. As they crept through the mist into the outer basin, two E-boats passed them returning from patrol, the subdued roar of their powerful motors contrasting with the chugging of the barge. Neither of the E-boats' crews bothered to look up at the rust-streaked vessel moving slowly the other way, and only the gulls seemed interested in their presence. They were only challenged once, and it was apparent that Canaris had planned the logistics of their departure perfectly.

Simon, self-conscious in his Wehrmacht uniform, stood with his back to the panelling that made up the rear of the wheelhouse and bridge. The only sounds other than the noise of their own engine and the wheeling, screeching gulls were the Oberleutnant's orders. As they passed the sea wall, and for the first time felt the gentle Channel swell, the Oberleutnant turned.

'She's designed for rivers, not the sea,' he said with a grin, 'but don't worry, Herr Hauptmann, you're lucky. The barometer's set high. For the next twenty-four hours, the Channel will be like glass.'

Simon thanked him. His accent made the wheelman glance, but he said nothing. The Oberleutnant, however, asked where Simon was from.

'Born and bred in Tanganyika,' said Simon. 'My father stayed there after the first war. I didn't come back to the Reich until just before this lot.'

The Oberleutnant seemed satisfied, and went back to his task of taking the barge to sea. After a while he pointed ahead.

'We shall round the Cap and anchor a little way off Octeville. With the English bombers you'll be safer out of harbour.'

Simon nodded. The wheelman grinned.

'My orders are to leave you there,' said the Oberleutnant. 'I have no idea what fun and games you're up to and I was told not to ask, but a word of warning. You're soldiers, not sailors, and this thing isn't meant for the sea, so don't take her too far out.' With a jerk of his thumb he indicated the engine grating behind them. 'Noisy, no power, but it'll keep going forever if you look after it. But you'll be lucky to get more than four knots, so watch the tides.'

'Fuel?' asked Simon.

'Full tanks,' said the Oberleutnant. 'Four, maybe five hundred kilometres. Rations for thirty-six hours, plenty of fresh water and emergency medical supplies, all in the galley.'

'Everything thought of,' said Simon. 'Thanks.'

'Don't thank me,' said the Oberleutnant, 'thank someone at OKW. They set it up. I'll tell you, Herr Hauptmann, your little disembarkation exercise was given the highest priority.' He pointed to the compass in front of him. 'They've even fitted a compass. Anyone would think it was the real thing and you were off to Dover! You've certainly got friends in the right places.'

Simon laughed and hoped he sounded as if he appreciated the joke.

'One other thing,' said the Oberleutnant. 'She's only just been requisitioned. There's still cargo in the holds. She's been carrying sodium chlorate . . . weed-killer, you know. So don't let any of your fellows go breaching the barrels. So far as I know, other than that it's harmless.'

'Acts as ballast, Herr Hauptmann,' said the wheelman helpfully, and the Oberleutnant nodded.

'With just your few chaps, it'll make her ride better. You don't want her too high out of the water, even if you are going inshore.'

Simon thanked them again. After a while the Oberleutnant said, 'It's a damned funny thing leaving navigation and seamanship to the Army. First I've ever heard of it, but I'm told you've

155

got both seamen and engineers?'

Simon might have said, 'Yes, a Highland major who's done a bit of yachting, one waterman RE, an ex-carrier driver and a REME mechanic'. But he didn't. Very casually he said, 'Oh, I don't know. You could look upon it as a river-crossing exercise on a somewhat grand scale.'

The Oberleutnant laughed. 'Not if the weather does change!'

Two kilometres north-west of Octeville they dropped anchor. When a pinnace arrived, the Oberleutnant took his crew of three down the rope ladder. Simon watched the pinnace pull away, then went forward and rolled back the corner of the tarpaulin that covered the hold. The fierce sunlight streaming down into the darkness picked out half a dozen men in field grey, six of the fifty-two British soldiers lying down there. After weeks of hiding, the light was blinding. Automatically they covered their faces.

'We're on our own!' shouted Simon, searching in the darkness for the Major or Cornford. 'We're anchored a mile and a half off the French coast. Rations and coffee in the galley.'

'Let's be having you!' shouted Cornford, and the men staggered to their feet. The Major came on deck, filled his lungs with the fresh sea air, then stared at the flat coastline. Simon pointed to distant cranes.

'Le Havre.' Then he turned and pointed to the northern horizon. 'Portsmouth and the Isle of Wight!'

The Major shook his head in delighted amazement.

'I still don't know how you did it, Manning, but whatever methods you used it's a bloody fine show. If you had a commission, you'd get the DSO!'

'We're not there yet, Major,' said Simon cautiously. 'One hundred miles to go in a barge designed for the Rhine. However, I'm told the barometer's set fair for the next twenty-four hours at least.'

The Major looked up at the sky.

'Clear as a bell,' he said with infinite confidence. 'Just a few little cumuli on the horizon, exactly as it should be! But not a mare's tail or a cirrus anywhere. We'll do it all right, don't you worry.' Then he shook Simon's hand and said, 'You've done your bit, now it's up to us.' He stared at the shore for a moment, then strode forward to inspect the whole of his new command.

They spent the rest of the morning and the whole of the afternoon organising themselves for the voyage. They did their best for the sick, and got their first taste in weeks of fresh air and sun. They cooked their first decent meal and even played a little rudimentary football. They watched minesweepers skating on the sparkling waters as they cleared the channel into Le Havre, and Bfl09Es taking off and landing at the airfield at Octeville. For the middle of a war, it was extraordinarily peaceful.

Hill had seen some odd messages in his time, but this came close to being the oddest. He was going to ring Sinclair at the FO, then remembered that Sinclair was now in the Navy. Sinclair had told him to contact Cuthbertson at the Cabinet Office, so it was Cuthbertson that Hill rang.

'We've news of a little bird that I'm told you're particularly interested in. A wanderer upon the face of the earth, one Simon Manning.'

At the other end of the line, Cuthbertson hesitated. Hill said, 'And it's pretty damned urgent.'

Cuthbertson told Hill to come straight round. Hill was there within twenty minutes. Hill settled in the chair, lit his pipe, then stared up at Cuthbertson.

'Your friend is being sent back. He is being cast upon the waves like our dear old Captain Bligh. He and his companions will have to fend for themselves across a hundred miles of open sea.'

Cuthbertson shook his head. 'I don't understand.'

'To be honest, nor do we. It's all very mysterious,' said Hill. 'But K tells us that Manning and his companions are leaving Havre this evening. Presumably en route for England.'

'Companions?' said Cuthbertson, puzzled.

Hill nodded. 'Oh yes, like Bligh he has friends.'

'In what are they leaving, for God's sake?' asked Cuthbertson.

Hill shrugged. 'We don't write each other letters, you know. I've told you all K said. Presumably they're leaving in some form of boat.'

Cuthbertson put his hand to his forehead.

'You don't look too pleased,' said Hill.

'It's such a damned silly message,' said Cuthbertson, 'and so bloody vague.'

'We'd love to have a word with Mr Manning,' said Hill quietly. 'After you, of course.'

Cuthbertson nodded and asked, 'Have you informed C-in-C Portsmouth, Southern Command, the RAF?'

Hill shook his head. 'Not yet. But we will.'

'In that case,' said Cuthbertson, 'we'll do it.'

Hill shrugged and got up. 'OK, but if you want to see your man again, make sure you do a decent job. See that it gets down to the man behind the gun. With all this Fifth Column and parachutists scare, HM Forces are pretty damned trigger-happy at the moment!' At the door, he turned and added, 'And don't forget when you've had your little chat with Mr Manning, we'd like to have ours. Find out what K's really up to, that sort of thing.'

Cuthbertson promised not to forget.

The moment Hill had gone, Cuthbertson asked for an outside line. It was some time before the call was answered, and when he he heard a woman's voice he was sure he was too late. Nevertheless, he asked for the Minister. The Minister had left the house at five the previous evening. His flying boat was due off at seven this morning.

'So by now,' said Cuthbertson, glancing at his watch, 'he'll be out over the Atlantic, halfway to Lisbon . . . ?'

The Minister's wife said he would, and volunteered the information that although Ambassador to Portugal was not a true reward for all her husband's long service to the Government and the Crown, he had every intention of making a success of it. Cuthbertson expressed a mixture of sympathy and hope and put the phone down.

At six in the evening a tug appeared. Simon was in the engine room when the Major called him on deck. The Major pointed westwards, just below the great red ball of the setting sun. A small grey vessel with a high bow, low stern and a tall, rakish funnel was materialising out of the haze.

'If I'm not mistaken, our tow and our final orders from the Hun,' said the Major with great satisfaction.

They had no glasses and could only wait. When the tug was

200 yards away, they heard the engine-room telegraph and saw the bow wave drop.

The tug came alongside, and the same Kriegsmarine Ober-leutnant called for the Major and Hauptmann to come aboard. Simon and the Major went down the rope ladder and were ushered into a tiny cabin. The Hauptmann of cavalry who had been Simon's escort on that night flight to Berlin was waiting. The Major saluted, the Hauptmann returned the salute.

'Sunset is in just over one hour, at 1920,' said the Haupt-mann. 'We shall begin the tow at 1930. We expect the tow speed to be nine to ten knots, and we shall tow you for the first five hours. That means that we shall drop the tow at 0030 hours. You will then steer north-northwest. Sunrise is 0435. By that time you should be well on the English side of the Channel, about forty miles from the English coast.'

'I hope to God they know we're coming,' said the Major, pointing at Simon and himself. 'We're in Wehrmacht uniforms, don't forget.'

The Hauptmann nodded. 'The British Intelligence Services were told this morning. We've had an acknowledgement.'

'Your own people?' asked Simon.

'The Luftwaffe and the Kriegsmarine have been told to keep clear of your course.'

The Major seemed satisfied. He held out his hand and said, 'We've a lot to thank your people for, Captain. Perhaps I may be permitted to do so on behalf of the men I command?'

The Hauptmann shook the hand, thanked the Major and asked that Simon should stay on board as liaison until the tow was slipped.

Brauer got back to Madame late. He was tired, angry and disgusted with himself. Added to that, the dry August days with the harvest lying in the fields had aggravated his hay fever, and his spirits had been further lowered from a meeting with his old comrade, Oberst Kretschmer. Kretschmer, now actual-ly designated Oberquartiermeister-England, had brought him up to date with all the arrangements for 'Sealion'. In spite of the optimism of the Party hierarchy some of the professionals were shaking their heads. The Kriegsmarine doubted the feasibility of the whole project. The Luftwaffe were meeting far more opposition than they had expected. Army planning and training were on schedule, 500 medium submersibles and fifty-two light floating tanks were ready, but before the afternoon was over Brauer had realised that elements at OKW and OKH were seriously doubting the practicability of any invasion should England continue to fight.

He had washed his hands and face from the bowl in his bedroom, and as he came out on to the landing Madame was waiting.

'Your Englishmen are on the sea,' he said coldly. 'By this time tomorrow they should be home. They are extremely fortunate men.'

Madame clutched his sleeve and kissed him on the cheek. The Oberst accepted her gratitude with icy restraint.

Madame hurried down to the kitchen and told her mother-in-law the news. The old woman displayed none of Madame's excitement. She was standing over the range, one hand on the mantelpiece. She turned her head, stared at Madame for a while as if not seeing her, then very quietly said, 'I hope when the Boche have gone, the people of the village understand.'

This time Madame did not fly into a temper. For the first time in many days she felt content. At last she had mastered the men at their own game. She smiled, said nothing and went on with her own work.

That evening Brauer did not ask Madame to his room to share his bottle of Dom Pérignon. Nor did he go to her bedroom. Well before midnight he got Haak out of bed and ordered him to drive north-east. They covered the seventy kilometres to Caen in little over the hour.

# CHAPTER 22

In his small rectangular room in the wooden hut that was his home, on the edge of Carpiquet airfield, six kilometres from the centre of Caen, Major Karl Ludecke sat on the bed, took off his boots and surveyed the hole in his socks. He was tired, and in spite of the mess party not in the best of spirits. In the last few weeks much of his *joie de vivre* had vanished. When he took the time for introspection, the reasons were evident.

The Stukas of Generalmajor von Richthofen's Fliegerkorps VIII were passing through traumatic days. After minimal losses in Poland, the Low Countries and France, things had changed dramatically. Attacks on shipping in the Channel and on British aerodromes had brought swift retribution. In the last six weeks they had lost sixty planes and crews, with another twenty planes badly damaged. Only five days ago, on the day the Reichsmarschall had proclaimed '*Adler Tag*', nine had been shot down on a single mission against the British airfield at Middle Wallop. Indeed, such had been their trouncing that two days later the Reichsmarschall had ordered that no less than three fighters must henceforth escort every Stuka.

Such losses, coming after the sweet success of the spring and early summer, would have affected anyone. In Ludecke's case there had been a further blow. Stukageschwader 77 at Carpiquet needed a new Gruppe commander. Ludecke had been chosen to boost their sagging morale. Ten days ago he had left his beloved Stukageschwader 2, the Gruppe he had first led into Poland, at St Malo. He was still in the same Fliegerkorps, Carpiquet was a fine flying field and he knew several of the Staffelkapitäns, but he badly missed the old faces. At Carpiquet he felt a new boy. He was also conscious that his present morale was hardly capable of lifting a Gruppe that had been so badly mauled. Low cloud to stop flying and a weekend in Paris were the tonics he really needed, but in the absence of that sort of luck the next best thing was bed.

He had taken his jacket off when his orderly tapped on the door with news of a visitor. Ludecke was not pleased. He threw a boot at the orderly and told him to get out.

'It's Oberst Brauer, Herr Major,' whispered the orderly round the side of the door. Ludecke got up, shook his head to clear it, put on his jacket and prepared to welcome his father-in-law. When Brauer came in, Ludecke saluted and poured him a glass of calvados. The Oberst accepted gratefully. For a moment they stood looking at each other, both with a glass in their hand, neither speaking — the Major in a state of semi-undress, the Oberst tired and worn.

'Is it Sophie, Papa?' asked Ludecke anxiously after a while, wondering whether his wife's father had news that had not reached him.

The Oberst seemed not to hear. Ludecke repeated the question. The Oberst suddenly shook his head.

'A special operation, Karl. An attack on a barge.'

'Where?'

'In the Channel at first light.'

Ludecke looked puzzled. 'I don't understand. Why hasn't this come down through the normal channels?'

Brauer did not answer directly, but sat down on the bed and said, 'A group of English fugitives are on a Kriegsmarine barge on their way to England. By first light they'll be in mid Channel north of Havre. It's a slow-moving vessel, barely able to maintain five knots. A perfect Stuka target.'

'Wasn't it very lax of the Kriegsmarine to allow the British to take one of their invasion barges?'

'They're wearing Wehrmacht uniforms. The barge was acquired by subterfuge.'

'Can't the Kriegsmarine sink it themselves? Surely they've got a spare E-boat?'

Brauer didn't answer.

'And what about my fighter escort?' asked Ludecke after a while.

Brauer looked surprised. 'This is only to mid Channel!'

'Have you been to mid Channel recently, Papa?' asked Ludecke with a grin.

Brauer shook his head.

'Then let me paint you the picture. The moment we take off,

162

the RAF will know. They'll plot our course to this point in mid Channel, and the controllers will alert the dawn patrols who will already be up there at 7,000 metres, waiting. Or they may, of course, pay us the honour of a special scramble. Whichever they do, we shall all arrive over your barge at much the same time. And if we don't have a fighter escort, we'll be lucky to see France again. Besides,' he added with a smile, 'the matter's out of my hand. The Reichsmarschall has pronounced that for every Stuka there must be three fighters. If I'm to take one Staffel there, there must be three Staffels or Messerschmitts!'

Brauer put his head into his hands.

'I'm sorry, Papa,' said Ludecke, 'but unless you can make the whole thing more official the Tommies will sail safely home.'

'The fighter escort . . . ?' said Brauer.

'In this Luftflotte, they're all supplied by Jagdfliegerführer 3, HQ, Cherbourg. On the other hand, if you had the authority you could approach one of the Jagdschwader direct.'

Brauer refilled his glass and said, 'There was another reason why I came to you, Karl.'

Ludecke waited. Brauer said no more. Suddenly Ludecke got to his feet.

'Please come to the point, Papa. We had a bad raid on the English airfields at Ford and Tangmere this morning. I'm tired, dead tired.'

Brauer turned his head and said, 'My honour as a German officer is at stake.'

Ludecke burst out laughing. 'Your honour, Papa! That could never be at stake!' He pointed to his father-in-law's chest. 'You have the old Iron Cross, First Class, and now the War Merit Cross First Class. After the invasion, you'll have the Knight's Cross!'

'I have been involved in their escape,' said Brauer flatly.

Incredulity and incomprehension filled the Major's face.

Brauer nodded. 'I can't tell you the circumstances, but against my will I had to make certain arrangements.'

'I'm sure it can all be explained,' said Ludecke cheerfully. 'Everyone knows you wouldn't deliberately aid the enemy!'

Brauer remained silent. Suddenly Ludecke began striding about the room.

163

'Supposing they do get back to England, what does it matter? A single barge-load of Tommies can't alter the war now. England is on her knees. Another week, maybe a fortnight, and there'll be peace.' He began speaking thoughtfully. 'There's been enough killing in this war already. Twenty . . . fifty . . . a hundred less Englishmen killed wouldn't be a bad thing. We shall need them to help make Europe safe against the Bolsheviks.'

'You say that because you went to school in England,' said Brauer accusingly.

Ludecke shook his head. 'Going to school in England for a year hasn't made me a traitor. It's just common sense. One barge-load of English soldiers won't rebuild their army.'

Brauer put his hand to his chest. 'It would be hard for me to live with the knowledge of all I have done.'

Again Ludecke shook his head. 'I'm sure there was a perfectly good reason.' He stared at his father-in-law for confirmation, but Brauer remained silent. 'All right,' said Ludecke after a while, 'I'll ask no more questions. But it still isn't as easy as you seem to think. If I take half a Staffel out there, even without a fighter escort it can't be kept secret. Six pilots, six observers to brief. They're not stupid. They'll know they've bombed an invasion barge, and if the men are wearing Wehrmacht uniforms, they might well notice.'

'Sophie told me in a letter that you once scored a direct hit on a French tank?'

'Very close,' said Ludecke modestly, 'a matter of a metre or two.'

'You have the B-2 Stuka,' said Brauer, 'you can carry one 500-kilo and four fifty-kilo bombs. Enough, if well placed, to sink an unarmoured barge.'

'There's still my observer,' said Ludecke.

'I can operate a machine-gun. I operated one in the trenches. I can certainly identify the target. And I've sailed, so I know the rudiments of navigation.'

Ludecke stared at the stern, tired face. 'Are you serious?'

'Perfectly serious.'

'We shan't have an escort, and we'll probably have a ground mist and sea fog. It won't be a joyride.'

Brauer nodded. Ludecke thrust out his hand and pointed.

164

'Give me that chart, and I'll ring the Met people.'

They came down from the bridge into the cabin. The Hauptmann of cavalry held up a bottle of calvados, said 'Sorry it's not Scotch,' and poured two glasses.

'How are your companions?' he asked, peering into his glass.

'Ever heard of Fred Karno's Army?' asked Simon.

The Hauptmann looked puzzled.

'Last war song of the British Army. Fred Karno had a sort of troupe of clowns.' He indicated the direction of the barge.

The Hauptmann smiled but said nothing. Simon sipped his calvados and the fiery liquid took his breath away. He was leaning against the bulkhead, when very quietly he said, 'Where's the catch?'

'Catch?' said the Hauptmann, puzzled.

'There must be a catch,' said Simon. 'No one believes in fairy-tale endings, not these days.'

'There's no catch,' said the Hauptmann.

'You said our people know we're coming?'

'They do.'

'No nasty twist?'

The Hauptmann shrugged. 'None. The English will presumably send an escort for you. As I've said, the Luftwaffe and Kriegsmarine have been ordered to keep clear of your route.'

'So we have a safe channel to Portsmouth?'

The Hauptmann nodded, smiled and said, 'Unless you hit an English mine.'

There was a pause, then Simon said, 'And what about the Gestapo? Surely they haven't just melted away?' He glanced round the tiny cabin as if expecting them to appear through the ventilator. 'A whole barge-load of English sailing from Occupied France, and the Gestapo conspicuous by their absence. That takes a lot of understanding.'

'You challenged the Abwehr to organise a boat. It's no good if the boat doesn't finish its journey.'

'I'd liked to have thanked Hopkins,' said Simon, almost to himself, then looking at the Hauptmann added, 'Perhaps you'd do it for me?'

The Hauptmann moved his head a little to the side and said, 'An unfortunate tragedy. His body was found in the river. He must have lost his way and fallen in. He had poor eyesight, you know, and wasn't a good swimmer.'

'Poor bastard,' whispered Simon, and felt like weeping.

They went on deck into a thick sea mist. The steel plates of the tug were icy cold and covered in water droplets. At any other time, the siren would have been blaring through the gloom. As it was, they were ploughing at ten knots into a white blanket. It was frightening to stand on the bridge and stare to the bow, where all visibility ceased, or to turn and see no sign of the barge they were towing, just a hawser reaching up into a void.

The Oberleutnant pointed.

'Sorry about the fog, but it hasn't always been as bad as this. It's really quite patchy.' Then he grinned and said, 'By the time you get back to the coast, the sun'll have burnt it off.'

Simon and the Hauptmann said nothing, just exchanged glances.

They were fortunate. They hit one of those better patches, just as the tug was dropping speed. When they cast off and pulled amidships of the barge to let Simon re-embark, the whole length of the barge was visible. As he stood waiting to grasp the rope ladder, the Hauptmann placed a soft, rolled bundle in his hand.

'The English flag,' said the Hauptmann, 'a present from the Abwehr, but please don't hoist it until we've gone.'

Simon thanked him. The Hauptmann indicated the rust-streaked side of the barge. There was a jolt. For an instant the two vessels clung together on the gentle Channel swell, then just as they began to part, Simon stuck his peaked cap more firmly on his head, grabbed the ladder and swung himself up and over the rail of the barge. The Major stood waiting. Simon remembered the bundle in his hands.

'The Union Jack, Major,' he said, handing the flag over, 'but not to be hoisted until the German ensign has disappeared.'

At the same moment that the Kriegsmarine tug was turning away from the barge and plunging back into the mist, a solitary Fleet Air Arm Swordfish, piloted by Lieutenant 'Billy' Hensman, RNR, and carrying in the third seat a special long-range fuel tank, was nosing its way slowly down the Brittany coast.

166

Hensman and his observer, now also acting as telegraphist/air gunner, had left Ford at 2100 hours as part of a flight of three, all armed with torpedoes. Near Guernsey they had alerted a flak ship, and in the ensuing evasive action lost sight of the dim wing-lights of the leader. They had carried on to the target area on their own, and now, after more than three and a half hours airborne, were beginning to wonder if the RAF reconnaissance information was correct. Other than the dark, rugged outline of France to port, the occasional searchlight a few distant bursts of flak, they could see nothing. Certainly not the Köln-class cruiser reported to be making northwards from St Nazaire.

Through the Gosport tube, the voice tube that acted as intercom between the crew, Hensman asked for a navigational check. The observer came back with the information that in fifteen minutes they would be passing through the eight-mile gap between Quiberon and Belle-Ile.

'How far back to base if we go on to St Nazaire?' asked Hensman.

The observer did a rapid calculation. '450 miles, Skipper.'

Hensman did his rapid calculation. At ninety knots, that would be the best part of five hours. With fog in the Channel and perhaps a diversion from Ford, it was just not on. Even with this massive tank filling the whole of the observer's normal position, he dare not risk staying airborne for more than nine hours.

'If we don't see anything in five minutes, we'll turn about,' said Hensman.

The observer gave an acknowledgement and prepared for the return journey.

Simon walked out of the shade of the wheelhouse. Somewhere to the east, beyond the fog, the sun was about to rise. But the fog was shallow. When he looked up he could see the washed-out blue of the sky. There appeared to be no clouds. A little wind ruffled the sea and blew a hole for them to see a quarter of a mile ahead. The tiny waves lapped against the barge's side, then the wind dropped and the fog closed in again.

Simon was no judge of a vessel's speed, but watching a small patch of oil twenty yards away it seemed abominably slow.

When he questioned their progress with the Major, Simon thought him sanguine to the point of foolishness. To seek a second opinion Simon scrambled down the ladder into the hot confines of the engine room, where the diesel thumped alarmingly and emanated a nauseating smell. Nipper Cole and the REME mechanic were equally pleased with their progress and assured him that they must be making a good six knots.

Fortified with so much hopefulness, Simon went back on deck expecting to see a welcoming vessel breaking through the mist. But the mist was their horizon and it was unbroken. Indeed, at that moment the fifty-two British soldiers on the Rhine barge seemed the only other people in the world.

He was straining his eyes, staring ahead, his mind full of the most contradictory thoughts, when Cornford joined him.

'A penny for them, sir?'

'I was ruminating on that strange characteristic of man that even at the moment of salvation he must necessarily experience a sense of anti-climax. It must be the Lord constantly reminding us of his penchant for giving while taking away.' Simon then asked the sergeant if he didn't also feel a sense of anti-climax.

'Can't say I do,' said Cornford, pushing back his Feldmütze forage cap, 'even though reveille was a bit early this morning.' Then he glanced into the hold, frowned and said, 'That's the burial service you quoted from sir: "The Lord gave and the Lord hath taken away." I'd steer off that if I was you.'

'Not good for morale?' said Simon.

The sergeant shook his head.

Simon scanned the mist for the hundredth time.

'It's all too peaceful,' he said after a while. 'If they know we're coming, why hasn't someone come out to meet us?'

'Probably on their way now,' said the sergeant cheerfully, 'but it's going to take a bit of a job to find us in this.'

Simon pointed upwards. 'If we can see the sky on and off, the RAF should be able to see us on and off. But I haven't heard a plane.'

'Maybe they're all grounded,' said Cornford.

'Maybe,' said Simon, and they walked back into the wheelhouse where the Major stood staring down at the compass.

'Are you certain, Major,' said Simon, 'that we are still heading for Portsmouth and not by any chance steering for the open Atlantic and the U-boats?'

'Good God, Manning!' cried the Major. 'What do you take me for? We've got a perfectly good compass and there's no wind to blow us off course.' He pointed straight ahead. 'We're still not much more than half-way over. You're too impatient, that's your trouble. Give the sun time, it'll burn the damned fog away soon enough.'

The Major went back to the single chart pinned to the wooden wall.

'What's the time?' asked Simon.

The sergeant took out his watch. '0415 hours, sir.'

Simon grunted, turned the collar of his Wehrmacht jacket up against the cold and gratefully accepted the steaming mug of coffee thrust into his hand.

# CHAPTER 23

As he moved his head from one side to the other, peering down beyond the leading edge of the wing, Ludecke felt exceedingly naked. There was little cloud to hide in, should he need to do so, and as he had feared, plenty of sea mist. He had taken off at first light, and hoped to intercept the barge fifty kilometres south-east of the Isle of Wight. His flying time to the target would be twenty-three minutes, and with his heavy load he would be climbing all the way. It wasn't a long flight and there was no hostile land to cross, but he was perfectly aware that from the moment his wheels had left the grass of Carpiquet he was engaged in a contest with the odds heavily against him.

As they had banked over the still sleeping city of Caen and seen the mouth of the Orne beneath them, Ludecke had grimly reminded Brauer that the Spitfires would now be alerted to their sortie. In fact, he was more pessimistic than he need have been. With the Ventnor Home Chain Radar out of action from the Stuka raids of the 12th and 16th, his solitary Ju87 was not reported until he had crossed the French coast and was twenty-five kilometres out over the Channel. It was then, with barely ninety-five kilometres to go, that two Czech Hurricane pilots at Tangmere were scrambled.

Nipper Cole came up from the diesel to get some fresh air, found it cold and put on his jacket. Simon put down the empty mug, and to keep his hands warm, put them in his pockets. The fingers of one hand closed around a sheet of paper. He took the paper out and remembered it as the sheet thrust upon him by the little Obergefreiter as they had embarked at Havre. By the faint binnacle light he began to read. When he started laughing, the others asked what was the joke.

'A satirical phrase-book for German invaders,' said Simon, 'presumably dropped by the RAF. "We are seasick, where is the bowl?" "Our ship is shuddering-sinking-burning-exploding!" "We've had enough!" '

He handed the leaflet to Cornford, who could make little of it. So Simon took it back and read some more. They were still laughing when the sound of an aeroplane engine brought them racing out on to the deck. At first they could see nothing, although it was evident that the plane was very low. Then for a moment, immediately astern, an archaic-looking biplane, all wings and struts, and with a torpedo slung beneath it, appeared out of the fog, tilted its wings slightly and disappeared again.

'A Swordfish!' shouted the Major in ecstasy. 'It's a Navy Swordfish!'

Those on their feet, whether on deck or in the holds stamped and shouted. Even the sick added something to the general cacophony.

Over the roar of the Pegasus engine and the whine of the slip-stream in his struts, Hensman heard nothing. He was stiff tired and the upper part of his body was numb with cold. He had been in the air, cramped in this cockpit, for more than seven and a half hours, and having missed his target was concerned only with getting back to Ford as soon as possible and certainly before the Messerschmitts were about. Neither did he get a glimpse of the barge as they passed astern of it: that was left to his observer.

'Good God, Skipper!' came the voice through the Gospor

tube. 'A barge! A bloody great self-propelled barge out there in the middle of the Channel!'

Hensman brought the Swordfish round in a right turn and got a glimpse of the barge's bow through a parting in the fog.

'It must be a bloody invasion, Skipper!' shouted the observer. 'We've arrived back in the middle of it. That barge is stuffed with Jerries!'

Hensman had flown Stringbags for three years. He had laid mines in the West Ems Channel, attacked E-boats off Ostend, had engine failure over the open sea, and when the *Courageous* had been torpedoed he had been lucky to have been plucked from an oily death. He had been trained to cope with emergencies and never be taken by surprise. Nevertheless, he had never expected to be one of the first two Englishmen to spot the German invasion. If it was the invasion?

'Any identification?'

'She certainly wasn't wearing a white ensign!' shouted the observer, then remembered that he had hardly noticed the ensign for it had been hanging limply from the stern.

Satisfied, Hensman turned the Swordfish for an immediate torpedo run out of the rising sun. His only fear, other than the prospect of having to face a sudden barrage of flak should the rest of the hostile fleet emerge from cover, was that the swirling, capricious mist would obscure his target at the critical moment.

'He's coming back!' shouted Cornford.

'Taking another look,' said the Major. 'Let's hope to God he doesn't lose us in this damned fog.'

Nipper Cole ran to the stern of the barge and tried to open the Union Jack. Deciding that wasn't enough, he hauled it down and ran back with it to the wheelhouse. Simon grabbed the other end and they held the flag out together.

Hensman needed to be down to sixty feet to drop his torpedo. He had been flying low in spite of the mist, so he had no need to dive his Stringbag. But for the visibility his run-in should be pure instruction-manual smooth, and the angle shallow.

He estimated the speed of the barge at not more than five knots, set what he believed would be the correct interception course for that speed, throttled back to eighty-five knots and settled slowly into the swirling banks of whiteness. He put his left thumb on the firing button and waited. Normally he would have dropped his torpedo at 2,000 yards; this time he might be lucky if he saw his target at 300 yards. At eighty-five knots he would have less than seven seconds to complete attack and evasion. They were very near their limit.

Hensman saw the barge when he was still 400 yards away. Although for a moment it disappeared again, he was able to give a gentle correction to the rudder to bring the bow in line with the torpedo aiming sight. Then he pressed the release button and the torpedo fell away. Relieved of its 1,610-pound load, the Swordfish tried to rise, but Hensman held the plane level.

There was no porpoising. The torpedo entered the sea with scarcely a splash, and ran straight and true. Hensman did not see the Union Jack held out on the deck below him, for he was too occupied slamming open the throttle and pulling the Swordfish up in a climbing turn and away from the debris of his disintegrating target. In any case, the deck of the barge and the figures waving frantically upon it were already obscured by the cylinders of his engine and the leading edge of his lower wing.

They heard the Swordfish low over the water and to starboard. With the dawn behind it and the mist around it, the plane was virtually invisible for most of its run-in. When at last those on the barge did see it, it was close, huge, its wings seeming to shade the whole sea, and the torpedo was in the water, racing towards them.

They stared at the glistening cylinder in stupid disbelief and helplessness. The Major ran back to throw the wheel over. One or two instinctively flung off their Wehrmacht jackets. But it was too late. The torpedo disappeared from their view to enter the barge between the main hold and the engine. There it exploded, deep in the bowels, to lift steel plates, wooden planks, lumps of machinery and men into a fearful, towering column.

As the debris rained down, Simon found himself huddled against the shattered wreck of the wheelhouse, staring at the tail of the departing Swordfish, from whose rear cockpit the observer was emptying his Lewis gun on to the tilting, splintered remains of the barge's deck. Simon shook his head and cried out, but no one in the plane or barge saw or heard him. He tried to move but seemed to have neither right arm nor shoulder. He managed to turn his head and saw men and the remains of men — some naked, others dressed in field grey — lying strewn around him.

Those were the very last things that Simon did notice. At that moment the fire racing through the stricken barge, just ahead of the engulfing sea, reached the sodium chlorate left as ballast. The ensuing explosion ripped the barge from bow to stern. Within half a minute nothing was left on the surface bigger than a plank.

No more than half a dozen persons actually saw that explosion and were not within it. They were Nipper Cole and three others, who had been thrown alive into the water by the detonation of the torpedo, and the crew of the Swordfish.

Cole, who while swimming for his life still wore that look of surprised innocence, was now astonished that the vessel that had been his home for the past twenty-four hours could disappear so utterly and so quickly. From his exceedingly low viewpoint, with his mouth awash, he could see nothing but the last traces of the explosive cloud.

For the Swordfish crew, already on their way back to Ford, the viewpoint was very much higher, and in spite of the limitations of their cockpits very much more comfortable.

'Her ammunition's gone up, Skipper!' cried the observer through the Gosport tube. 'She's just disappeared. It was like a conjuring trick. One minute she's there, the next she's not!'

Hensman gave the thumbs up, and peered ahead for his first sight of Sussex.

Ludecke had climbed all the way to 3,000 metres, and was trying to distinguish glistening mists from glistening sea when he saw the two explosions ahead and to starboard. Through the arc of the propeller he saw first the tall, dark column thrown up by the torpedo, then a few seconds later the large, white cloud that signalled the explosion of the sodium chlorate and the end of the vessel. He shouted to Brauer behind him, then with a touch of the rudder brought the Stuka towards the lingering cloud of gas and the hole blown in the mist. They circled slowly.

'If that's your barge,' Ludecke called out, 'someone's been here before us.'

From his position in the rear cockpit, Brauer searched the whiteness. Even as he looked, the sun and early morning breeze were thinning the mist. He saw an oil slick and bits of debris floating lazily on the calm, glassy surface. The only other vessel, a tiny speck that caught the first of the sun's rays then disappeared again, was about eight kilometres away and appeared stationary.

'It could still be down there somewhere,' said Brauer. 'The mist's clearing. We're over the right spot. If we just hang on for a . . .' He stopped and stared, fascinated by the holes that had suddenly appeared on the Stuka's wing, the dents in the metal, the instant transformation from dark green camouflage to silver. Then he heard the machine-guns. He shouted a warning at the same moment that he grabbed butt and trigger of the MG15, and with all his muscles tensed, scanned the bare sky above him. He felt the Stuka shudder under the impact of more bullets, and was crushed into his seat as Ludecke flung the plane into a vertical turn. He saw a Hurricane coming lazily up beneath him, but couldn't bring his gun to bear before the fighter slid below the Stuka's tail. Then they were diving down to the protection of the thinning remains of the sea mist.

Ludecke had dived many times upon his targets, always with his Jericho trombone screaming, his airbrakes out and the bomb under his belly extended beyond the arc of the propeller by the trapeze cradle. This time his dive was an emergency one, accompanied only by the shrieking of the slipstream, the roar of the Jumo engine and the two Hurricanes seeking to get him back in their sights. When he tried to lower the cradle to jettison the bomb, it was jammed. He jettisoned the wing bombs, pulled gently back on the stick to decrease the angle at which the large 500-kilogramme bomb would fall, and caught the full force of eight machine-guns.

The bullets tore through Brauer, slapped against Ludecke's back armour and ripped into both his legs. They ruptured the port inner-wing fuel tank and shattered the control pulley to the rudder. They punctured the tank in front of the instruments, and the cockpit was sprayed with oil. Out of control, the Stuka rolled on to its back. Ludecke shouted at the inert Brauer to bail out, then struggled to get out himself. He opened the canopy, but with legs shattered, his feet remained jammed in the rudder bar pedals.

With the large black bomb still firmly clutched between its spats, and its pilot hanging upside down in the cockpit, his hand inside his flying jacket clutching not the ribbon of the Iron Cross, First Class, but the small gold crucifix that hung around his neck, the Stuka dived vertically into the sea.

The tiny black speck that Brauer had spotted and towards which they had dived was His Majesty's Drifter *Betsy Ann*. Six months ago it had been fishing for herrings in the North Sea. Now, armed with a single Lewis gun of 1914-18 vintage and equipped with an almost equally aged wireless transmitter, it formed part of the Auxiliary Patrol, along with four hundred other drifters and trawlers. Positioned forty miles from the coast, the very outpost of Britain's defences, it shared with the two Czech pilots the sight of the final plunge of Ludecke's Stuka. As the plane hit the water and disintegrated into a thousand pieces, the *Betsy Ann's* captain, Lieutenant Ross Sinclair, RNVR, led his motley crew in a rousing 'Hurrah!'

Hensman landed at Ford soon after five, expecting to find the airfield in a state of intense excitement. Instead, there was a distinctly lethargic air over this little piece of Sussex, more in keeping with the nearby cathedral city of Chichester than a naval air station in the front line. The hangars, blasted from the Stuka attacks of the 18th, were still smoking; the Lewis gunners were standing by their sandbagged emplacements; his ground crew welcomed him back with as much joy as could be expected at that hour; but there was nothing more. Certainly not the tension he would have anticipated with an invasion fleet less than forty miles away.

He made his report and was shocked at the blasé way it was received. He went into breakfast and told his story to the other two Swordfish crews. They were not impressed. In the afternoon he had to accept the truth. There was no invasion. That evening the Intelligence Officer put him in the picture.

'Billy, old chap. The latest on Jerry is that he hasn't yet concentrated enough shipping for a full scale invasion, but they're holding exercises all along the coast. You clobbered a barge-load that lost their way in the fog. Bloody good show! The CO's putting you in for a DSC. Have a drink!'

# CHAPTER 24

Behind his sandbagged position on the cliff-top, Corporal Barnard peered eastwards awaiting the dawn. The night had been dark and seemingly endless. Few stars had been visible, and then only for brief periods. There had been an air raid somewhere over to the west, and at least one German aircraft had flown over the island and alerted the Portsmouth guns. But the searchlights had only confirmed what Barnard already knew. The sky was largely cloudy. An hour and a half ago, one of his section had come out of their billet in the hotel with a mug of tea. They had squatted behind the breastwork, shared a cigarette and listened to the lapping of the sea. That visit, and the dog that had run down the path and made his heart jump, were all that seemed to have happened on land during the last four hours.

He stamped his feet, leaned upon the sandbags and waited. 150 feet below, just beyond the now deserted boarding houses and esplanade, was the beach. He supposed, although he had never had a holiday here, that at this time of year the sands should have been lined with rowing boats and canoes, and the now departed huts filled with deck-chairs.

He would like to have known the place in peacetime. It must have looked grand with all those fairy lights in the chine and the gardens, the pier lit up, fireworks on Regatta night, yachts in the bay, and the hydrangeas. The hydrangeas were in flower now. He could just make them out, the nearest not more than ten feet away. The locals were probably right when they said it used to look like the South of France.

Dawn when it came was serrations of the palest green wedged between sea and cloud, and suggested that Tuesday, 27 August 1940 would at least start as another overcast day. Other than those bands of washed-out colour, the first tints of the day that Barnard was conscious of were the trace of red in the cliffs to his right, the flesh of his hands, the rusty brown of the endless row of anti-invasion scaffolding that lined the beach, and the blue of the hydrangeas.

Only two ships were visible. A destroyer making for Portsmouth and a trawler crossing the line of the Nab Tower. There was no invasion fleet, and Barnard gave a sigh of relief. He always seemed to get the pre-dawn watch, but perhaps that was because he was now a veteran. After Dunkirk, most of the platoon were new. He looked over the cliff-edge on to the slate roofs below. A thin wisp of smoke rose from a chimney to his left. A section of Sappers were billeted down there. Later in the morning they would be out laying more beachmines.

As the long dark night faded, Barnard turned down the collar of his greatcoat and wondered what the day would bring. Guard duties, rifle training and an air raid or two, probably. Yesterday afternoon, Portsmouth had caught it. They had made the useless gesture of standing by the Lewis gun. The RAF had done better with a score of 47 to 15.

An object moving gently with the waves, a few yards out from the water's edge, caught his attention. He had no binoculars, so could only screw up his eyes and peer. When the object eventually came to rest a hundred yards to his right, opposite the mouth of the chine, the light was sufficiently good for him to realise that there was something very familiar about the shape. When his platoon sergeant arrived, Barnard pointed.

'Down there, Sarge, where that trickle of fresh water ends. Came ashore fifteen minutes ago. Reckon we've seen something like that before.'

The sergeant's tired eyes followed the pointing arm. His weary mind leapt back three months to the jetsam of Dunkirk.

'A body,' he said slowly, almost stupidly. 'You're right, Barney lad, you're right! It's a bleeding body!'

They went down the twisting road that joins the southern end of the esplanade with the cliff, to the barbed wire that heralded this seaside no man's land. Beyond them lay the mines, the scaffolding, the grey sea, and the body.

They got the sapper corporal out of bed, and with the aid of his grubby plan and a prodding bayonet, set out for the water's edge. Fortunately, the mines laid upon this beach had not yet shifted, and they reached the new wormcasts either side of the body without mishap.

The body lay on its back, legs open, arms out, stomach extended to an obscene hillock. The flesh was white, puffy and nibbled. It was not clad in khaki battledress. For all its washed-out state, both tunic and trousers were still easily identifiable as the field grey of the Wehrmacht.

'An airman, poor bastard!' said the sapper corporal, pointing to the eagle over the right breast. 'And looks as if he's been in the drink for a good long time.'

The sergeant shook his head.

'Wehrmacht,' he said with great authority. 'That's army, like us.' He pointed to the stained piping of the collar patches and the piping and numbers on the shoulder-tabs. 'I reckon they were once white. That's infantry. 9th Company 1,072nd Regiment.'

The sapper corporal bowed to this superior knowledge and tried to turn the head with the point of his bayonet, but the skin was too soft to stand such treatment. The sergeant untied his own gas-cape, and opened it on the sand beside the body. 'Lift him gently,' he said, and they did. With the sapper corporal once more in front, prodding the way, the little procession made its way back through minefield and scaffolding to the esplanade. There, on the dry, wind-blown sand that covered the hard roadway, they laid their dripping bundle.

Barnard stared down into the gas-cape. Three and a half months ago he had seen only one dead body, that of his father, who had anyway died peacefully. Since then he had had a surfeit. Nevertheless, this dead German fascinated him. The body now rested with its face upwards, towards the sky. Although it was swollen and pockmarked where sea creatures had nibbled it, and was becoming difficult to identify, there remained something familiar behind the tattered, swollen horror.

178

A distant memory of a walk down a dirty side-street made Barnard crouch beside the body and pull back the sodden right tunic sleeve. He was not disappointed. The skin was flabby and bulbous, but as guaranteed, the dye that made up the tattoo was indelible. The bulldog and the two Union Jacks draped either side of it were not the least disfigured.

Barnard raised his head.

'You know who this is, Sarge?' he asked in a hoarse voice. 'It's Nipper Cole of the carrier platoon.'

The sergeant came closer and peered.

'Pull the other one.'

Barnard removed his hand, which had been obscuring the tattoo.

'That tattoo. I was with him when it was done.'

The sergeant stared for a long time.

'Christ, Barney,' he said at last, 'what the hell's he doing dressed up like that?'

Corporal Barnard shrugged. He had no idea, and was too tired to think of one.

The sergeant opened the ambulance doors and the CO of 'A' Company, the 5th Wessex, saw the body lying on the stretcher. In spite of the ravages of the sea, he too recognised the uniform. So did two civilians walking along the pavement. The sergeant pulled back the right sleeve, the CO saw the tattoo and grunted. The two civilians tried to see what was happening but were moved on by Barnard. The sergeant slammed the ambulance doors shut and went back to the office with the CO.

'It's Private Cole all right, sir,' said the sergeant cheerfully. 'Corporal Barnard was with him when he had the tattoo done. Some back street in St Omer.'

'What do we know of him?' asked the CO after a while.

'Not much, sir. He was still quite a kid. Eighteen or nineteen, hence the "Nipper". When he first came to the Battalion he was in "B" Company. He showed considerable mechanical aptitude and got transferred to the carrier platoon.'

'Last seen?' asked the CO.

'During the retreat, sir, when we was part of "Holtforce". On the 21st, I think it was. Just south of Arras, sir, when Battalion HQ and the carrier platoon had that brush with the panzers.'

The CO nodded. The 21st would be forever engraved on his memory.

'And he was reported missing?'

'Yes, sir,' said the sergeant, 'along with Sergeant Cornford, Lance-Corporal Church and half a dozen others. We saw at least one carrier brew up.'

The CO thanked the sergeant and told him to make sure that Corporal Barnard kept his mouth shut. The sergeant saluted and withdrew. When he had gone, the CO picked up the phone. This was one for the Brigade Intelligence Officer.

# CHAPTER 25

They had both travelled on the nine-fifty from Waterloo but had not seen one another. They had met as they had walked through the red-capped Military Police to the grey-painted paddle steamer. They were together by the rails as they had watched Portsmouth Harbour with its purposeful-looking warships and its still, silent barrage balloons slip slowly into the distance. They were still together in the bowels of the vessel, watching the pounding connecting rods of the aged reciprocating machinery, and they came up on deck together. But it was not until they rounded an anchored fleet tanker and saw the spire of All Saints, Ryde, ahead of them that Hill said, 'You wouldn't by any chance be going to 314 Brigade HQ would you?'

Cuthbertson looked up from the foaming, churned water with its little diamonds of intense green, and said, 'As a matter of fact, yes.'

'A body washed up on the sands of the Isle of Wight,' said Hill, looking up at the August sun, 'and we at once have such a mystery it even lures the Cabinet Office.'

'Oh, I don't know,' said Cuthbertson urbanely. 'They're falling out of the skies pretty fast just now. One German airman's body is hardly a phenomenon these days.'

'Ah,' said Hill, 'but it's not an airman's body, is it? If the uniform is to be believed, it's a soldier's body. An infantryman's!'

'He could have been a passenger in a plane that was shot down,' said Cuthbertson.

Hill shook his head. 'He was a Schütze. A private. The lowest of the low. Not the sort of chap to get rides in aeroplanes.'

After a moment Cuthbertson said, 'With the Hun busy on invasion exercises all along the coast, and the RAF bombing him every night, some of the Wehrmacht are bound to be caught.'

Hill turned from the rails, stared at the long, snaking wake of the ferry and said with great sarcasm, 'What do you reckon, then? They were rehearsing for the Christmas panto, and Private Cole of the 5th Wessex was dressing up as a Schütze when a tidal wave caught him?'

'Not proven, as they say in Scotland,' said Cuthbertson quickly.

'Oh, come off it!' said Hill. 'The tattoo's been identified. It was done in St Omer!'

'No doubt Germans are also now being tattooed in St Omer,' said Cuthbertson.

'With a bulldog and two Union Jacks?'

As they walked up the gangway, Hill offered his car and Cuthbertson accepted. They got into a green Austin. As the ATS driver slipped the car into gear, Hill said, 'Still no word of your fellow, Manning?'

Cuthbertson shook his head. 'Strange business that. We're inclined to think your message was a hoax.'

Hill lit his pipe. 'K doesn't usually play tricks or waste precious communication facilities with leg-pulls.' After a moment he asked, 'You warned everyone?'

'Everyone,' said Cuthbertson, 'right down to the GOCs of the coastal divisions. Of course, we couldn't give details, we didn't have any.'

For a while they were silent, then the M16 man turned in his seat and said, 'Odd business that Swordfish attack. A German barge so far out that it was on *our* side of the Channel.'

'Fog,' said Cuthbertson firmly. 'Funny things can happen in fog. We checked with the Admiralty. They wouldn't have had a compass. Jerry probably had no idea he was steering north. Thought he was heading back to Deauville.'

Hill took his pipe out of his mouth and whistled tunelessly. Neither spoke for the rest of the journey.

314 Independent Infantry Brigade HQ was in a manor house approached up a steep winding lane, and surrounded on three sides by an ancient beech wood. The sentry at the lodge, the brigade sign, the anti-gas paint and gong on the wooden post, and the cluster of military vehicles parked outside, betrayed the army presence. In a dark, panelled sitting room, now bare of everything but an army table, chairs, bed and maps, and in the presence of the Brigadier and his Intelligence Officer, Cuthbertson and Hill were brought up to date. In the last few hours, three more bodies had been washed up within the Brigadier's command. All were in Wehrmacht uniforms, all had infantry Waffenfarben.

'Identity discs?' asked Hill.

'None, sir,' said the Intelligence Officer, 'and that's the funny thing. You know Jerry has that aluminium alloy disc with the perforation? Like us, you take one and leave one on the body. In their case, they tear a piece off. Well, none of them had anything. Not even a pay-book. In fact, their pockets were empty.'

Hill stroked his chin, then turned and stared at Cuthbertson. Cuthbertson looked up at the moulding of the ceiling.

'We've got a body for you, if you'd like to see it?' said the Brigadier breezily. 'Bit of a mess, I'm afraid, been in the water quite a time, you know. What the damned gulls don't peck, the mackerel nibble.'

They went outside to a truck whose canvas hood was down. The Brigadier opened the hood, and Cuthbertson and Hill peered into the dim interior. The body was very swollen; the uniform, stretched to bursting, was that of a Gefreiter. The stench was most unpleasant.

'I've got the MO's preliminary report,' said the Intelligence Officer as they went back into the house. 'The bodies aren't too badly decomposed. Two show distinct signs of burning.'

'Do the locals know about this?' asked Hill.

The Intelligence Officer nodded. 'One was spotted by a civilian. He led our chaps down the cliff to get it. Tongues are already beginning to wag, I'm afraid.'

'The tattooed one this morning,' said Cuthbertson. 'Could there have been a mistake?'

The Intelligence Officer shook his head. 'He was identified by a man from the same battalion. We know who the poor devil was. A Private Cole. He was reported missing on 21 May.'

'But the identification was solely on the tattoo?' asked Cuthbertson.

'Not exactly. The man who first identified him thought he recognised him. That's why he looked for the tattoo.'

They had lunch in the mess and listened to the speculation. No one in the brigade knew of the Swordfish attack, and neither Hill nor Cuthbertson mentioned it. They were having coffee when the Intelligence Officer was called to the phone. He returned with the news that a fifth body was coming ashore near Atherfield Point.

They jumped into a pick-up, and drove down to the Military Road. They stopped the car, walked across a field, and guided by a white tape through the minefield, scrambled down a sandy chine to the shore. The body, in much the same state as the others, lay above high-water mark on a bank of shingle and dried seaweed. Four soldiers, including the NCO who had marked the path, were staring down at it. Their expressions suggested that it might have come from Mars.

Cuthbertson looked and turned away. Hill bent down and began a careful examination. There was nothing in the pockets, and like the others this man was from the infantry. When Hill pulled up the right sleeve he found that the skin had been tattooed but the design was unintelligible, partly through the large irregular pockmarks that seemed to have been caused by burns. Hill was surprised at the state of these marks, for the wounds seemed to have partly healed during life. Only the MO's report could tell him more, so he turned his attention to the torso. He sent the watching military away to get a stretcher, then opened the tunic collar. Inside were bandages and the thick string of identity discs. He lifted the head and slipped the discs off. They were British.

As they scrambled back up the chine, Hill came close to Cuthbertson and said, 'This one was certainly British. Freeman, W.J. Freeman. Number 1896784. I'll have his rank and unit by tonight.'

After dinner they walked out on to the lawn and stood under the beeches.

'Sapper William James Freeman, 63rd Chemical Warfare Company RE,' said Hill, staring straight ahead. 'GHQ Troops with the BEF. The Company seems to have been badly knocked about.' He paused for a moment, stared at Cuthbertson and said, 'I don't know much about tides and winds, but my guess is that there are more to come. Some will presumably miss the island and end up on the Hampshire and Dorset coasts. Perhaps not for a day or two.'

'If you're right,' said Cuthbertson, 'it's a devilishly tricky situation!'

Hill laughed. 'In your business, I'd have thought you'd have got used to making categorical denials?'

Stung, Cuthbertson glanced at his watch. Hill shook his head.

'You can run away if you want to, I'm staying here. There's going to be a lot to clear up. But if you do go back, keep your mouth shut. For a while anyway.'

'The PM . . .' Cuthbertson began, when Hill cut him short.

'I'm not asking you anything, am I?' he said aggressively. 'I'm not checking up on whether you really did let HM Forces know that your chap Manning was on the way home with his friends. I haven't the faintest idea how five British soldiers got themselves into German uniforms, and I'll probably never know. Nor do I know whether that Swordfish had any part in the story, or whether the poor sods we've been picking up just set out to swim across. All I do know is that it'll serve us no good whatsoever if it gets about that a load of British Tommies, dressed as Germans, are being washed up on the south coast. On the other hand' — he broke into a rare smile — 'it won't do us any harm at all if it's the *Huns* that are being washed ashore!'

'The bodies,' said Cuthbertson, 'if they were Germans . . . ?'

Hill shook his head. 'Forget the International Red Cross and all that stuff! We've just got to lose them, that's all. Send them back where they came from. Get the Navy to bury them at sea.'

'You can arrange that?' asked Cuthbertson anxiously.

Hill raised his eyebrows. 'Oh yes, trust Uncle Hill to get you out of trouble. That is, if I can get to them quick enough. The question is, how many more were wearing identity discs? Or have we been lucky in finding the only chappie who kept his?'

It was a fortnight later when Hill burst into Cuthbertson's office with the full statistics.

'Forty-five washed up all told,' he said briskly. 'All the way from the Isle of Wight to Cornwall. Of that lot, we can identify seven as positively German. All from the Luftwaffe.' He pushed a piece of paper on to Cuthbertson's desk.

Cuthbertson scanned the names on the paper.

'The other thirty-eight?' he asked.

Hill shrugged. 'Officially, soldiers drowned while attempting an invasion, or caught during disembarkation exercises. Take your pick. Unofficially all British, all from the same vessel.'

'That's stretching it a bit, surely?'

Hill shook his head. 'The bodies went into the sea at much the same time. Uniforms are all from an identical batch. Shoulder-tabs show 9th Company of the 1,072nd Infantry Regiment. A figment of the Abwehr's imagination. There was nothing in any pocket. When you're dealing with this number, however careful you are, someone will keep something in a pocket. There's only one answer. They were issued with the uniforms just before they sailed.' Suddenly he burst out laughing. 'It's a real K trick. Smells of him!'

'And if someone asks questions?' said Cuthbertson. 'Burial places, names, units?'

Hill shook his head again. 'Grey area, old man. Men reported missing. Before this war's over, there'll be hundreds of thousands of them.' He took out his pipe, lit it and said, 'The invasion rumour is spreading like wildfire. It's burning brightly in the villages of southern England, consuming Europe and now it's got to America. The Hun's had one hell of a bashing! No one wants to kill a piece of propaganda like that.'

After a while Cuthbertson smiled. Hill leaned forward in his chair and said, 'I've done all the dirty work. Just to put the record straight, why didn't you want Manning back?'

'Policies change,' said Cuthbertson carefully. 'In Manning's case, events overtook him.'

'We sometimes have people like that,' said Hill. 'Pity, but there it is. However, if, and I'm just saying if, the people we've been picking up were your man and his friends, then his part in the propaganda war will have been considerable.'

Cuthbertson got up and walked to the window. Two barrage balloons were as dazzling as mirrors in the afternoon sun.

'I think he would have been pleased to know that,' he said at last. 'Although he wasn't in the Forces, Manning seemed to believe in the power of the sword.' He was still facing the window when he said, 'There was another factor. The possibility that Manning had become an Abwehr agent. They badly need to build up their network here, particularly with their invasion project. We had those four spies landing last week, the German and the three Dutchmen. They'll hang before the year's out. We wouldn't have wanted that for Manning. We were all too fond of him.'

When he turned, Hill had gone.

# EPILOGUE

It was a Sunday in October when Cuthbertson took the single sheet with it précis of the Abwehr file to his parents' house in Berkshire, tore it into scraps and burned the scraps in the garden incinerator. By then the invasion story was becoming a legend.

In America it was reported that hundreds of flat-bottomed barges, crammed with Germans in full field equipment, had emerged through the mists of the Channel to be annihilated by shore batteries, the RAF and the Royal Navy. In Europe, where there had been no fighting for several months, Paris hospitals were supposedly filled with badly-burned German soldiers, and long ambulance trains had steamed into Berlin. In the next year, 1941, the Free French Information Service numbered the Germans drowned at 30,000, and by then the terrifying effects of petrol burning on the surface of the sea had been added to the destruction wrought by more conventional weapons.

If the invasion rumour spread swiftly, the British and Allied condemnation of Nazi atrocities in the occupied countries was much more tardy. It was not until 17 December 1942, after more than three years of war, that Eden shocked the House of Commons with his 'Jewish statement'. As he said in his memoirs, 'It had a far greater dramatic effect than I had expected.' By then, of course, several million had died.

Another casualty of the war was Canaris. Hero or traitor, depending upon viewpoint, he was arrested after the July bomb plot. He avoided the infamous People's Court, and for many months, along with Hans Oster, was kept alive by Himmler. On 9 April 1945, however, within four weeks of the end of the war, and with the Allies less than a hundred miles away, he was dragged naked from his cell in Flossenburg concentration camp and hanged.

# A selection of bestsellers from SPHERE

## FICTION

| | | |
|---|---|---|
| PALOMINO | Danielle Steel | £1.75 □ |
| CALIFORNIA DREAMERS | Norman Bogner | £1.75 □ |
| NELLA | John Godey | £1.75 □ |
| RAILROAD | Graham Masterton | £2.75 □ |
| HAND-ME-DOWNS | Rhea Kohan | £1.75 □ |

## FILM & TV TIE-INS

| | | |
|---|---|---|
| WHOSE LIFE IS IT ANYWAY? | David Benedictus | £1.25 □ |
| FORT APACHE, THE BRONX | Heywood Gould | £1.75 □ |
| ON THE LINE | Anthony Minghella | £1.25 □ |
| SHARKY'S MACHINE | William Diehl | £1.75 □ |
| FIREFOX | Craig Thomas | £1.75 □ |

## NON-FICTION

| | | |
|---|---|---|
| YOUR CHILD AND THE ZODIAC | Teri King | £1.50 □ |
| THE PAPAL VISIT | Timothy O'Sullivan | £2.50 □ |
| THE SURVIVOR | Jack Eisner | £1.75 □ |
| THE COUNTRY DIARY OF AN EDWARDIAN LADY | Edith Holden | £4.50 □ |
| OPENING UP | Geoff Boycott | £1.75 □ |

*All Sphere books are available at your local bookshop or newsagent, or can be ordered direct from the publisher. Just tick the titles you want and fill in the form below.*

Name _____

Address _____

Write to Sphere Books, Cash Sales Department, P.O. Box 11, Falmouth, Cornwall TR10 9EN

Please enclose a cheque or postal order to the value of the cover price plus:

UK: 45p for the first book, 20p for the second book and 14p for each additional book ordered to a maximum charge of £1.63.

OVERSEAS: 75p for the first book plus 21p per copy for each additional book.

BFPO & EIRE: 45p for the first book, 20p for the second book plus 14p per copy for the next 7 books, thereafter 8p per book.

*Sphere Books reserve the right to show new retail prices on covers which may differ from those previously advertised in the text or elsewhere, and to increase postal rates in accordance with the PO.*